ROCK-A-BYE COWBOY
ROCKY ROAD RANCH
BOOK 3

LEXI POST

All rights reserved.

No part of this publication may be sold, copied, distributed, reproduced or transmitted in any form or by any means, mechanical or digital, including photocopying and recording or by any information storage and retrieval system without the prior written permission of both the publisher, Oliver Heber Books and the author, Lexi Post, except in the case of brief quotations embodied in critical articles and reviews.

PUBLISHER'S NOTE: This is a work of fiction. Names, characters, places, and incidents either are the product of the author's imagination or are used fictitiously. Any resemblance to actual persons, living or dead, business establishments, events, or locales is entirely coincidental.

Rock-A-Bye Cowboy Copyright 2025 © Lexi Post

Cover design by Dar Albert

Published by Oliver Heber Books

0 9 8 7 6 5 4 3 2 1

ACKNOWLEDGMENTS

For my husband, Bob Fabich, whose service to the Air Force, Fire Service, and Coast Guard I will never stop touting. Putting others before self is a motto he lives by daily.

Thank you to my sister, Paige Wood, who had such great insights and gave me excellent ideas on making a good story better.

Thank you to my stepson, Army Veteran Rob, for sharing his experiences of being deployed in Afghanistan and Syria. A true hero, like his dad.

My reader group, Lexi's Legends, came through for me as usual. A big thank you to all of them and to Pamela Reveal for Jackson's daughter, to Donna Antonio for Jackson's raccoon, and to Patricia Way for the ranch. I want to also extend a special thank you to Veronica Westfall and her mom, Rosalie. "Rosalie" is the perfect name for the Dunn matriarch.

I can't end my gratefulness without thanking my amazing critique partner, Marie Patrick, who has encouraged me while writing this book and read everything I've thrown at her, no matter how rough, helping me to bring it together. My friend, you are one in a million.

AUTHOR NOTE

This story was inspired by a very old Greek play by Euripides titled *Orestes*. This play, like many Greek plays, is complicated. However, the themes of the play are guilt and punishment of the guilty, in this case, Orestes, who has killed his mother because she killed his father. Caught between politics and family anger, both Orestes and his sister, Electra, are voted to be put to death, so they decide on revenge before they die. Just as all mayhem breaks loose, the god Apollo arrives on the scene, sending Orestes to Athens to face the first court trial, where Apollo foresees Orestes not being put to death but exiled for a year and Electra marrying Orestes' best friend. That's the most important part, though it is very convoluted.

But what is striking are the themes of guilt and vengeance versus justice. Orestes is hounded by the three Furies of mythological fame, and they work hard to drive him insane with guilt as they are goaded on by his mother's ghost.

So, what if Jackson Dunn, while still very young, believes

AUTHOR NOTE

his actions caused his brother's death? Would he also be driven crazy by his perceived guilt? To what lengths would he go to seek the meaning behind what happened and his just punishment? And when, if ever, would he seek the help of family and friends, as Orestes did, to truly live? Perhaps a caring woman could help the healing process along.

MR. RIGHT CHARACTERISTICS LIST

1. She preferred a tall, average-looking man of slim build, not too muscular (no gym rats).
2. He shouldn't have any emotional baggage.
3. He couldn't have any children or an ex-wife.
4. He preferably had a desk job with good earning potential.
5. He was willing to talk.
6. He had a sense of humor.
7. He didn't have a family who interfered with his life.
8. He couldn't be in the military or a first responder (she didn't need a hero).
9. He had to be open to forever.
10. He should be willing to admit when he was wrong, even if grudgingly admitted.
11. There had to be chemistry between them (she wanted passion in her life).

CHAPTER 1
FOUR PEAKS, ARIZONA, AUTUMN

"OW! WILL YOU SLOW DOWN?" Danielle Hubbard rubbed the top of her head after hitting it on the SUV's ceiling.

"Fine. You really need to chill, Dani. We're on vacation."

She gave Kaitlynn a scowl. "My idea for my vacation was to spend it at home eating ten gallons of ice cream and getting twelve hours of sleep a night with no men in sight. Not being jarred around on a supposed driveway to this aptly named Rocky Road Ranch to rough it for two weeks."

Kaitlynn, thankfully, slowed the car to a crawl over one seriously large hole that could have made a perfect duck pond during monsoon season. "Ice cream? You broke up with Mr. Right Number Ten?"

Damn, she forgot she'd told Kaitlynn about him. She shrugged, though the sting of being second to his work still hurt, hence the need for ice cream. "He was a long shot anyway. Far too busy running his father's business to have a social life. To be honest, I thought that could be a benefit. You know, not being together too much but being able to take vacations whenever you want? I had even figured out what I could do to help the business."

Kaitlynn stopped the vehicle, though it was hard to tell since they were going so slowly now, and looked at her. "You can't tell me you were thinking of leaving Mayes Mineral Drilling. You're the only other woman at the whole freaking company! What would I do? You do realize this is all about me."

She couldn't help but grin. "Of course it is. I figure they'd hire someone else, and if the person wasn't another woman, then I'd just have to hang with you once a week so you could bitch about the boys."

"Okay, as long as you were thinking of me. Though I'd much rather come into the office and bitch." She started the car, crawling along once again. "Then maybe you'll get lucky on this vacation. At least here there're real cowboys. You won't find any good men in your ice cream." Kaitlynn smirked, obviously thinking she'd scored a point for coming to a dude ranch.

"Doesn't matter." Dani crossed her arms. "I said I would give it five years or ten men, whichever came first. Well, it's been four and half years and ten men, so I'm done."

Kaitlynn laughed. "You can't be done done."

"I am done, done as in no more men for me. I will now plan for being alone the rest of my life." Saying it out loud made it sound so depressing.

"What about your Mr. Right list? It took you two years just to get that compiled."

"Yeah, and a lot of good it did me. Obviously, there is no

Mr. Right for me." She'd done so much research on personality traits and compatibility tests, read psychology books, and even studied reality television shows. "I'm thinking what I value in life is just not what men in general value."

Kaitlynn snorted before coughing. "Heck, I could have told you that. Look at the men we work with."

And that was exactly what had motivated her to create her list. The last person she wanted to end up with was a guy like them. "Exactly my point."

"I don't know. You've had some pretty decent relationships with that list. Maybe the right one just hasn't come along yet."

She shook her head. She'd given her search a fair shot, more than fair. "Nope. I'm done."

Kaitlynn smiled slyly. "What if one of the cowboys on this ranch meets every criterion on your list? Will you just ignore him?"

"I burned the list, so I wouldn't know." That wasn't entirely true. She'd spent so long on that list that she knew it backward and forward.

For the second time, Kaitlynn stopped the car and looked at her. "You didn't."

"I did." She uncrossed her arms and pointed. "I think we're almost there."

Kaitlynn looked ahead, and a wide smile filled her face as the car started forward again a bit faster. "I see me some cowboys."

Luckily, Kaitlynn was easily distracted. "What's your plan for this vacation?"

Her friend slowed a bit over another bump. "Plan? It's

vacation. There are no plans. Just have fun. But if a cowboy wants to snuggle on a cold night, who am I to say no?" Kaitlynn wiggled her eyebrows but kept her eyes on the road, or rather, above it, where there were some cowboys.

As soon as they parked, Kaitlynn jumped out and headed toward the small crowd, her hips swaying in her tight jeans, obviously more than ready to start her vacation.

Dani wasn't so excited. She spent every workday with men. If she couldn't have a girls' vacation, she wanted to be alone in her big soaking tub at home, preferably with scented candles. But that's not where she was.

Exiting the SUV, she stretched her long legs before begrudgingly walking past what appeared to be a rather large adobe residence to join Kaitlynn. Her friend had somehow managed to get in front of everyone. Dani stayed in the back, easily seeing over the mother of two children standing in front of her.

A number of cowboys and a few cowgirls were milling about, and behind them was a barn. Between that and the end of the house, she could just make out white wooden fencing, which was exactly what she would expect on a cattle ranch. Not that she'd ever been to one, nor had she planned to. Unfortunately, when Kaitlynn won the free vacation and begged her to come, she couldn't turn her down.

"Howdy, y'all."

At the greeting, she turned her attention to the five ranch people standing in a neat line, the others having disappeared into the barn. They made the silhouette of a mountain. On each end was a woman in western wear, a blonde on the left and an auburn brunette on the right, both shorter than she was. Next to each of them stood a cowboy. The one standing beside the blonde was tall and lean. The one on the opposite end was a little shorter but broader. And dead center of them all stood a cowboy who was taller and broader than anyone and looked about as happy to be at Rocky Road Ranch as she was.

She studied him, as he was far more interesting simply because he was the only one in the dirt yard who seemed unhappy. He had his gray cowboy hat pulled down low, and his thumbs were hooked in his front pockets. Unlike the men on either side of him who wore button-down shirts, he wore a green T-shirt that looked two sizes too small, accentuating his mounded chest and bulging arms. That particular physical characteristic was one from her Mr. Right list to avoid. Number 1 was a man of slim build who was not too good-looking so she wouldn't have to worry about other women fawning over him, and she especially didn't want a gym rat. Her older sister had found that out the hard way. Guys built like the cowboy in the T-shirt spent way too much time on themselves. If she couldn't compete with a family-owned business, she'd never be able to compete with the camaraderie of the gym.

"Welcome, everyone. My name is Tanner Dunn."

She moved her gaze to the lean cowboy who'd spoken.

"My family and I will be hosting you for the next couple weeks. This is my wife, Amanda. These are my brothers, Jackson and Brody, and at the end there is Hannah, Brody's soon-to-be wife. They're getting married on Christmas Eve."

"Congratulations!" one of the guests called out, and Hannah beamed with happiness as everyone clapped.

Obviously, *she'd* found her Mr. Right. Maybe finding love was easier among like-minded people. Dani's gaze flitted back to the man called Jackson. The only thing they had in common was that neither wanted to be there.

Tanner waited for the applause to die down. "You are our very first guests. We're excited to have you and your opinions on our operation. You will have the full experience of staying on a working cattle ranch. All we ask is that you give us feedback."

"On everything." Brody Dunn rolled his eyes as he spoke.

Tanner laughed. "Yes, everything. We want to know what is great and what needs work. You will have a questionnaire on your bunk at the end of every day, but you don't have to wait to fill it out." He pointed to the adobe residence. "We have a box over there on the porch where you can put in your thoughts, and we certainly welcome any suggestions. If you don't like writing your suggestions down, you can tell any one of us your ideas, and we will be sure to get them added to the rest of the feedback. This is a new venture for us, and we are looking forward to making your vacation enjoyable."

"So, basically, we're your guinea pigs." Kaitlynn put her hands on her hips.

Brody laughed. "They figured you out, Tanner." He turned to Kaitlynn. "You're absolutely right, miss. Your payment for this vacation is not in money but in thoughts. Not a bad deal, I'm thinking."

Kaitlynn nodded in agreement before a man responded. "You have some pretty good-looking guinea pigs here."

Kaitlynn's head whipped around to the man standing

behind her, not a cowboy but one of the guests. "Well, thank you."

So much for a cowboy cuddle. It looked like Kaitlynn would be snuggling with a guest before long.

"Now, folks, you'll each be assigned a bunkhouse, and my ranch hands will help you get settled." Two cowboys and one cowgirl started to file out of the barn. "My righthand man is Layne, and he'll be happy to show the Wilson, Saunders, and DeGrasso families where they'll be staying."

Dani studied the heavily mustached man with longer hair than the rest, though that wasn't saying much. He was as tall as Tanner but broader and looked a bit older, maybe in his thirties. He had a winning smile as he tipped his hat. "Howdy, folks." The three families joined him, the kids a bit in awe.

Tanner continued. "Nash here, who knows everything there is to know about cattle and will be happy to tell you, is going to show all the gentlemen to their bunkhouse."

Nash lifted his hat and reset it on his head. In appearance, he was the opposite of Layne. He looked younger than Tanner and sported shorter light brown hair. He appeared friendly and approachable. "Right this way." He motioned for the men to follow him.

Tanner waited for the men to file out before addressing everyone who was left. "And, ladies, you'll follow Vic, our resident cowgirl and all-around horse handler, to your bunkhouse. If you would all gather your suitcases, you can get settled in before chow time."

Brody once again interjected. "That's six o'clock. But

don't worry, you'll hear the dinner triangle. When it sounds, you can head over to the clubhouse."

Dani remained where she was as people started to move toward their vehicles to get their suitcases. She was curious as to why Jackson hadn't said a word. What was his problem? There was only one way to find out.

Moving forward, she was heading toward him when he suddenly turned on his heel and disappeared into the barn. Other guests were talking to the Dunn couples, so she followed Jackson.

Stepping into the building, she noticed two things right away: the scent of hay and the lack of anyone visible. Did he leave out the other end, which was wide open? She ambled forward when she heard a voice and halted.

"This is bullshit. I should let you loose on everyone. That'll show them what Havoc is all about. The last thing I need is to babysit a bunch of civilians."

She raised her eyebrows. Civilians? Maybe following the scowling Dunn brother hadn't been so smart, after all. She turned, intending to leave as quietly as she'd come.

"I know you're there."

At his words, she looked over her shoulder. Was he talking to someone else?

"Show yourself, or I'll sh—shit."

She grinned as she turned back around. "You'll shit?"

Jackson Dunn came out of a stall near the end on the left and stalked toward her.

She knew he was tall from seeing him outside, but inside, heading right for her, he no longer appeared to be part of a mountain silhouette but the entire mountain itself.

"You're supposed to be with Vic."

Not a little off balance, a rarity for her, she smirked. "Well, isn't that a how-do-you-do."

His angular jaw tensed even as his brows lowered. She couldn't quite see the color of his eyes, but his dark hair was definitely cut very short, and it looked like he wore a silver chain around his neck, though what was on it disappeared beneath his T-shirt, barely discernable. "Miss, this is an active cattle operation. It's important that you don't wander into areas where there are no staff. That could be dangerous."

Though every word was polite, he'd lifted his head enough for her to see his intense whiskey-brown eyes, proving he was more than irritated. If anyone knew about safety, it was she, which got her back up. "So, you're saying you aren't trained staff and being in the barn with you is a risk?"

A small tick started beneath his left eye. If she hadn't been looking so intently, she would have missed it. His jaw worked as if he was attempting to unclench it. "Riskier than you can imagine."

She'd expected a smart-ass reply, but his answer surprised her so much, she lost her thoughts for a moment. There was really no reason to goad the man. She'd just been curious. She shrugged. "You could just say you want to be left alone since you want no part of your brothers' operation. I'll be happy to leave you to your sulking."

Without waiting for a response, she turned on her heel and headed for the open barn doors. She'd almost reached him before he spoke.

"Our operation." The words were ground out in a growl, causing her to stop in her tracks.

There was more to this man and family than it had appeared when they first arrived. She was such a sucker for a mystery. Without turning around or uttering another word, she continued outside, only to be stopped a few steps later by the cowgirl named Vic.

The woman was short, but she had swagger. Her black ponytail was so straight, it looked ironed—something Dani would have to do to get hers that straight for two minutes.

"Do you need help with your gear?"

Dani looked down at the shorter woman, who was not intimidated at all that Dani stood almost a foot taller. "No, I didn't bring that much."

Vic's blue gaze seemed to size her up in one glance. "Smart. Let's get it so you can settle in with the other women."

She glanced around to see that everyone else had dispersed, so she gave a quick nod and headed for Kaitlynn's vehicle. Luckily, it wasn't locked. Typical Kaitlynn. Grabbing her backpack, she slung it over her shoulder, and then slammed the door closed.

"That's it?" Vic stared at the backpack.

"Yeah. The website said you had washers and dryers, so I didn't bring much. Just T-shirts, sweaters, jeans, and one skirt. Why? Do I need more?"

Vic grinned, which lit up her face and made her appear a lot more approachable. "Nope. Just never met a woman who packed as little as I do. Come on. I'll show you to your bunkhouse."

Feeling as if she'd just been given the stamp of approval from someone who knew their shit, she happily followed Vic past the house and the white fencing she'd seen earlier, which looked to be a corral. They walked to a rectangular log building that made up part of an open square of other structures. The one across the way was a carbon copy, but the two at either end were two-story log buildings, with one having large windows and a glass door.

Vic pointed to the one with glass. "That's the clubhouse, where you'll eat tonight's dinner. It's nothing special, but there'll be some barbeque nights and some more complicated meals."

"Complicated?" Dani stopped behind Vic in front of the bunkhouse with the apt name of *Fillies*.

The cowgirl scrunched her nose in distaste. "I prefer a good steak and mashed potatoes over anything else."

"Ah, got it." Most likely, the Dunns wanted to impress their guests. She wasn't into complicated foods herself, but she was always willing to try something new. After they strode up the steps to the porch, she stopped. "Why are everyone's suitcases out here?"

"I told those ladies they could check out the clubhouse or unpack. They decided to go to the clubhouse. Is that what you want to do too?"

She shook her head. She was more curious about where she'd be sleeping.

Vic nodded in approval and opened the door. "Here's your home for the next two weeks." She pointed to one end. "The bathrooms are down there. You can choose whatever bunk isn't taken."

Dani looked around the large room with adult bunk beds along one side and comfortable-looking chairs and loveseats, and end tables on the other. A cast-iron wood stove took up space in the middle of the wall opposite the bunks. "Why do I feel like I'm in a college dorm?"

Vic shrugged. "Don't know nothing about that." Vic leaned in and lowered her voice. "But I suggest you shower at night or early in the morning because there are only three showers."

She widened her eyes at that. "Do you live in something like this?"

"Hell no. I live in a house like normal people. Working at the Rocky Road is just my job." Again, the cowgirl grinned.

Dani searched the space. "There are no closets?"

"No, but there are hooks on the walls between the bunks, see?" She pointed to the five-foot space between the floor-to-ceiling bunks. "I suggest taking a lower bunk. You'll have space under it for your boots and phone."

Since Vic seemed to know what she was talking about, Dani dropped her backpack on the bunk bed across from the door for easy access to outside if she needed some alone time.

"I don't know when the other women will be back, but you may want to unpack. Claim your space. If you have any questions, I'll answer them now."

It was on the tip of her tongue to ask about Jackson, but she shook her head. "Thanks. I appreciate the advice."

Vic gave a quick nod and then left.

Not sure when the rest of the women would return, she quickly unpacked, then went out on the porch and rolled Kaitlynn's suitcase inside. She knelt down and opened it.

The top piece of clothing was a pink hoodie. Kaitlynn could be such a girly girl when not at work. Dani set the hoodie on the top bunk to make sure Kaitlynn got it, then closed the suitcase and rolled it into the space with the three empty hooks.

Happy with having staked her claim to a space, she stepped out onto the porch. The sun had started to set, and the colors in the sky were dazzling. Yellows, oranges, and some reds already streaked between two mountains. She loved the Arizona sunsets but always seemed too busy to stop and enjoy them. Maybe she'd get some good relaxation on this vacation, after all. Maybe she'd refuel her soul and make some decisions on how she wanted to enjoy her life without a husband.

She stepped over to a rocking chair that was surrounded by suitcases and pulled it from the mayhem and sat. The clubhouse lights showed the movement inside now, and she could see Kaitlynn talking to a male guest in her usual animated fashion. Dani smirked at the trouble Kaitlynn would have finding a private place for a quickie, but if anyone could do it, Kaitlynn could.

Feeling a little more comfortable with her surroundings now, she found herself looking forward to meeting the other women. Maybe she'd have a girls' vacation, after all.

CHAPTER 2

JACKSON WOKE at the sound of his infant daughter's gurgle. Rolling over, he reached to turn up the nightlight and make sure she was okay.

She lay on her back, her eyes closed, her fist pressed to her mouth as she slurped at it in her sleep. Relieved that nothing was wrong, he turned down the light and lay on his back too, but not before noticing it was just after 04:00.

Clasping his hands behind his head, he stared at the ceiling, forcing himself to think of the chores he had in the morning before taking Tabitha to the doctor for a checkup. He was paranoid about his daughter. The fear that he would do something wrong and she would die was strong, too strong. He'd seen so many people die—men, women, all the children.

On the one hand, he resented that she was his, while on the other hand, he wanted to be around her constantly to protect her. He was a psychological mess. Why the Army psychiatrist had allowed him out into the civilian world was a mystery. It seemed having PTSD, a baby he hadn't known existed, and a desire to stay in Syria was enough to get a man honorably discharged. Who knew?

Then again, the Army had ulterior motives for getting him out. Major Gabriella Rossi had pulled one over on them as well as him by hiding her pregnancy, and the Army wasn't happy. Because she was dead, they'd taken the brunt of their anger out on him. Even as he thought of the woman who was the mother of his child, his stomach clenched. Gabby had used him for her own purposes: to get pregnant. He'd been an idiot. Even though she was a superior officer, the fact that she was a gorgeous blonde with all the full curves he enjoyed had swayed him. That and her golden tongue. Disgusted with himself, he rolled on his side to look at his daughter in her new crib.

She slept peacefully, no longer sucking on her fist. He envied her. She had no idea she'd been born in a war-torn country to parents who were, at best, acquaintances. She was unaware that her mother was gone and her father fucked up. It seemed like she should somehow have that running through her brain synapses, but she was blissfully ignorant. And he wanted to keep her that way. He just didn't know how.

The heavy-duty watch on his wrist vibrated, telling him it was time to get up. Quietly, he rose on the other side of the bed, watching Tabitha for any sign she was waking. He opened the door of his room wide and waited a moment to make sure she was still sound asleep. Then, leaving it open, he stepped across the hall into the bathroom. He was showered and ready for the day in thirteen minutes.

Back in his room, he silently dressed in a pair of Army green sweatpants and the same colored T-shirt. Tabitha had been sleeping until almost 05:30 lately, which gave him some time in the morning. After slipping on a pair of sneakers, he opened the app on his phone that communicated with the baby camera monitor he had set up in his room, which allowed him to keep watch and hear any noises. Then he quietly slipped out, closing the door gently.

As he walked down the hall toward the kitchen, he watched his daughter on the app, making sure her breathing was even. Her little lungs were so small, her breaths seemed too short, but the doctor at the base had assured him she was normal.

"Good morning, Jackson. Coffee's almost ready."

He looked up from his phone to find Amanda Hayden, Dunn now, setting out cups next to the coffee maker. He still didn't understand how his oldest brother could have married a Hayden, but then again, he didn't want to understand. It was enough to just get through the day with his sanity intact.

"So, what do you think of our first set of guests?" Amanda poured coffee into a cup and slid it over the island counter toward the first stool that was near him.

He clipped his phone to his sweatpants and accepted the cup but remained standing. "I only met one, so I couldn't tell you."

She smirked. "One? Wow, that's one more than I expected you'd talk to."

He ignored her sarcasm as he ignored everyone's. He used to enjoy it and give as much as he got, but it seemed juvenile now. He took a sip of the steamy brew. It wasn't as strong as he liked it, but it would do. "I'm going for my run. Tabitha shouldn't wake until after I get back."

Amanda waved her hand. "No worries. If she wakes, I'll be sure to get her."

He stiffened. Now the fact that a Hayden was his brother's wife mattered. "Is Isaac not up yet?"

Amanda's smile didn't quite reach her eyes. She wasn't stupid. She was well aware of his prejudice against her. "Not yet. He had the night off last night. I'm sure he'll be up soon since your father likes to be dressed before breakfast."

That was a subtle hint that Isaac was his father's certified nursing assistant and not a nanny. That might be true, but Isaac doted on Tabitha and made a better protector. "Good. I'll talk to Isaac about officially becoming Tabitha's nanny. I'm sure you can find another CNA with all your contacts." The last word came out in a sneer.

Amanda's eyes narrowed, but he ignored her. Everyone knew the Haydens were a greedy bunch. He took one more gulp of the hot coffee before heading out the front door.

Continuing down the porch steps, he breathed deeply before stopping to stretch his arms over his head. He looked up at the dark sky and took another deep, cleansing breath. He dropped his hands and turned to head down the ATV road into the ranch but caught himself before he took a step. That way led past the stable, the corral, and the bunkhouses. There was little chance the city folk would be up yet, but he wasn't taking any chances.

Instead, he turned toward the Rocky Road's infamous one mile driveway when he heard a sound behind the barn. It sounded like scratching on plastic. That was no guest, at least not the human kind. He strode over to the barn and opened the door before he switched on the overhead light. The sound stopped, so he waited. After less than a few minutes, it started again.

What the hell? Quietly, he moved past the stalls, stopping when the sound stopped. When he was almost to where they kept the ATV, a panicked screech sounded on the opposite side of the barn. Rushing forward, he found one of the square plastic trash barrels rocking. He leapt forward and held it steady to keep it from tipping over. Whatever was inside wanted out in the worst way.

His mind quickly catalogued the various critters it could be, all of which could do damage to a man but nothing he couldn't handle. When a soft whimper sounded from inside, he had a feeling whatever it was had worn itself out. With no warning, he threw the cover over the side and jumped back.

Nothing emerged.

Cautiously, he stepped forward and looked into the trash can. A young raccoon looked up at him as it pressed itself into the corner.

"Well, look who's here. How'd you get locked in the barn?"

The raccoon stared at him as its body shook with fear. It was a well-fed raccoon, so it knew where the food sources were, but he wasn't fully grown yet.

"Not to worry. I have no bone to pick with you. I'm just going to tip this over, and you can leave. But not here. I have a feeling you don't want to be in the barn ever again." He closed the lid, and a tiny whimper escaped.

The sound tugged at his heart, as it was so similar to a

sound his daughter made before she started to cry. Actually, the raccoon's screech was eerily similar to Tabitha's crying.

He tipped the trash can just enough so it would roll on its two wheels and brought it outside. After turning off the lights and closing the barn door again, he opened the trash can lid. It was darker outside, but the raccoon's eyes reflected the ambient light. "You ready?"

It didn't make a sound, so he slowly tipped the can until it lay on its side. "Okay. You can go home now."

When the critter didn't immediately run out, he tapped his hand on the bottom of the trash can to encourage an exit, but the raccoon remained inside. He could just tip it out, but the fear emanating from that animal had him rethinking that.

"Okay. I'm going for a run, and you can leave whenever you want. Got it?"

He didn't expect an answer. Even as he thought about it, he was sure the Army psyche doc would have something to say about him talking to a raccoon or even letting one leave on its own. After four tours overseas, he was done with seeing innocents hurt, so screw the shrinks.

He walked away so the raccoon could see he was leaving and started out of the dirt yard in a jog. Though he'd grown up on the ranch, he'd rarely run down the driveway, so he took his time. No sprinting on this route. Luckily, he didn't need to work up a heavy sweat since it felt to be in the mid-fifties.

He kept scanning the dark desert landscape, foregoing the actual drive to run beside it where the terrain was smoother. The hour or so just before dawn was his favorite time of day. It was when everything was calm and preparations for an attack or a convoy could be made without distractions. He always thought best at this time of day.

It was his third week back home, and he still felt as if he didn't belong. Everything had changed on the ranch. His brother marrying their enemy's daughter, his dad half paralyzed from a stroke, Tanner turning the ranch into a vacation destination, and his youngest brother, Brody, heading out to become a wildlife manager for the state after his Christmas Eve wedding. It didn't feel like home anymore, except when he was out working. Then, for a little while, he could forget about all the changes.

After reaching hard-packed Mesquite Road, he turned around and headed back the way he'd come. He needed to just focus on two tasks: caring for his daughter and working the ranch. He craved routine. Hiring Isaac, if he'd agree, would be a start, a step forward, something the Army psychologist had told him he needed to do. With no one telling him what he had to do every day, he had to start deciding that for himself. Then again, Tanner had a big say in that, which was also weird since he'd always taken his orders from Dad.

The sky was starting to lighten, not so much that anyone inside would notice, but for people like him who ran in the dark, the difference was obvious. Ahead on the other side of the drive, it looked like a saguaro cactus was moving. Great. Just what he needed, hallucinations on top of everything else that was wrong with him. He moved his gaze away from the walking plant and focused on where he was running. Unfamiliar territory meant he needed to keep a higher alert status.

As the terrain grew easier to discern, he swept his gaze

ahead again, hoping there were no more walking cacti. But instead of relief, he tensed as his steps slowed. "What the fuck?" Though he said the words under his breath, they sounded loud in the stillness of the early dawn.

One of the guests was walking down the driveway. Did they despise the accommodation so much they were walking home? He didn't want company, never mind one who was a guest at the ranch. He'd just continue jogging by and nod if they said anything. But as he grew closer, the silhouette became familiar. Damn, if it wasn't the woman from the barn. Though he faced the lightening sky and couldn't see her face, he would bet his truck he was right.

He was barely fifty yards away when she appeared to notice him because she suddenly stopped.

Just jog by and nod. When he was within fifty feet, she walked across the driveway. "Hey, Jackson. Looks like I'm not the only early riser."

Just jog by and say "morning." No need to stop. He drew closer, and she stepped past the driveway and right into his path.

Shit. He slowed to a stop. "What are you doing out here?"

She shrugged. "I don't sleep well in strange beds. Rather than wake anyone, I decided to come out for a walk."

"Don't do that. It's dangerous."

Her brows drew together. "That's why you're out here jogging? Because it's dangerous?"

"No, I ..." A small part of him was telling him he should be polite, but he didn't have it in him. "I'm out here so I can be alone."

Instead of taking the hint, she nodded. "I can understand that. Living alone makes that easy, but when you're part of a family, I imagine that gets a little trickier."

Family? He wasn't getting away from family. He was running down the goddamn driveway because he didn't want to run into guests! "It's too dangerous out here. You can't see where you're going, and there are rattlesnakes, tarantulas, and wild burros."

"I know. I was watching for the snakes and spiders but didn't realize you had burros on your ranch. I hear they can be ornery. Isn't the ranch fenced in?"

Maybe he should just let her keep walking. But as much as he wanted to, his childhood upbringing refused to allow her to walk alone down the drive. "Only where the cattle are. Come back to the ranch. You can hang out in the clubhouse. The cook is probably in there, and you could talk to him if you need company."

"I don't need company. I'm content being alone, but I will come back with you since I'm less familiar with burros than I am with spiders and snakes."

Relieved she was going back toward the barracks, he forced himself to walk with her instead of jogging on ahead. As long as she walked in silence, he could cope with that.

She immediately spoke. "I grew up in Buckeye, so I know a bit about the desert. I moved to Show Low for a job opportunity."

He didn't respond, instead unclipping his phone to check on the monitor in the hope that she'd stop talking.

"My family is scattered all over Arizona. My older sister teaches at ASU in Tempe, and my younger sister is up in

Flagstaff. She's a paramedic. My mom moved to Glendale about three years ago. It's a little weird at the holidays because she's in an apartment now, so we have to rotate gatherings between the three girls."

Comfortable that his daughter still slept, he reclipped his phone but remained silent. Was the woman's dad in the picture? Not that it mattered. Still, as she granted his wish and remained silent, the not knowing niggled at his brain like a stone in his boot, irritating the hell out of him. Determinedly, he clenched his jaw, refusing to learn any more. That stone could just keep scratching at his brain as far as he was concerned.

They reached the dirt yard, and she halted, turning toward him. "Thank you for educating me on the dangers around here, Jackson." She held out her hand. "By the way, I'm Danielle, but people just call me 'Dani.'"

He grasped her hand out of habit; however, his response was anything but. "What about your father?"

Her grip loosened, and she withdrew her hand from his, then began playing with a thin bracelet on her other wrist. "He's gone. I think I'll head to the clubhouse now. Maybe the cook will tell me what to expect for meals this week. I like planning ahead." In the growing daylight, she smiled before striding toward the barn.

Gone? What did that mean?

It wasn't until she started to bend down toward the green garbage can on the side of the barn that he remembered the raccoon. Just as her hand grabbed the top to pull it up, the damn critter ran out, causing her to screech and fall back on her ass as the raccoon made a beeline for him.

He figured it would run around him and head into the brittlebushes near the fencing on the west side of the house. But the next thing he knew, it had run up his leg, around his back, and up onto his shoulder.

"What the fuck?" He started to reach up to throw the critter off.

Dani started to laugh. "I never figured you for the owner of a pet raccoon. Maybe a pet mountain lion, but a raccoon?"

He stilled at her words. "Pet? This thing isn't my pet."

The raccoon started to chatter loudly. Or at least it seemed loud in the quiet early dawn.

She rose and brushed off her ass. "Well, I'm not going to tell him or her that. He's already mad at me as it is. I'll leave you to your furry friend and see what's cooking in the clubhouse. See you around."

As Dani walked between the buildings and disappeared from sight, the raccoon's vocalizations quieted. It really did seem that the critter didn't like her, which might be a stupid thought, but it made him feel like he and the raccoon had something in common. They didn't like strangers on the ranch.

"Okay, fella, you can get down now."

Obviously, the raccoon didn't understand English because not only didn't it move, but it grabbed the back of his head as if it were planning to hang out while he walked.

He had to admit he wasn't too sure how to get the animal down without getting scratched or upsetting it. Too bad Brody was living at Hannah's, or he'd just go in and wake him up and ask what he should do. Looking around for somewhere to deposit the critter, he spotted the bench on the porch.

"Okay, buddy. We're going over there to sit, and then you can get down. Got the mission?"

Of course, the raccoon didn't make a sound, but as Jackson started to walk, he felt it hold onto the back of his head. If he had a full head of hair like Brody, that would be fine, but with his almost-shaved head, it was a little painful. He'd felt far worse, so he just ignored it.

Once on the porch, he sat slowly and leaned back. Now the raccoon could easily climb down. Unfortunately, it didn't seem inclined to move, but its hand on his head had loosened its grip. He patted the bench seat. "Come sit here."

The animal sniffed in the general vicinity but didn't move.

He looked at his watch. Tabitha would be waking up soon. "Come on. I know you can climb that far." Since the raccoon was on his right shoulder, he held his arm out so it made a slide to the seat. When the raccoon still didn't move, he used his other hand to push it gently in the direction it needed to go.

It finally got the message and climbed down to sit next to him and investigate his watch. Carefully removing his hand, he rose. "I'm going inside now. You better go home. I'm sure someone is looking for you."

Just then, the front door opened three feet away, and the raccoon scooted back up onto his shoulder. "Well, fuck."

Tanner turned at his exclamation. "Is that a raccoon?"

"No, it's an elephant. Of course it's a damn raccoon."

"Hmph. Looks good riding shotgun on your shoulder.

When you get back from Tabby's doctor's appointment, I'll need you to help Layne finish the petting zoo fencing. We set it up on the east side of the birthing enclosure."

As Tanner started down the steps, Jackson pointed at him. "Her name is 'Tabitha,' and you need to go back in the house and get me one of Cami's balls."

Tanner turned to face him. "I don't have to do anything. This isn't the Army. This is a ranch and a friendly one at that. It's about time you remembered that."

Jackson ground his teeth and refrained from shouting because he could feel the raccoon tensing on his shoulder. "Fine. Would you mind terribly retrieving one of Cami's balls so I can give this critter something to occupy his time with before my daughter wakes up and wonders where I am?"

Tanner's shoulders slumped when he finally realized the gravity of the situation. "Of course. I forgot what time it is, but you explaining certainly makes sense." Tanner strode back up the steps and into the house.

Jackson unclipped his phone and checked on his daughter. She still slept, but that could change at any moment. After returning the phone to his waist, he turned his head toward the raccoon but could see only the belly. "You do know you're causing me a lot of trouble, right?"

The damn thing started scratching his head. "Hey, stop that." He covered his head with his hand, but the critter tried to get its nose under his fingers, which actually tickled. "Okay, okay, but no scratching."

The raccoon sniffed at his head, then crawled around his neck to his left shoulder. At least it wasn't super big, but it was definitely an adult and well fed at that.

The front door opened again, and the critter gave a low growl.

Great. Just what he needed, a raccoon bodyguard. "Just leave it on the bench here." He backed up so the raccoon didn't attack his brother.

Tanner shook his head after placing the ball on the seat. "I hope you don't plan to keep that thing."

Even though he'd thought of the raccoon as a "thing" himself, coming from Tanner, the word choice bothered him. "I haven't decided yet. We just met." He didn't bat an eyelash as Tanner stared at him.

"Just keep it away from the guests." Tanner strode away between the barn and house and out of sight, no doubt heading to the clubhouse to see how the cook was doing.

"Okay, I have something for you." He moved back to the bench and sat, but the raccoon was on the wrong shoulder. So he picked up the ball.

The raccoon made a grab for it, and he quickly stretched his arm out. "You want this?"

The critter crawled over his head to his other shoulder.

Remembering what happened the last time he'd coaxed the animal to get down, he lowered his arms and dropped the ball on the porch. It rolled a few inches and stopped.

Immediately, the raccoon crawled down to the bench and lay down, reaching for the ball with his hand.

Jackson stood and stepped away. "Have fun with that. It's all yours. Cami has plenty."

As the raccoon continued to reach for the ball that was just a bit too far, Jackson moved to the other end of the porch and jumped off before striding back in front to jog up the stairs and into the house.

Tabitha would be awake any minute now. As he headed down the hall, he passed by the window where the bench sat and saw that the raccoon was still there but had somehow managed to grab his toy and now sat like he lived there. Good for him.

Now, if only he could feel as comfortable in his own life, it would be a rosy world, but since he didn't, he'd just have to make do.

CHAPTER 3

DANI SMILED as she listened to the conversation between Kaitlynn and one of their bunkmates. Kaitlynn was enthralling the woman with her adventures at the Rockhaven drill site. That one had been a bear. If Dani remembered correctly, she'd had to reschedule multiple times because the guys were ignoring the safety protocols, complaining that they took too long. The men had been quite vocal about it, too.

Not like Mr. Jackson Dunn, who didn't like to talk at all. Getting words from that man was like getting water from a stone or any of the other common idioms. He was tight-lipped, closemouthed, and as silent as they came. Number 5 on her Mr. Right list was "willing to talk." There was nothing worse than trying to get a man to talk. She had wanted someone who would be her partner in everything. That didn't happen without conversation.

It still hurt that her plans for the future had not panned out. Yes, she was only twenty-seven, but she'd accomplished everything else. She had a job she enjoyed, owned her own home, was on her way to a comfortable—

"Dani, is that the truth?"

Startled from her mulling, she looked toward Kaitlynn. "I'm sorry. I didn't catch that."

Kaitlynn rolled her eyes. "Monica doesn't believe me that I left Axel on the site."

"Oh, she did. And guess who had to drive out and get him."

Monica, a woman in her early twenties with very short brown hair and dark brown eyes, grinned. "You did."

Kaitlynn nodded. "Yup. Dani's our safety officer, and she said it wasn't safe leaving him in the middle of the desert in triple-digit heat. Wimp."

Dani shook her head. That was when she and Kaitlynn had become friends. She'd asked Kaitlynn to have drinks with her, thinking she could talk sense into her, only to end up completely siding with her. "Wimp or not, OSHA would have shut us down, and I'd be out of a job."

"Crap, what time is it?" Kaitlynn jumped up from her chair.

Monica looked at her phone. "It's almost time for dinner. We have about ten minutes."

"I gotta go."

In an instant, Kaitlynn had crammed her new straw cowboy hat on her head and was out the door.

Dani was quite sure Kaitlynn was meeting someone, though who was anyone's guess. She'd been flirting with guests and ranch hands alike. "Monica, do you suppose we should wander outside and see what they're grilling for our dinner?"

Monica rose and placed the book she'd been reading on her bunk. "According to the archery instructor, it's supposed to be ribs, corn on the cob, baked beans, green beans, sweet potatoes, salad, cornbread, watermelon, and cookies."

"Holy crap. I'm going to gain twenty pounds staying here for two weeks."

"No, you won't. I hear we need to eat a lot tonight for the cattle work tomorrow. I can't wait! What did you do today?"

She couldn't help smirking. "I went to a lecture on staying healthy and then sat in the hot tub."

Monica's eyes rounded. "There's a hot tub?"

She nodded. It definitely helped to go exploring. She was never one for guided tours. "Let's go see how the feast is coming. If it's as good as what the cook prepared for breakfast, we are going to get full fast."

"I agree." Monica opened the door, and they stepped out.

There were three other women sitting on the porch, and they joined them on their trek to the center of the open square. Dani felt like she was part of a ranch tour already. That would never happen. If she was going to be stuck on the Rocky Road Ranch for vacation, she was doing what she wanted.

The yard between the four buildings was already lit with lanterns, and four large picnic tables were laid out with checkered tablecloths, but not the cheap plastic kind. That was a nice touch. She scanned the crowd slowly converging, looking for Kaitlynn, and spotted Jackson in a serious conversation with Brody. Now that she thought of it, she hadn't seen the man smile. He was a mystery to be solved, and she added it to her mental list of to-do items while at the ranch.

"Hey, Dani, there you are." Kaitlynn hooked her arm with her as if she'd been looking for her.

"Yup, here I am." She lowered her voice. "And where were you, or should I say who were you with?"

Kaitlynn's gaze shifted toward a guest in a new black cowboy hat, probably bought at the little half-empty gift shop in the corner of the clubhouse. "Nowhere in particular, but the kisses were excellent."

She held her hand up. "Spare me the details."

Kaitlynn laughed as she guided them toward the end of one of the picnic tables before letting go. "I had the best day. Can you believe they let me handle a gun and even shoot it?"

Dani widened her eyes in pretend shock before frowning. "I really need to talk to their safety officer."

"Oh, please. You're not at work. Let it go."

Kaitlynn was right, but safety came naturally to her. She found herself checking the fencing around the pool, the strength of the steps to the bunkhouse, and even the roughened floor of the shower to keep people from slipping. "I know, but it's only day two. It will take a while."

"Okay, folks, grab a plate and help yourselves." Tanner rang the iron triangle on the porch of the clubhouse, and people started to line up.

As Kaitlynn immediately headed to the line, Dani waited. There was no rush since she hadn't done anything strenuous to work up a big appetite. She probably should do something tomorrow to at least get a look at the ranch. Maybe a hike or a horseback ride, depending on what they were offering.

Her gaze wandered from the line in front of the buffet to the man now standing alone, scowling. She followed his line of sight and found Brody talking to Tanner's wife, who shrugged her shoulders before turning to join her husband. Brody turned and looked at Jackson and shook his head.

She was almost as far away from Jackson as she could get and still be in the yard, but she swore she could see every muscle in his body tense from his pectorals to his neck—though, to be fair, his lower half was covered in jeans and boots.

Almost as if her gaze had triggered his senses, he turned and looked straight at her.

It was the movement more than the look that had her tensing. Surely she couldn't have done anything wrong. She was a guest.

That's when he started toward her.

Well, if she'd done something wrong, she was about to find out. Though his long, angry stride took less than ten seconds to eat up the ground between them, she still felt as if she were waiting for her boss to go off on her, as he did on occasion, which just had her planting her feet and crossing her arms.

When he got to her, he halted but didn't say anything. No surprise there. So she did. "Hello, Jackson."

He gave a short nod.

"Are you joining us for dinner?"

Irritation flashed in his eyes before he unclenched his jaw. "I am."

Since he didn't say anything more, she didn't either, taking the time to study him and give him a taste of his own medicine. He really was a big man, and when he gritted his teeth, which she was positive he was doing, his angular jaw looked chiseled out of stone. So did his torso, for that matter. How did he find time to work out while ranching? He must do so, because his brothers weren't nearly as built.

"What?" The word came out in a growl.

"Nothing. Why?" She had a feeling they could have an entire conversation with one- and two-word sentences. She was game.

"You're staring at me."

Well, there he had to go and ruin it with four words. "Yup." She bit down hard to keep from grinning.

His brows lowered. "Why?"

Oh, good. He was playing again. She shrugged. "I'm trying to figure out why you're scowling."

He scowled harder, and she bit down to keep from laughing outright. "I was told I have to eat with the guests or starve."

"Maybe you should fill two plates and squirrel one away. Then you could skip the crowd tomorrow."

His face relaxed as he studied her. "I eat two platefuls at dinner."

That was interesting. "If you want, I could fill a second plate so it's not so obvious."

"And will you hide my dinner for tomorrow in your bunkhouse?"

"There's no refrigerator in there. You can't eat ribs that have been at room temperature all night."

Shaking his head, he held his hand out toward the dwindling line of people as others started sitting at the table with their plates. "Let's see how much we can carry."

She uncrossed her arms and started forward. Jackson fell into step with her, walking neither ahead nor behind. She wasn't sure what to make of that, so she ignored it as they reached the picnic table with the spread, and she took a plate. Despite the fact that everyone except the Dunn family had already filled their plates, there was still enough left to feed them all again tomorrow.

She turned and gave a plate to Jackson. "One or two?"

"Two."

She handed him a second one before moving forward. She filled her plate with more than she expected. It just all smelled so good. When she couldn't fit anymore, she stepped away to head back to her table, only to find him waiting for her, two full dinner plates in his hands. She laughed and then headed back to the picnic table.

She took a seat across from Kaitlynn, and Jackson slid in next to her at the end.

Kaitlynn's gaze immediately devoured him. "Well, hello."

Not wanting Kaitlynn to get too excited, Dani made the introductions. "Kaitlynn, this is Jackson Dunn. Jackson, Kaitlynn Salkowski."

"Oh, you're one of the owners." Kaitlynn leaned forward as if to impart a secret. "The sights on this ranch are truly breathtaking."

Dani stifled a groan as Kaitlynn gave him her signature soft-eyed look.

Jackson just nodded, continuing to chew the mouthful he

had taken just as Kaitlynn had leaned in. Had he timed that purposefully? She'd bet he had. He may not say much, but he wasn't dumb.

Kaitlynn smiled coyly at Jackson. "Tell me. Do you give private tours of the ranch?"

Dani held down a smirk. Asking yes-or-no questions of Jackson was going to get Kaitlynn nowhere fast.

Jackson actually didn't even answer. He just shook his head before taking another mouthful of pork ribs.

Dani felt the need to protect him, so she switched topics, which always worked. "Kaitlynn, you said you were at the shooting range. How'd you do?"

Kaitlynn chuckled even as she shook her head. "Well, let's put it this way. If someone needed me to keep a crowd of enemies at bay, I'd be their woman. But if I needed to pick off an active shooter, I'd be worthless."

"So you missed the target." Dani gave Kaitlynn a sympathetic look.

"Not necessarily. I hit a lot of targets. They just weren't mine." Kaitlynn laughed before giving Jackson a wink. "I'm much better with bigger machinery."

Dani quickly explained. "Kaitlynn works on one of our drill teams. We mostly mine copper."

Jackson actually looked curious, but before he could ask a question, Kaitlynn beat him to it.

"What's that you're wearing around your neck?" Kaitlynn was back to focusing on what she considered a potential bedmate. It wasn't that she slept around. She just didn't like not having a lover for very long, and she had dumped her last one about three weeks ago. "Why do you keep what's on your necklace hidden?"

"It's a gift from Uncle Sam." That Jackson answered was a surprise in itself, though it made complete sense. That he was military would explain his fitness and bulk over his brothers'.

Before Kaitlynn could say something stupid, Dani jumped in. "They're dog tags. He's military."

"*Was* military." The words were spoken low, as if he were embarrassed by that fact.

"Oh, then you're a cowboy and a hero." Kaitlynn set her elbow on the table and cradled her chin in her hand. "Did you ever see any action?"

Dani felt the tension emanating from Jackson at Kaitlynn's question. Shit. Something bad must have happened. Still feeling protective, she spoke before he could respond. "You know, I meant to get some watermelon for dessert. Jackson, would you be willing to get some for me?"

Jackson immediately rose. "Sure."

As he strode away, she turned to Kaitlynn. "You need to leave him alone."

"What? Don't tell me you're interested? I thought the big muscular ones were a no-go for your list."

"They are, not that it matters because I burned the list. And no, I'm not interested. I just know from talking to him that he's not happy about this whole dude ranch venture his family has started and is not interested in guests."

Kaitlynn's eyes widened. "You got that much out of him?"

She nodded, seeing no reason to explain she overheard him talking to his horse.

"Hmm, that's too bad. He has great potential."

Dani nodded to the man Kaitlynn had been kissing. "What about him?"

Kaitlynn looked to her right, where there was a long line of people sitting between her and the man on the opposite end of the table. "You mean Artie? He has possibilities—more than I thought. He's from Pinetop, so a lot closer to me than any cowboy working here would be. But it's only day two. There are six men in the singles bunkhouse, and I've barely scratched the surface of getting to know them."

"You do realize that this isn't a dating service, right?"

"Oh, but it could be."

"Not really." Dani waved her hand toward the other tables. "There are kids around."

Kaitlynn shrugged. "But that makes it more exciting, having to keep any shenanigans out of sight."

"'Shenanigans'? Where'd that word come from?"

Kaitlynn grinned. "Artie."

"Here you go." Jackson set down a plate with watermelon and two chocolate chip cookies. "I have to get back to work. Ladies." He gave a short nod and strode away.

"He'd drive me crazy with all that chatter." Kaitlynn laughed before reaching across and snagging a cookie.

Dani stared at the plate, surprised by the thoughtfulness of the added treats. She'd been determined to avoid the cookies after the healthy living lecture earlier but was touched that Jackson had added them. Picking one up, she bit into it and barely stopped herself from sighing. They were exactly how she liked them, crusty on the outside, gooey on the inside, and still warm.

She stopped chewing for a moment. Did that describe Jackson as well? She turned to see where he had gone, but he'd already disappeared. Turning back, she took another bite, mulling over the mystery of Jackson Dunn. He had effectively failed to meet another of her Mr. Right criteria: no military, police, firefighter, or other heroic professional. But the fact that he admitted he was a veteran did help explain a few things about him, like his taciturn demeanor, his overly developed physique, and his serious ways.

The question was, did that also account for his angry mood? Or, more importantly, why was she so determined to find out?

CHAPTER 4

JACKSON PULLED out the final clump of dirt with the post-hole digger and then stepped aside. "You need help with that post, old man?"

Layne's dark bushy mustache twitched before he grabbed up the post and settled it over his shoulder. "I thought they taught you respect in the Army."

"They did—for superior officers." He looked around. "I don't see any around here."

"Wiseass. I can still have you fired."

"I wish." He gave an exaggerated sigh. After his mom passed, he'd spent every spare moment at Layne's house until he graduated high school. He'd liked getting lost in the mix of Layne's large family, plus he'd looked up to Layne, who was eight years older and always seemed to have his shit together when the world was falling apart.

Layne placed the post in the hole and held it. "Then what would you do?"

He started shoveling the dirt around the post. Layne

always seemed to ask the tough questions. What would he do? He had no idea. He'd thought he'd die fighting for his country to make up for what happened to his brother.

He leaned on the shovel. "I don't know. I didn't have a plan for the future." He certainly hadn't expected to have a baby, ever. It was a good thing Isaac knew babies and was able to watch Tabitha.

"You knew you'd be getting out of the Army eventually, right? Or did you expect to stay in and move up the ranks?"

"Fuck no. I went as far as I wanted. Once you get to major, what's called a staff sergeant on the enlisted side where I am—I mean, was—you end up doing more paperwork and babysitting than really helping. It gets political. I just wanted to fight the bad guys and protect as many of my guys as I could."

"Did you?" Though Layne's voice sounded casual, his gaze was keen.

He was so used to people not knowing him well, it was easy to forget that Layne knew him better than even his family. "Yeah, I did." He set the shovel aside and grabbed up the post-hole digger.

"Then that means you can let go of that brick house of guilt over Devlin's death that you've been carrying all these years."

He stabbed the post-hole digger into the ground with all the frustration he felt before pulling up dirt and thrusting it in again. No matter how many men he saved, it didn't make him feel better. Even the horrors he'd seen in Syria didn't mitigate his role in his brother's death.

"Don't go too deep."

At Layne's comment, he halted. Damn, if he hadn't already. "Couldn't you have said something sooner?" He pushed some of the dirt back in until he gauged the hole to be as deep as the others.

"I was waiting for your answer."

He looked over at Layne. "My answer is no."

"Shit, Jackson. If you didn't get that off your back after all these years, you need some professional help because, man, you're messed up."

He snorted as he retrieved the shovel. "Tell me something I don't know."

"I'll tell you what you don't know. How to build a future for you and your daughter. It's not all about you anymore. Whether you like it or not, you need to make some decisions, whether it's to raise her here on the ranch or buy your own place in a neighborhood where she can grow up with other kids." Layne paused. "Unless you want to give her up for adoption to two people who have their act together."

"No!" His answer was immediate and based on instinct alone. "She's *my* daughter. The DNA tests proved that. I may not have wanted her or planned on her, but she's here, and she's *mine*."

"I'm glad to hear it. That means you'll get yourself some professional help and learn what you need to know to raise her. Now, fill this hole in so we can get this done before the end of day."

He shoveled the dirt against the pole, Layne's words digging deep into his mind. His friend was right, as usual. It was now about Tabitha. If he could focus on her, he might be able to find some balance in civilian life.

Packing in the dirt, he stepped back. "That post's not going anywhere."

"Good. Now, get digging. I'll go grab another one." Layne headed for the pile of posts on the trailer.

Jackson turned in the opposite direction toward the line of spray-painted X's on the ground. Quickly, he picked up his tools and brought them to the next post position as a distant line of horses drew closer. "Fuck." Just what he needed, a bunch of city dwellers gawking at him and Layne working. Driving the post-hole digger into the ground, he turned his back to the approaching riders.

Layne walked up and set the post on the ground, holding it upright as he waved to the group. "Howdy, folks. Miss Amanda."

"Hello, Layne. Can you explain to everyone what you and Jackson are working on?"

Jackson continued to dig, not in a hurry to be social.

"Of course." Layne sounded far too happy to oblige. "You see, folks, the Dunns here have decided to add a petting zoo pen for our guests as another activity. So we are setting the posts that will hold the fenced enclosure. It will need different fencing because it's not for cows."

"What will be in it?"

Jackson recognized the voice as belonging to Dani's friend Kaitlynn.

Layne responded smartly. "Well, miss, what would you like to be in it?"

"I don't know. Maybe goats and a burro. Any chance you could have a bobcat?"

Amanda replied to Kaitlynn before Layne could answer.

"We welcome all suggestions. If you all could write down your ideas on your comment sheets this evening, we can start planning."

Just when Jackson thought they'd all move on, a man's voice added to the conversation. "That looks like hard work. Son, would you like to help?"

Jackson pulled out the last bunch of soil, happy to hand over the post-hole digger to anyone who wanted it, but he didn't turn around.

A young male voice answered his father. "No thanks. I thought we were going to see the petroglyphs."

Amanda chuckled. "Don't worry, we are. But if anyone would prefer to help set posts, you're welcome to join them. Right, Layne?"

"Absolutely. We're always looking for a few good men."

"And women?"

Jackson turned at the sound of Dani's voice.

Layne coughed over his stumble. "Miss, we are happy to have anyone."

"Good answer." Amanda nodded before urging her horse, Breeze, forward, the group following behind as they moved down the ATV road.

As Dani drew even with where they were working, she halted before dismounting and walking her horse toward them. She wore a pair of worn black cowboy boots, blue jeans, a light maroon sweater, and a straw cowboy hat, fitting in more with the ranch now. For the first time, he noticed how attractive she was. She didn't have the fair features and extra curves he usually went for, but there was something in her walk. Confidence? Contentment? It actually reminded him of Layne in a weird way. He pointed toward the departing riders. "You're going to miss seeing the petroglyphs?"

She shrugged. "I'm sure I can see them another day, if I want. I'm not great with following the leader."

"Good thing you weren't under my command, then." He frowned, imagining having to keep her in line and pretty sure it would be a futile endeavor.

"No worries about that. I was destined for other things, like keeping risk-takers safe." She tied her horse's reins to a large mesquite tree nearby.

Layne strode over. "I'm guessing you two have already met. I'm Layne." He held out his hand.

Dani stepped forward and shook it. "It's nice to meet you, Layne. You're the second-in-command of the ranch, from what I understand. So I expect you're the one I should talk to about how I can help here."

"You really want to help?"

She crossed her arms over her chest. "No, I thought I'd just stand here and look pretty."

Jackson liked her comment but kept silent, curious about how this would all play out. Layne expected to get the holes done and was still getting used to having Vic around, their one female ranch hand. He was all about women roping and helping on a cattle drive, but he did have a few old-fashioned ideas.

"You're doing a damn fine job at that, too." Layne certainly didn't disappoint, but Jackson had a feeling what his friend meant as a compliment would not be taken in quite that way.

Dani's brows rose before her gaze raked over Layne, from the top of his white cowboy hat to the square toes of his cowboy boots and back. "You know, Layne, I'm thinking you do a better job than me at looking pretty, so why don't you hand over the pole and give Jackson and me something to gaze at while we work."

Layne's jaw dropped, and his mouth opened, but nothing came out.

Secretly pleased at how quickly Dani came back at Layne, Jackson dropped the hole digger and lifted the shovel. "I don't like the idea of anyone just standing around. Dani, would you mind shoveling in the dirt while Layne holds the pole? That would allow me to go to the next spot and start digging."

She turned toward him and uncrossed her arms, her lips twitching. "I suppose that's a better idea." Walking toward him, she held her hand out, and he gave her the shovel. She looked back at Layne. "You coming?"

Jackson didn't wait to see what Layne's reaction was, as he didn't want either of them to see how amusing he found them. Though it was probably the first time he'd been amused in a long time.

He stopped at the next X on the ground and started digging. Halfway down, he glanced toward the other pole to find Layne stamping at the dirt around it and Dani with her arms crossed again.

Jackson went back to digging. What kind of woman came to a dude ranch on a free two-week vacation and then skipped a leisurely ride in favor of fence work? She also seemed to know a little about horses since she'd dismounted easily and tied her mount to the nearby tree.

When he finished the hole, he found Dani standing nearby, and she clearly had something to say. He leaned on the hole digger. "What?"

She jerked her head toward the area where Layne had gone to retrieve another post. "Your friend there needs to learn something about women. Like coming into the twenty-first century."

He shook his head. "That's not going to happen."

She lifted her chin and locked her hazel gaze on him. "What about you?"

"Me? You mean, as in what I believe women can do?" At her nod, he continued. "Trust me, I've seen women outperform men more than once in the service. From mechanics to marksman, I've seen them leave some of my men in the dust."

"Did you command any women?"

"I did, and I reported to a couple as well." He'd even slept with one far above him. At the reminder of Major Rossi, his daughter's mother, he stiffened. She'd betrayed him in the worst way and didn't even know it, nor ever would.

"Was it hard taking orders from a woman? Did you ever send women into combat?"

Dani's questions, as innocent as they were, didn't sit well with him. It wasn't her fault, but he couldn't stomach the emotions roiling around in his gut. "I have to dig another hole."

Her eyes rounded at his brusque response, but he kept walking. Yes, he was an ass. It was who he'd become. Then why'd he feel like a heel at her reaction?

He stopped at the next X and stabbed the post-hole digger into the dirt. He pulled the dirt out and continued to punish the ground for his own issues. Even though he finished the hole quickly, he wasn't quick enough to avoid her coming over as Layne left to get another post.

"Hey, I'm sorry if I touched on a sore subject. I'm not used to being around men who are willing to lay down their lives for our country. The men at my work are a bit more, shall we say, self-focused."

He couldn't seem to get himself to apologize for his own behavior, though he knew he should. "You said you had drill teams that mine copper?"

She relaxed, resting her foot on the shovel head. "Yes. Mayes Mineral Drilling is the company. I schedule the teams and serve as the safety officer. Sometimes I'm their best friend, and sometimes they treat me as their worst enemy. That doesn't bother me much. It's when I have to piss off the boss that things get dicey. He doesn't like being told he can't do something."

"And they all listen to you?"

"Eventually." She sighed, shaking her head before stepping off the shovel. "Sometimes it takes some yelling, and in the worst times, I have to threaten to call in OSHA. The guys are a bit easier because they know my whole purpose is to keep them safe. Sometimes, I think they give me a hard time just for the fun of it."

Obviously, she was a woman who stood her ground. She also didn't feel the need to always be with her friend, which he also respected.

Layne strode up. "I'm going to move the posts down, so

they aren't so far away. You want to hold the post while I do that?"

"Sure." Jackson set down the hole digger and steadied the post once Layne had it in. "Okay, let's pack it in."

Dani immediately started shoveling, quickly packing the ground in before stomping on it and adding another shovel of dirt. "There. How many more do we have?"

He scanned the area between where they were and the birthing enclosure, which is where Tanner had decided the petting zoo area should start. "I'd say about eighteen or so more. But you can leave anytime. You're a guest."

"Oh, I don't want to leave. I'm just trying to figure out how much of my day I can spend avoiding everyone else. This wasn't exactly my plan for vacation."

She seemed to think a lot like him. He probably shouldn't ask, but he found her a lot more interesting than digging holes. "Then why did you come to the Rocky Road?"

"My friend Kaitlynn. She won the vacation and begged me to come with her. She's the only other woman at the company, and she kind of depends on me. At first, I held out, but when she found out my plans had fallen through ..." Dani shrugged.

Being loyal to a friend was a good quality. "What were your plans?"

Immediately, she stood straighter. "Just a trip down to Rocky Point, Mexico. But the man I was seeing decided he couldn't get away, which turned into, he didn't really have time for me. So then my plans were to get twelve hours sleep a night and eat ice cream for dinner."

He wasn't sure what to say to that. Obviously, the guy

was an asshole. And he couldn't remember the last time he had twelve hours of sleep, nor did he want it. If he slept too long, he had nightmares about the children in the war zones. "If you want, Tanner could order you some of Mrs. Silva's ice cream. She makes it herself and has a little shop in Four Peaks."

At first, she looked askance at him before laughing. "You know, I'm going to add that to my suggestion card tonight. Any particular flavor you recommend?"

"Rocky road."

"Rocky ro—oh, I get it." She smiled.

She really did have nice lips, not too full, but not too thin either, and perfectly shaped. He just needed to not stare at them. "I'm sure we'll be stocking that flavor on the ranch soon. My favorite is cheesecake ice cream."

"I do like a good cheesecake. Should I request that specifically?"

"Yes. Mrs. Silva only makes it around the holidays, so now is the only time to get it."

"Are there other flavors I should request that are only made—"

His phone interrupted her, and he quickly answered it. "Yes."

"Didn't you get my text?" Brody sounded exasperated.

Jackson frowned. "Obviously not. What is it?"

"Tabby just woke up, and she's not happy."

"Tabitha? I'll be right there." Ending the call, he stuffed his phone in his pocket and started toward his horse.

"Hey, where you going?" Dani's voice stopped him in his tracks.

He turned toward her and pointed west. "I have to get back to the house. My daughter just woke up."

"Your daughter?" Dani's surprise brought her voice an octave higher.

"Yes." He didn't have time to explain even if he wanted to. He needed to get back. Dani was just a guest anyway. On the ranch for two weeks, then gone. Spinning around, he jogged toward Havoc, the need to see what was wrong with Tabitha urging him on. By the time he'd mounted, his heart was racing in a near panic.

Havoc immediately set out at a gallop, as if understanding his urgency without being told.

Just this morning, the doctor said Tabitha was in perfect health. If something were wrong with her, he'd get a doctor in the city. It was his duty to take care of her. He just wished he knew what the fuck he was doing.

CHAPTER 5

DAUGHTER? Jackson had a daughter? Dani tried to wrap her head around that news. The stiff, overly built, grumpy military veteran had a daughter?

"Now, where'd Jackson go?" Layne strode up with a post in his arms.

"He got a call, then left in a hurry. He said it was about his daughter."

Layne set the post in the hole. "Ah, that explains it. She probably spit up or something and now he thinks something's wrong." The cowboy chuckled. "New fathers are so clueless."

She started to shovel in dirt. "How old is his daughter?"

Layne shrugged. "Not sure exactly. Maybe a month, six weeks. Pretty young."

"Where's the mom?" It was none of her business, but she had set out to solve the mystery of Jackson Dunn, and this was part of it.

"Dead."

She stopped shoveling and looked at the man. "Dead?"

"That's how he puts it. The mother was Army too. I don't know how she died, but they were both in Syria, and then he was sent home with Tabitha." Layne eyed her. "I wouldn't bring it up. He wasn't happy about coming home."

She stamped on the ground around the post before adding more dirt. "I wasn't planning to. Actually, I'm surprised he spoke as much as he did today." She stepped back to view the post. It looked good to her.

Layne stamped it down again, then picked up the post-hole digger and started toward the next spray-painted X. "Yeah, he wasn't always like this. He's changed."

Swallowing her irritation at Layne for having to add his own stamping, she kept focused on Jackson. So he hadn't wanted to come home? Who didn't want to come home from being deployed to a war zone? Especially with a baby?

Obviously, if she wanted to know more about Jackson, talking to Layne could prove helpful. They seemed like they got along well, and since Jackson was gone, she strode to the trailer with the posts and brought one over.

Layne looked up, and his eyes widened. "You can't carry that."

Seriously? "Hmm, I just did. They're not that heavy."

His brows furrowed, as if he were trying to process that she could lift a fence post. Finally, he went back to digging.

"What was Jackson like before?"

A smile tugged at Layne's mustache. The man always seemed to be in a good mood. "He was always challenging guys, daring them to do this and that. He broke a few bones over the years but seldom lost any challenges. Even after his last deployment, he was still causing a ruckus, challenging people to ATV races, to running down a rockslide, to push-up contests, even one-handed billiards at The Stampede."

Layne stopped and took the post from her, setting it in the hole. That was her cue to shovel, but she'd left the shovel at the last pole. So she ran back and got it. "It sounds like his horse was named after him."

"Maybe."

"You said he's changed, though. How?"

Layne opened his mouth and then closed it. Finally, he spoke. "You don't have to help me. I can call another ranch hand."

She kept shoveling. "Really? How many are sitting on their thumbs enjoying the afternoon?" She stamped down the ground again, hoping Layne wouldn't tell her to go back to the bunkhouse.

"No, but you're a guest."

"True, but I didn't pay for this vacation, and honestly, I'd rather do this than play cornhole."

"Now *that* I can understand." Layne didn't stamp down her dirt this time. "Okay. You grab another post, and I'll dig another hole."

She handed him the shovel. "Works for me."

For the next two hours, she helped Layne set the posts. Her reward, if she could call it that, was to learn more about the Rocky Road Ranch and Jackson specifically. He was an enigma, but her curiosity was more than that. It had taken eight posts and a stop for a bottle of water with Layne for her to figure it out.

Jackson was simply not like any man she'd met. The guys at work were very talkative and generally coarse in their conversation. The men she dated generally had desk jobs except the one police officer she'd dated before starting her Mr. Right list. So it was actually not a surprise that she was curious about Jackson. She'd never met a man who met so few of the items on her list of requirements. The man even had an ex, though she'd passed away, and a daughter! That was a definite disqualification. In fact, no ex-wife and no children came in at Number 3.

Not that she was sizing Jackson up as a potential partner. It was more the fact that because she wasn't looking anymore, she had the freedom to just enjoy peeling off the layers that made the man. Since she wasn't invested in the process, it was much more fun.

She guided her horse into the barn, where she found Vic talking to a ranch hand named Ernesto. It looked like a serious conversation until Vic saw her. The woman patted Ernesto on the back. "Just tell her you're sorry and mean it. Then change your behavior. That you have a wife who puts off her family to spend more time with you is a good thing."

Ernesto didn't look convinced, but he nodded anyway.

Dani dismounted, the conversation hitting a cord in her gut, reminding her of her last breakup.

Vic strode up and took the horse by the reins. "Where've you been? Your group came back an hour ago. Amanda told me to go find you. She said you'd stopped to help Jackson and Layne."

Though Dani didn't like being babysat, she did like that the family had the guests' safety on their radar. "That's where I was. Jackson had to come back here a couple of hours ago because of his daughter, so I helped Layne finish."

"You're a guest. You don't have to do that."

Tired, sweaty, and not a little hungry, she snapped. "I thought this was a dude ranch where the guests get to see what it's like to work on a ranch, not play stupid cornhole."

Vic's eyes rounded, and she started to grin. "Good point. Be sure to add that to your feedback today. That's what I had thought this place was supposed to be about too, but I just work here. Your input means something."

Appeased by Vic's quick support, Dani shook her head. "Sorry. I'm just sweaty, dirty, and a little tired."

"Go shower up. You have over an hour before chow."

She groaned. "Any chance there's some food set out in the clubhouse?"

"Actually, there is. They leave stuff out all day for those who are wandering around. I don't know what it is, but there's sure to be something."

That news brightened Dani's mood immediately. "At this point, I don't care what it is. Thanks." She walked by Vic and headed out of the barn past the corral and between two bunkhouses.

Guests in the quad, as she referred to it, were playing cornhole and thoroughly enjoying themselves. Maybe the ranch had to cater to both types of guests. Not everyone was like her, as she well knew. She'd be sure to mention that both types of activities were good.

She opened the glass door of the clubhouse and was hit with a blast of cold air that made her shiver. Scanning the large room, she spotted a table with what coffee urns and headed that way. When she reached it, she found iced tea and cold sodas had also been set up. But what drew her were the snacks, which included fruit, granola bars, and chocolate chip cookies. She should grab a couple bars and go shower, but the cookies were too enticing. Lifting one, she felt it was still warm and immediately took a bite. "Hmm."

The clubhouse door opened, and she turned to find Jackson, who stopped as he spotted her, then moved forward. "How was Layne doing with the fence posts when you left?"

She smiled smugly, quite proud of herself. "We got them all in."

His brows shot up. "We? As in you and Layne?"

"Yup. All done. He said you and he would be running the fence in a couple days. Something about you having to care for your daughter every other day." She paused. "Is your daughter okay?"

He didn't meet her gaze. "It was a false alarm. She just had gas, but then she wouldn't go back to sleep. I need to find someone who can care for her daily while I'm out on the ranch."

She didn't know a lot about baby care, but her older sister did have two young ones. "How old is she? I have no kids, but I would think for the first few months, it's more important for you to take care of her than to be putting up fences."

His scowl was immediate, and she braced herself for his anger. "Who said that? Was it a doctor? No one told me that."

"I know very little myself, but I think babies need to bond with their parents."

He looked away again, obviously completely uncomfortable. "She only has me. Isaac is taking care of her when I'm not. He's my dad's CNA." He turned back and stared straight at her. "Does that mean Tabitha will bond with Isaac?"

The intensity of his stare had her stepping back. "I'm not sure. But you could look it up." She pulled her phone out of her pocket.

"Come with me."

Before she knew what he was about, he'd grabbed her hand. "Where are we going?"

"We need to get Tabitha from Isaac."

We? She thought about trying to resist, but the panic in his voice made her want to help, especially because she'd caused it. She should have just kept her mouth shut.

He didn't let go of her hand until they entered the ranch house. He dropped his cowboy hat on the entry table, probably out of habit, as he strode by.

Hoping to be more helpful than she had been, she followed, barely noticing the décor as he silently moved from one room to the next, his rubber-heeled cowboy boots not making a sound, while she had to walk on tiptoe to avoid her boot heels touching. She wasn't sure why he was being so quiet, but her best guess was that Tabitha might be sleeping.

In a room off the kitchen, they found a man in maybe his mid-fifties sleeping in a wheelchair. She hadn't seen him before. Next, Jackson moved through the kitchen with its giant eat-at island counter, then through a family room with sliding glass doors to a private pool area before heading down a hallway.

She wasn't even sure he knew she was still there, his focus was so intense. He stuck his head in every room that had an open door, even a bathroom, before coming to one that was closed. He didn't knock, nor did he walk in. Instead, he stood to the side of it, listening, before slowly turning the knob. The door opened inward on well-oiled hinges, and Jackson moved his head just enough to look inside.

Whatever he saw had him moving so fast that one minute he was there and the next he'd slipped into the room. Poking her head around the corner, she found an interesting tableau. Jackson stood with his arms held out in front of a bald-headed man with a goatee, who sat in a rocking chair holding a sleeping baby. She had to be Tabitha. The large bald man, presumably Isaac, was in his mid-thirties and looked quite surprised. But without a word, he rose, equal in height to Jackson, and deposited Tabitha into her father's arms.

The difference in how they held the baby was surprising. While Isaac had held Tabitha cradled against his chest, Jackson kept space between him and his daughter, though he supported her head and body appropriately, almost as if it were how he was taught.

As Isaac left the room, he noticed her and motioned her down the hall. When they got to the family room, he addressed her in a whisper. "Why are you in the house?"

Though the man's stature could be intimidating, he had a kind face that took away from his giant presence, unlike Jackson. She pointed down the hall. "He asked me to come."

Isaac's brows rose. "Jackson?"

She nodded.

"Asked for help?"

"Not exactly. He more demanded I come with him. He was worried about Tabitha bonding with you."

Realization dawned in the man's eyes before he

nodded. "He should be." Isaac studied her a moment. "If you can help him with that, you would be helping them both."

She looked down the hall, feeling a bit uncertain as to how involved she wanted to get. This was serious stuff, and she was just on vacation and too curious for her own good.

"That little girl in there needs all the help she can get."

At Isaac's whispered words, she remembered Layne's comment about Tabitha's mother. *She's dead.* Damn. She'd always been a sucker for children's charities. This was just an up-close-and-personal kind of charity. Besides, what else was she going to do, eat chocolate chip cookies?

Nodding, she gave Isaac an uncertain smile, then turned and headed back down the hall. What's the worst that could happen?

She peeked into the room to find Jackson sitting in the rocker as stiff as a board, still holding his daughter as before, only now his arms rested on his lap. Even she knew that wasn't going to work for either of them. Were his shoulders made of ironwood that he could sit like that?

So as not to startle him, she moved slowly, but his head snapped around immediately.

She gave him an encouraging smile as she stepped around him to stand at his side.

He watched her like she was the enemy, which was unnerving, but she'd never backed down from a dare yet.

She patted his arm and mouthed the words, "Bend your elbows."

Giving her a short nod, he bent his elbows, bringing his daughter closer to him.

She pointed to Tabitha's head and then touched the rock-hard bicep near his armpit.

He seemed at a loss as to what she suggested. So she put her arms under the baby's torso and lifted her to the right position.

She wasn't sure whether it was instinct or he just suddenly understood, but he moved his arm to hold Tabitha so her head rested in the crook of his arm.

Tabitha turned her head toward Jackson, opening and closing her mouth before settling in. The baby was adorable, as most babies were, as well as well fed and chubby in all the right places, including her rounded cheeks. Her hair was a very light brown, though there wasn't much of it, and her nose was such a tiny little thing, it was amazing she could breathe, but she appeared to be quite content. Tabitha's delicate, soft little stature was a stark contrast to Jackson's large stiffer-than-a-fence-post body.

Dani smiled. The baby looked very content, though Jackson looked harder than a cliff she'd noticed on one of the nearby mountains. She wasn't sure she could do anything about that. He may just have to get used to his daughter. Unless...

She stood in front of him and motioned for him to rock, but he didn't get it. Probably didn't even realize he sat in a rocking chair. She moved back to his side and whispered in his ear, "Rock gently."

He didn't make any sign of acknowledgement, but he did start to rock, just a little.

She gave him a thumbs-up and a smile. He was a little stiff for a rock-a-bye cowboy, but it was a start. Pleased that he and his daughter were in a better place than when she'd walked in, she started to leave.

A soft whistle, like the quietest of bird calls, filled the room. She turned at that to see Jackson had made it. He stopped and mouthed the word "wait."

Not sure why but always curious, she came back and bent next to him to whisper in his ear. "What?"

He turned his head toward her. "When do I stop?"

"Never stop showing her you love her." At her own words, her heart tripped over in her chest as memories assailed her. "But for now, just until you're tired, then lay her in her crib and be here when she wakes."

She couldn't say any more, her throat closing as she fought the tears welling up. Quickly, she turned and quietly left the room, getting halfway down the hall before the first tear slipped down.

She let herself out and stepped onto the porch. Despite her blurred vision, she made it to the bench and sat, taking deep breaths to get a hold of herself. She hadn't lost it over her dad's death in years. It had to have been seeing Jackson with his baby in his arms.

That and her father's final words, so much like those she spoke to Jackson. "Tell my girls I will love them forever." He'd said them to a co-worker who'd passed them along. When her mom told her and her sisters, she'd cried, mostly because her daddy was gone, but years later, as a teen, she'd finally understood exactly how powerful those words were. And it wasn't until she hit her twenties that she'd realized her dad hadn't meant just his three daughters but her mother too. It was then that she'd started her Mr. Right list.

Wiping away the tears that had made it past her defenses, she purposefully let her thoughts stray. Her dad hadn't been home much since he'd worked on an oil rig in the Gulf, but when he was, he focused on his family. She hoped Jackson would be able to focus on his daughter as her dad had.

That was why she'd looked for men who had good earning potential, or at least good financial sense. She wanted a man who was not gone for months at a time. What was the sense in having a husband she rarely saw? She stilled. Yet that was exactly what her mom had had, and the reason was obvious. They had needed the money to support their family of five.

Movement between the vehicles parked in the yard interrupted her thoughts. She rose and stepped back in the shadows as a cowboy hat moved behind the cars, then stopped at Kaitlynn's SUV. Concerned, she quietly walked down the steps. Unfortunately, she lost her vantage point. Deciding on an immediate course of action, she strode toward Kaitlynn's vehicle. As she came around a pickup truck, she halted.

The man in the cowboy hat was getting in Kaitlynn's vehicle! Instantly, she started forward, only to stop when she could see the SUV. The cowboy wasn't alone, and from the pink bra on the woman inside, Kaitlynn wanted him there.

Dani turned on her heel and headed back the way she'd come. If she'd been thinking straight, she would have realized a ranch hand or guest wouldn't be stupid enough to steal a car from the Rocky Road Ranch. It wasn't like they could get away with it by speeding down the rutted obstacle course that was the driveway.

She shook her head at herself and at Kaitlynn. At least her friend was enjoying the vacation so far. Her steps slowed as she reached the bunkhouse. Actually, she was enjoying her time as well, but for a completely different and even opposite reason. So far, everything she'd learned about Jackson had him failing to meet every one of her Mr. Right criteria, and she found him fascinating.

Anxious for her shower now, she opened the door and stepped into the coolness of the air-conditioned structure.

Brody Dunn looked up from his phone as he sat opposite the door. "There you are. I was hoping we could have a chat before dinner."

She looked longingly toward the end of the building where the showers were located before pasting on a smile. "Sure. Is it about my feedback?"

"Uh, no. I won't see any of that until after everyone leaves."

She moved to the chair opposite him, which gave her a perfect view of her own bunk. "Then you want my feedback in person? Are you doing this with all the guests?"

The usually cocky cowboy looked away. "No, it's not really about your stay here."

"Really?" That got her curiosity going. "Then what did you want to talk about?"

His gaze returned to her. "I wanted to talk about Jackson."

Now that was a surprise. "Okay. What about him?"

Brody seemed to be having a tough time deciding what to say. Since he was a bit too full of himself, she didn't help.

Instead, she waited, which was no small feat considering the showers were so close.

Finally, he spoke. "Today, Jackson came back to the house to take care of Tabby and talked about you."

"And what did he say?" She thought back on their conversation and couldn't think of anything earth-shattering.

"It's not what he said. It's that he talked about you."

"I'm not sure I follow."

Brody rubbed the back of his neck before continuing. "My brother hasn't said much to us beyond conversations related to his daughter or to tasks that need to be completed. But today, he talked about you. Not just about you but about your job, your helpfulness, and that you remind him of the women he worked with overseas."

"I'll take that as a compliment."

"It's more than a compliment. It's a breakthrough."

She hadn't seen Brody be so serious. "I'm guessing this is a good thing. I'm glad I could help."

As if she'd said the words he'd been waiting to hear, his face lit up. "You are? Then would you be willing to help a bit more?"

She stiffened. First, Isaac had asked her to help Jackson with his daughter, and now Brody wanted ... what? "That depends."

"Listen, I know I shouldn't even be asking you, but I was wondering if you'd check in on Jackson once in a while. It doesn't have to be every day. You're on vacation, and I shouldn't even impose on you, but ..."

"But what?"

"I want to help my brother. He's not the same person he

used to be. Something happened on his last deployment that changed him."

"That's not surprising."

Brody shook his head. "But it is. This was his fourth deployment. He's always come home no worse for his experiences. This time is different. He won't talk to any of us about anything beyond what I mentioned. But he's talking to you. I don't know why, and I don't care. I just want him to be ... I don't know, happier."

"If I do check on your brother, I'm not going to come back to you and tell you everything. If he's not talking to you, then there's a reason."

"I don't care. This is about helping him. I understand I may never have my old brother back, but there has to be a way to get him to feel better about life, his life. I don't know."

She had to admit she was surprised that Brody was so concerned, but then again, Jackson was his brother. Besides, she already found Jackson to be the most interesting part of the Rocky Road Ranch. "Okay. I'll check in on him once in a while."

"That's great." Brody's wide smile was back, and he rose from his chair. "Thank you." He held out his hand.

She rose and shook it. "Don't expect any miracles. I'm on vacation."

"I know. I appreciate it." He let go of her hand and moved toward the door. He stopped before opening it. "Ah, heck."

"What's wrong?"

"I forgot I was supposed to get Dad a few of those chocolate chip cookies from the clubhouse. He loves those things."

At the mention of the patriarch of the Dunn family, she had to ask, "Is that your father in the wheelchair?" She hooked her thumb over her shoulder toward the ranch house.

"Yeah. He had a stroke earlier this year. He's improving every day. He just doesn't think it's a good idea to be wheeling about among the guests. I better go snag a couple of those cookies and hightail it back to the house before dinner is served. See you later."

He gave a short wave as he opened the door, then slipped out.

She watched him stride across the quad toward the clubhouse, a bit confused about who he was, though even more curious about Jackson now.

So he wouldn't talk to his family, but he talked to her? Definitely something to think about—after a shower.

CHAPTER 6

JACKSON KNOCKED on the doorframe of his father's office, though his father wasn't there. Instead, Tanner sat at the desk, frowning at the computer. It was odd not reporting to his own father, but the stroke had done some serious damage. It made sense that Tanner was in charge. At least their dad was getting better and did use the computer now.

Everything felt odd since he'd never expected to live at the ranch again. Then again, he hadn't expected to find an empty key ring on his windowsill that morning either. It had to be the raccoon. He was going to have to look out for the little guy and give him a name. Maybe even make him a warm place to sleep. It might be unseasonably warm at the moment, but the winter chill would hit any day now. That is, if he remembered correctly. It'd been a long time since he was home for any length of time.

Tanner looked up and relaxed back into the chair. "Hey, thanks for dropping in. I need a break from working on these orders. Brody usually does them, but he had to take a group on a hike. What's up?"

"I can't work the ranch anymore."

Tanner's brows lowered as he sat forward in his chair once again. "Why?" The worry in his voice was obvious.

Jackson moved to the side of the desk so he wouldn't have to look over the computer to see his brother. "It was brought to my attention yesterday that I need to spend more time with my daughter at this age so she bonds with me instead of with Isaac. I've been doing some research, and it's vitally important to her ability to interact with others in the future, especially because she has no mother."

"I see." Tanner looked away, clearly not sure what to do.

This gave him the perfect opportunity to make his own suggestions. "I thought since I'll be regulated to the house for the most part, I could help sift through all those feedback cards and tabulate results for you. I'm not great with budgets, but if there are other tasks I can do here, I'm willing to help. I just have to put Tabitha first."

Tanner rose. "That would be a great help. If you're not available to help put up the fencing for the petting area, I can move Nash to help Layne, then I can have Ernesto with Waylon. That means I'll have to have Amanda ride the fence line with Brody, though. But Brody and Hannah are supposed to lead another hike tomorrow. So I'd need Amanda and Vic to ride the line. Vic was helping with the other guest activities, but I can handle it alone."

Jackson shook his head. "Just move Vic to helping Layne and leave everyone where they are."

"But you know how Layne is." Tanner didn't elaborate, but Jackson knew what he meant.

"He and Dani put in over half the posts after I left. So he's capable of learning to work with a woman."

"Dani? We don't have a Dani on staff."

Surely Tanner knew about the guests being allowed to help. That was the whole point of the dude ranch thing. "Danielle is a guest here. They can choose to help with ranch activities, remember?"

Tanner settled his hip on the desk, his eyes wide. "Layne worked with a female guest to set fence posts?"

"That's what I just said."

His older brother lifted one eyebrow. "I bet he was biting his lip the whole time. He wouldn't be as polite with a ranch hand. I don't want to scare Vic off. She's dependable and knows her shit."

Jackson nodded. "Exactly. And she's got more backbone than our bull, Old Glory. Layne's not going to scare her off. Fuck, Tanner. You're as bad as Layne. I saw women in combat run circles around some of the men. Stop playing nursemaid."

Tanner smirked. "That's your job now, right?"

"Yeah, I guess it is."

Tanner patted him on the shoulder. "I'm going to let Layne and Vic know the change in plans." He strode to the door and stopped, turning to point to a pile on the desk. "Feel free to start entering those. They're the last two nights of suggestions. I haven't even started looking at them yet. You'll find a file folder in the computer labeled 'Feedback.' It's in another folder labeled 'Dude Ranch.' I set up a spreadsheet, but if you have other ideas for tabulating comments, I'm wide open to them. I expected Brody to be doing all this, but he's leaving in four weeks, so it's all yours." With that, Tanner left the room, a soft whistling floating down the hall behind him.

A little surprised he'd received no pushback, Jackson walked behind his dad's desk and sat. It was a strange feeling. All his life, his father had run the ranch from this very spot. No one had been allowed in the room until they turned eighteen, and even then, only when his dad was present. Here he was, sitting at the helm of their new operation, not a place he'd ever expected or wished to be. So much had changed. He scowled at the computer with its screen saver picture of the ranch.

He didn't like change. Everyone, from his superior officers to his men, knew that. Layne knew it and even Tanner did to a degree. Feminine voices down the hall reminded him that women now invaded the house, something else different that he didn't like. Yet here he was, making a change himself—his duties for his daughter. On the one hand, he still didn't like having to make the change, but on the other, he liked being in control of it.

Sitting back, he studied the room. If he moved one piece of furniture, he could put Tabitha's carrier seat and port-a-crib in the room with him. He'd read that everything he could do to be with her, from changing and feeding her to just talking to her, could help them bond.

Though the Syrian nanny Gabriella had hired had tried to show him what to do, he didn't understand Kurdish. When he'd had asked her to come to the US, he could see her answer was very clear. Something about being tortured for eternity before she'd do that. He should be thankful to her for that. Now it meant his daughter would bond with him and not her. He rose and moved the round table against the wall to make room for the port-a-crib and carrier seat. Then he strode to the door and ran right into Dani. Instinctually, he grabbed hold of her shoulders to keep her from falling.

His nostrils filled with her unique scent, and he noticed her taller height was perfect for him. She fit his body in all the right places. He didn't want to let go, but he forced himself to set her away, though not too far. He kept his hands on her shoulders. "You okay?"

A smile tugged at her lips. "Yes. Walking into you is like walking into a brick wall. Thanks for grabbing me."

She stepped back, and he released her, though he didn't really want to. "Were you looking for something?"

"I was. I was looking for you. I didn't see you anywhere, so I thought I'd check in here. How's it going with Tabitha?"

"Better. I need to thank you for pointing out what I needed to do. After I put her to sleep last night, I did some research. You were right. I owe you."

"No need. I'm glad I could help. I'm sure you'll have a handle on everything now."

From the tone of her voice, it sounded as if she were ready to leave, but he didn't want her to go. He wanted to share what his plans were. "I'm not sure about that. Maybe you could give me your opinion?"

"You mean the ranch hasn't had enough of all my opinions already?" She held up her hand. "Oh, that's right, the suggestions are all anonymous. I'm always happy to share my opinion. Who isn't?"

Curious as to what she might have said in the feedback, he made it a goal to figure out which cards were hers. But for now, he could see what she thought about his idea. "Come in." He stepped back and held his arm out so she could enter.

She stepped past him. "This looks like an office. Oh, is this the center of the operation?"

He walked past her to stand next to the desk. "Yes. This was my father's office, but Tanner has taken over, though Dad still comes in from time to time to work on the finances. And as it turns out, I'll be spending more time in here than out on the ranch."

Her smile of approval had him standing straighter. "Over here, I thought of putting Tabitha's infant carrier and the port-a-crib so she can be with me when I'm working. This way, I can talk to her while I'm in here. What do you think?"

"I think that's an excellent idea. Tabitha is very lucky you're her dad and that you can adapt your work situation to be with her."

Her smile faltered, and he noticed immediately. "Is something wrong?"

She shook her head, though her smile disappeared altogether. "No. It just brings back memories of how much my own father wanted to be with us but couldn't."

Her explanation reminded him that she'd said her father was *gone*, which could mean a number of things—divorce, death, abandonment. He leaned his ass against the desk, ready and willing to listen, or rather, wanting to listen. "What did your father do for work while you were growing up? I noticed your boots and hat aren't new. Was he in the cattle business?"

"I wish. No, he originally worked on an oil well in New Mexico but was laid off. Despite all the rigs in the state, he couldn't find another job. I think he was blackballed. He always spoke his mind and was very protective of his crew. I expect his bosses didn't like that. So, when I was about five, the closest rig job he could find that paid him enough to keep us housed and fed was in the Gulf of Mexico."

"That's a haul. Did you eventually move to Texas?"

"That was the original plan, but my parents dragged their feet. They'd both grown up in Buckeye, but there was just no work for Dad there. There were five of us, including him. So he took the job and a twenty-eight-day-on/twenty-eight-day-off schedule. That way, he was gone a month, and then we'd have him for three weeks before he went back. When he was home, it was amazing because he didn't have to work at all, and we'd spend a lot of time with him doing fun things. It was hardest when he had to work during the holidays, and some years, he'd trade schedules and work two months just so he could be home for Christmas."

She didn't say anything more, but she played with a bracelet on her wrist as she stood staring past him with a small smile on her face, probably lost in happy memories.

After a moment, she turned her gaze on him. "This time of year, as we get closer to the holidays, always reminds me of him. He gave me this bracelet our last Christmas Eve together." She held up her arm, revealing small, uneven white stones of some kind. "It's made with freshwater pearls. Though I was a bit of a tomboy growing up, he wanted me to have something special from him when I dressed up. Eventually, I got too big for it and had extra chain added so it would still fit."

She lowered her arm. "I was ten when he gave it to me. I thought I was something special that year. My older sister was a teen and more interested in boys, so I got to help Dad wrap gifts on Christmas Eve, though he hid this bracelet from me. We had so much fun and laughed. That was my last Christmas with him."

He knew that feeling, as he'd been able to help his parents set up for Christmas when Brody was still young. "Did your parents divorce, over moving or the long-distance marriage?"

"No, of course not. They loved each other so much, nothing could have separated them except my dad's death."

Her immediate defense made it clear he'd completely misstepped. Apparently, he wasn't the only person who'd grown up with loving parents. "I apologize. What happened to your father?"

"There was an explosion on the rig. My father had told them repeatedly that they needed to change out the annular preventers, the valves, but they never got it done. In the end, one valve released, there was an explosion, and my father was badly burned. He was medevacked to the closest hospital, but he died before my mom could get there. We were devastated." She crossed her arms, as if giving herself comfort from the pain.

He wanted to help her feel better but didn't know what to say. "I don't know how that must have felt, but I can tell that it still hurts. We lost our mom to severe asthma, but it was a slow decline. Still, none of us, meaning me and my brothers, expected her not to come home from the hospital. Losing a parent sucks."

She cocked her head. "Thank you for putting it so succinctly. That's it exactly. It sucks."

"I'm not that good with words."

She placed her hand on his arm. "No, you are good with words. That's exactly what I thought. You know?"

He nodded. "I know."

She gave him a soft smile. "In a couple of years, you will have so much fun playing Santa for Tabitha."

It hadn't even occurred to him how close Christmas was. "I haven't bought anything for her yet."

Dani moved her hand to his face and cupped his jaw. "Relax. You will, and it will be the best Christmas ever because it's your first with her."

Her touch comforted him, and her words soothed. His chest grew tight with gratefulness. Maybe because his new role as a father, a role he'd never expected to live long enough to have, had made him soft. Or maybe it was something else. Either way, what he was feeling toward her was difficult to resist. He set his hand against hers on his cheek and looked into her unique eyes, filled with greens, blues, and browns. She was a very interesting woman. He let go of her hand and rose. "Come. I want to move Tabitha's port-a-crib in here."

"When you make a decision, you don't waste time, do you?" She followed him down the hall.

At his bedroom door, he held his finger to his lips. He opened the door and walked in quietly, only to find his daughter looking at him. "Tabitha, you're awake already?"

He immediately checked her diaper. It was dry. "She's only been asleep for an hour."

"Does she usually sleep longer?"

"Yes. I'll come back later."

Dani nodded and tiptoed out of the room.

As he closed the door, he paused and looked at his daughter once more. She had her fingers in her mouth. He shut the door softly and turned to find Dani watching him.

"You're going to make a great father."

"I think about the years and years ahead of me, trying to get things right with Tabitha. I'm going to make a terrible father." He shook his head as he started back down the hall toward the office.

"Why do you say that?"

He stepped behind the desk and looked at her over the computer. "Because I have no idea what I'm doing. I never wanted to be a father. I planned to die long before that could possibly happen."

CHAPTER 7

DANI STARED at Jackson with her mouth open. It was rare for someone to say something she couldn't respond to, but his statement was so unexpected and so heartbreaking that she found herself stunned.

He, however, just sat down in his chair, as if his words were as normal as saying the weather was pleasant. "I should get started on my work." He lifted a large stack of comment cards.

She closed her mouth, trying to decide what question to ask first.

He typed something into the computer and then pulled a card from the top. After typing something else, he looked up. "Thank you for your help today. You'll enjoy the storytelling tonight around the campfire. Mr. Jeffries knows more about Four Peaks than anyone I know."

She was being dismissed? "Jackson, you can't just tell me you thought you wouldn't live long enough to have children and leave it at that."

He waved her off. "Forget I said it. It doesn't matter now."

She stood there as he continued to look at comment cards and type. Ignoring her. Obviously, he wasn't going to say another word. Pissed, she left the room and the house. Stalking past the barn and corral, she went in search of Brody. He had asked her yesterday how his brother was doing. That was another big no on her Mr. Right list. Number 7, to be exact. Any man she married couldn't have a meddling family, and clearly, Jackson did. She was quite sure he'd failed to meet half the characteristics on the list already, not that she even had a list anymore. It was burnt to ashes for a reason. Too bad she couldn't forget all the criteria.

In the clubhouse, she bypassed the group learning to line dance and went to the kitchen to ask the cook whether he knew where Brody was, only to discover Brody was on a hike on the west peak. She toyed with the idea of saddling a horse and riding out, but she didn't know the area well enough. She should never have agreed to Brody's request.

Maybe a soak in the hot tub by herself was in order. She left the clubhouse and headed for her bunkhouse. Once inside, she changed into her bathing suit, threw on a Rocky Road Ranch robe, grabbed a towel, and headed for the pool area. Unfortunately, there was a water volleyball game going on as music blared from speakers at the hot tub end.

Monica shouted at her from the pool. "Join us, Dani. We need more players if we're going to kick these guys' butts."

"Sorry. I have other plans." She pointed to the sun, as if she planned to lay out, and kept walking until she'd left the pool area and found herself in raw desert. Flip-flops weren't the best footwear in this area since she was well aware of the spiders and snakes that could be hiding in plain sight.

Then she noticed a familiar fence. If she weren't mistaken, that was the fence around the Dunns' private pool. She followed the fence to an open door that let her into the family's empty pool area, which included a small hot tub. It wasn't as big as the guest pool area, but it was much, much quieter.

She unfastened the bracelet her dad had given her and put it in the pocket of her robe. Then she dropped her towel on a lounge chair, took off her robe, and carefully folded it so the bracelet wouldn't fall out. Finally, kicking off her flip-flops, she stepped in. After all, Brody had asked her to check in on Jackson and Jackson himself had requested her help. Even Isaac wanted her to help with Tabitha, so in her opinion, that gave her the right to use their hot tub.

Kaitlynn would think her crazy for enjoying peace and quiet alone, but it was her happy place. Smiling, she closed her eyes, focusing on the gentle flow of the warm water around her. Her serenity lasted about three minutes before she heard the sliding glass door of the house at the other end of the pool. She opened her eyes to see Isaac wheeling out Jeremiah Dunn, the patriarch of the family.

Isaac leaned over and said something to Jeremiah before going back into the house.

Immediately, safety alarm bells went off in her head. A man in a wheelchair alone by a pool was a disaster waiting to happen.

But he wasn't alone. She was there. So when Jeremiah

started wheeling down the patio toward her, she stood, ready to rush over if needed.

He stopped a few feet from the hot tub. "Who are you?" His tone wasn't friendly.

She sank back onto the seat of the hot tub. "My name is Dani. I'm a guest, but Brody sent me over. I'm a friend of Jackson's."

It took the man a moment to process her connections. His green eyes were sharp, and he had a full head of hair that was very similar in color to Brody's. Both men had brown hair with blonde streaks, though she could see there was a little gray starting on the sides of Jeremiah's temples. He wasn't a large man, but he was broad, so she imagined he'd been a force to be reckoned with when he was healthy.

"What Jackson needs is a psychologist, not a friend. We have to get Dr. Navarro over here. She helped me. She can help Jackson."

Obviously, that was someone Jeremiah believed in. "Have you asked Jackson if he'd like to talk to her?"

Jeremiah's brows lowered, reminding her of the very son they spoke about. "I don't care what he likes. It's what he needs."

Wow, she was immediately reminded of her mother telling her she had to clean her room because she 'said so.' "I think if you could tell him how this doctor could help him, he'd be more likely to agree."

"Jackson doesn't agree to anything. He just does, whether he should or shouldn't. He has to be handled like he acts."

That was an interesting outlook. "He seems to be thinking a lot about his actions with Tabitha."

Jeremiah's face immediately softened. "Tabby is special. She needs more time with her grandfather."

Dani had heard that people's personalities could change after a stroke. Had Jeremiah changed, or had he always been so self-involved? "What Tabitha needs is to be loved by her father. The rest will come eventually."

Instead of getting angry, Jeremiah nodded. "That's what my Rosy always said. As long as you have love, everything else will fall in line. She was one smart woman." He paused. "Maybe you're smarter than I first thought."

If that was supposed to be a compliment, it failed. "Do you know why Jackson didn't expect to live long enough to have children?"

Jeremiah laughed, causing her to question his comprehension. He ended his laughing with a snort. "I used to say that kid had a death wish. He started out fine, but around seven years old, he started taking risks and daring others to do stupid shit. It was as if he had to take over where Devlin left off." The last words were spoken softly, as if the thought had just occurred to him.

She opened her mouth to ask who Devlin was, but Isaac came out the sliding glass door and headed their way.

He had a frown on his face as he squinted in the sunlight. "Jeremiah, what are you doing—oh, hi, Dani. I didn't see you there at first."

"Hello, Isaac. I just needed a bit of downtime away from the noise." She hooked her thumb over her shoulder to indicate the general direction of the guest pool.

"You can use this one all you like." Jeremiah gave Isaac a

sullen look. "No one else uses it except me—and only under protest."

Isaac held up his hands. "I'm just the CNA. You'll have to talk to Amanda about your physical therapy in the pool." He dropped his hands down. "I would think you'd be thankful for this pool. Your upper body strength has increased exponentially since you started water therapy."

Jeremiah raised his arm and showed off his bicep.

She made a show of widening her eyes. The man did have some good upper body strength, so he probably had never been in danger by the pool, after all. But compared to Jackson, who had biceps the size of his father's head, Jeremiah was not so impressive. "I'd say you should keep up those workouts in the pool."

Jeremiah beamed. "Isaac, this is one smart woman."

She barely kept from rolling her eyes.

"Okay, Jeremiah. Stop flirting, and let's get you inside. It's time to get ready for dinner."

The older man frowned at Isaac before turning toward her. "What'd you say your name was?"

She hadn't actually given him her full name. "My name is Danielle Hubbard, but people call me Dani."

"It was nice to meet you, Dani." Jeremiah turned his wheelchair around and started wheeling himself back toward the sliding glass door, grumbling all the way.

She could easily see where Jackson got his grumpiness and his soft side from, if Jackson's efforts with his daughter could be considered soft. She waited until the two men had disappeared inside the house before getting out and drying off. Instead of relaxing, she now had even more questions. It was time to find Brody Dunn and get some answers.

Throwing on her robe, she slipped into her flip-flops, grabbed up her wet towel, and headed back the way she'd come. She walked quickly past the guest pool, which had emptied out considerably, with just a few people standing in the shallow end chatting. One of them looked like Artie, but Kaitlynn was nowhere in sight. If it was Artie, he looked downright scrawny.

But that might be because she'd been around Jackson so much. Walking into him had certainly been a surprise, not to mention the zing of excitement she'd felt as he held her to him to keep her from falling. She'd thought him a brick wall, but his body had a little give, and the mounds of muscle had been titillating.

It shouldn't be that much of a surprise because, she had to admit, she'd always liked strong men. She just didn't like men who spent so much time at the gym building muscles they didn't use. Jackson had apparently used his in the Army and now used them around the ranch. Still, part of criterion Number 1 on her Mr. Right Characteristics List was that the man be average-looking. She didn't want a husband that every woman swooned over. Jackson, if he stopped being so closemouthed around the guests, would find himself the central attraction of the ranch.

She opened the door to her bunkhouse and stepped inside, happy for the warmth now that the day was cooling. But she needed some information, which meant finding Jackson's younger brother. She'd done Brody a favor, so he needed to cough up some information.

She finished pulling on her cowboy boots and opened the door but closed it quickly when she felt how cool the air had become now that the sun had dipped behind one of the four peaks. She grabbed her short brown leather jacket and shrugged into it before continuing out the door. Her first question would be about Devlin.

Even before she reached the clubhouse, she spotted Brody talking to Tanner by the fire pit, where the cook was already starting dinner. According to the day's schedule of activities, they were having rib eye steaks before Mr. Jefferies entertained them with historical stories about the area around a campfire while they toasted marshmallows and made s'mores. It all sounded very nice, but her vacation was leading her down much more interesting paths.

She strode up to Brody, and he immediately stopped his conversation with Tanner, giving her a welcoming smile. He and Jackson were like polar opposites. "Hi, Dani. How was your day?"

She gave him a half smile in return. "It was interesting. You'll have my full report on my comment card tomorrow."

He glanced at Tanner before looking at her uncertainly. "I'm available now if you'd like to fill me in."

Now that was interesting. Had Brody not informed his brother that he wanted her to look in on Jackson? "I don't want to interrupt."

Brody immediately shook his head. "No interruption at all. Tanner was about to make a call anyway."

As if he'd already forgotten he'd said he'd make a call, Tanner's brows rose before he pulled out his phone and walked away, already punching in numbers.

"Did you not tell Tanner you asked me to check on Jackson?"

Brody shrugged. "I don't tell him everything. Besides, he has very specific ideas about guests and family, but then again, he doesn't realize you're the only guest Jackson has talked to or that he's talked to you more than any of us."

She'd given that circumstance a bit of thought. "He may find it easier to talk to a stranger who will be gone in a couple weeks than with a family member he will have to live with."

"That's a good point." Based on how his stance relaxed, Brody was relieved by her observation.

"But what about Layne? I understand they were best friends from way back. Hasn't Jackson talked to him?"

Brody's gaze didn't meet hers and instead seemed to find the wrapped raw meat on a large tray nearby to be more interesting. "Layne's never revealed anything Jackson shared with him, not even when we were young, when Jackson would go to his family's house after school to hang out."

She digested that piece of information. That meant that what Layne had shared with her was also because he figured she'd be gone in another week or so. The more she thought about her position on the ranch, the more she liked it. Who knew her vacation on a dude ranch could become so interesting?

Brody's gaze came back to hers. "So how was Jackson? Tanner told me he's quitting his duties as a ranch hand to take care of Tabby. That's a big change. When he first brought her home from his deployment, he seemed afraid to touch her, though he did because he refused to let Amanda care for her."

She let the inference that only women knew how to care for babies slide. "He wants to bond with Tabitha. She's his daughter, and after doing some research, he decided that she's more important than putting up fencing for a petting zoo."

"That's still a big change in only a couple of weeks."

Two weeks? To say she was shocked by that was an understatement. "Jackson just came home from overseas two weeks ago? With Tabitha?" Even as the realization of what Jackson had been facing hit her, her sympathy for him rose.

Brody rubbed the back of his neck, clearly concerned. "Yeah. He hasn't explained her or her mother except to admit she's his. Did he say anything to you?"

She shook her head. Had Jackson impregnated a Syrian woman? She knew from Layne that the woman was dead. What if they had been in love and she'd died during an attack? That would explain how protective he was of Tabitha. "He hasn't said anything to me about her, and if he had, it wouldn't be right to tell you. But he did say that he didn't expect to live long enough to have a child. According to your father, that's because he likes to take risks, but it didn't start until he was seven. Your dad said Jackson was trying to be like Devlin. Who's Devlin? Was he a childhood friend who moved away and Jackson started acting like him?"

Brody stiffened, as if expecting to be hit or something. "Devlin was our brother. He was older than Jackson but younger than Tanner."

There had been another Dunn boy? "What happened to him?"

Brody's gaze wandered from her. "There was an accident, and he died when he was eight."

The ramifications of such a loss swept through her, sending her back to the day she'd lost her father. She'd been ten and thought the world had ended. "And Jackson was seven."

Brody nodded before finally looking at her.

"So Devlin took risks. How deep did Jackson's risk-taking habit go?"

Brody shrugged. "I don't know. After that, Jackson was always over at Layne's when Dad didn't insist he be here to help with chores."

Now that she knew Devlin was Jackson's brother and the kind of boy he'd been, Layne's account of Jackson being a daredevil connected more than a few puzzle pieces together for her. But it seemed the more she learned about Jackson, the more questions she had. Why had he copied his brother? "Were you there for the accident?"

"I wasn't. Listen, I didn't mean for you to be dragged down by my family's history. Thank you for helping me out. I appreciate it. Don't feel obligated to check in with Jackson anymore. You're on vacation, and I overstepped."

Oh, no, he wasn't getting off that easily. She was hooked now. "It's no trouble. Actually, your father invited me to use the family pool."

"My father?"

"Yes, your dad came out and visited with me today while I was in your private hot tub. He said I was a smart woman because I said the same thing Rosy used to say. I'm guessing Rosy was your mother?"

"Yes, 'Rosalie' was her full name, but—wait, what did you say that my mother used to say?"

"Something about the most important thing being love and the rest would follow. We were discussing Tabitha and Jackson."

Brody looked surprised, but he didn't say anything.

"Is something wrong?"

"Nope. Nothing's wrong at all. I'm glad you got to meet my dad. If you'll excuse me, I need to find my wife." He took two steps and stopped, but he couldn't hide a satisfied smile. "Any time you want to spend looking in on Jackson and Tabitha is okay by me. It's your vacation, after all, and if that's what you'd like to do, that's great." And with that, he took off, not quite running to the clubhouse but definitely in a hurry.

That was an odd reaction to her explanation of what she'd said that was like what Rosalie had said. Shrugging her shoulders, she headed for one of the large picnic tables now filling with guests anxious for some chow and conversation. She would have to make a point of telling Kaitlynn how much she was enjoying her vacation, especially after complaining about coming so much in the first place. She'd just be careful not to say why. No one, not even her friend, needed to know exactly how fascinating she was finding the Jackson Dunn mystery.

CHAPTER 8

JACKSON QUIETLY CLOSED the door to his room. Tabitha was asleep for her afternoon nap, and he was free to get back to work, except he didn't want to work. Walking by the office, he continued into the family room and sat in his dad's old wingback chair, facing the sliding glass doors.

Yesterday, after Dani had come over in the morning to show him some ways he could interact with his daughter, he'd discovered—by chance—that she'd returned in the afternoon to enjoy the family's hot tub. He didn't tell his family, as Tanner had made it clear that guests needed to stay in the designated areas. He shook his head. That didn't work with Dani. She was always wandering about and had only participated in a couple of activities all week.

That's because she'd been helping him with Tabitha. He was more than grateful. He didn't trust Amanda since he'd grown up with her as the daughter of his family's enemy, and Hannah was far too busy planning her Christmas Eve wedding. He was pleased Dani continued to visit him. Otherwise, staying inside the ranch house all day would have driven him insane by now, and it had been a total of only four days. During his first deployment, he'd learned that depending on help from another was not a weakness but a strength, especially when it meant survival. By his last deployment, he'd taught that same acceptance to dozens of men and women in theater.

Even as he thought of his last and final deployment, he expected the usual anger. It came, but it wasn't as gut-wrenching as it had been the first two weeks at home. Now, it was more of a sharp flash that dissipated slowly. He wondered about his reaction. Could it have to do with Tabitha?

Usually, he'd talk to Layne about such things, but he hadn't seen the man since the day they had put in posts for the—his attention was caught by movement in the opening of the fence at the other end of the pool. Waiting for the figure to come out of the shadow, he watched as Dani walked to the hot tub. Dropping her towel on a lounge chair, she untied her robe and added that to the pile before quickly moving to the hot tub.

She was much thinner than his usual type. He liked a woman with more weight. Smaller women made him feel like he might hurt them. Not that Dani was thin in her bikini. She had all the curves of a woman in her prime, plus she was tall. That must be why he found himself attracted to her. She didn't seem delicate.

She slipped out of her flip-flops and dunked into the hot tub up to her neck, hiding her body from his view. Not that he should be spying on her private time. She'd already given up a lot of her vacation time to help him be a better father. Which is why he sat inside, indecisive about joining her.

He wanted to.

He picked up his phone and looked in on his daughter. She lay sound asleep, innocently unaware of his doubts and turmoil. He'd been in said turmoil since he learned of her, but now, watching her sleep, safe in his father's home, eased his anxiety.

He was well aware of where his PTSD came from. It was one of the reasons he didn't want to be around the guests. He rubbed his eyes with one hand, trying to keep the memories from surfacing. Overseas, he'd grown inured to seeing dead men and women, but the horror of seeing the school where they'd slaughtered the children had been too much. And it wasn't the only place where he'd seen children killed. His own forces had killed two children who carried bombs. It made him physically sick.

The image of the young girl, maybe nine years old, took over his mind. Her dark eyes were fierce despite her smile. She carried a basket overflowing with bread. But the basket wasn't filled with bread, according to the radio. Their drone sensors had detected an explosive. Go back! Go away! Don't come closer! He yelled, and she paused. The hope that she would turn died as she shook her head and ran toward them.

The gunshot stopped her in her tracks. She teetered for a moment before falling backward, the bomb going off, but his attention was caught by a man running away from the scene. With rage filling him, he didn't think. He lifted his gun and shot the man multiple times. Children were to be protected, not sent on suicide missions.

He opened his eyes, and the tick under his left eye started. His heartbeat raced, making it hard to breathe. Desperately, he looked around, ready to attack the next person with a gun. But there was no one. He knew better than to trust his sight. Picking up his radio, he found it to be his phone. Touching it, the image of a sweet sleeping baby stared back at him.

A baby. His baby. His daughter. Safe. She was safe.

He stared at the image for a long time, focusing on his breathing, trying to get his mind to calm. He stared at Tabitha sleeping. He would always protect her with his very life.

Looking up, he tried to remember what he'd been doing. Tabitha was asleep, and he was ... was going to Dani. He rose from the chair and strode to the sliding glass doors. His mind focused on only one thing now. Dani. He wanted to be with her. He wanted to touch her. She was but yards away in the water. He strode toward her.

"Hi, Jackson."

He didn't respond. Instead, he started to undress, toeing off his boots and dropping his shirt to the ground.

"Are you joining me?"

After unzipping his jeans, he dropped them as well. He was wearing his swim shorts. Had he planned to swim? His mind couldn't seem to focus.

"Jackson, are you okay?"

He looked at her. "Dani."

She nodded as she rose. "Yes. What's wrong?"

He didn't know. He was confused. Tabitha. Dani. Home.

"It's okay." She held out her hand. "Come in."

He stepped to the edge and took her hand. It was soft but

strong, and he grasped it like a lifeline as he descended the stairs. The warm water swirled around his legs, making him feel off-balance. Grasping her to him with his free arm, he closed his eyes and held her against him. Her scent triggered a memory of holding her as he did now.

Safe. The word floated through his brain, taking hold.

She released his hand and wrapped her arms around him tightly.

He lowered his head to bury his face in her hair. She smelled of comfort. She felt right. Everything was going to be okay. It was never okay, but that's how he felt in her arms. Lifting his head, he moved his hand from her back to her chin and gently tilted her head so he could see into her eyes. They were almost all blue like the sky in the early dawn hours when barely any rays of sun hit the horizon.

His movements were instinct, his actions not under his command as he lowered his lips to hers.

Peace. The word flitted through his consciousness as he moved his mouth across her soft lips, and when they opened, he dipped his tongue in to taste the sweetness inside. The sheer relief and contentment that filled him took him by surprise. He'd forgotten these feelings. He wanted more of them. When her tongue moved against his own, he groaned, the sound coming from deep inside him, from a place he didn't know existed. He wanted more, but did he deserve her? Reluctantly, he broke the kiss.

When he opened his eyes, he found her studying him.

The thought that he should apologize settled in his head, but he didn't know why.

"Jackson, do you know where you are?"

Her question helped him focus, and he looked over her head. He was in the backyard of his family's house. "Yes."

"And do you know when it is?"

He frowned. When? He tried to think. He was home from his last deployment in Afghanistan. No, that wasn't right—Iraq. He shook his head, trying to think.

She stroked his bare back, settling his thoughts.

He was home from Syria, and he had a daughter. "Yes. I'm home. I came home from Syria with my daughter."

Her smile eased his nervousness. "Yes. And Tabitha is napping, right?"

He turned his head to look at his jeans where his phone was clipped. "Yes, she's napping." Everything settled into place in his head again. He turned back to look at the woman in his arms. "And I'm here with you."

"Yes, you are." She looked a bit unsure.

He didn't want her to be unsure. "And I enjoyed kissing you, Dani."

Her confidence returned. "I liked kissing you as well. Would you like to sit?"

Though he knew where and when he was now, he hadn't comprehended that he was standing with her in the hot tub. "Yes. In a sec. I need to check on Tabitha." He let her go and reached for his jeans. Unclipping his phone, he checked on his daughter. Seeing that she still slept, he turned back to Dani and sat next to her, setting his phone on the concrete nearby.

She took his hand, as if she knew he needed it.

He intertwined their fingers, her presence balancing him. "Do you want to talk about it?"

"What?"

"Your episode." Her eyes, now with a bit more green, showed no judgment, only curiosity.

Did he want to talk about it? That was the question the psychologist asked when he arrived back in the States carrying a baby and a diagnosis of PTSD. He'd said there was nothing to say. He'd just wanted to come home. But then he'd gotten home, and everything was totally changed.

She just gazed at him steadily.

It must be her eyes. They were mesmerizing, with their multitude of colors, and, at the same time, soothing. "I was somewhere else. Not home. The last time I seemed to travel back to Syria in my head, my father had the news on, and a child had been killed in a car accident. The father had been driving drunk and crashed into a tree. The car burst into flames. While the father stumbled out, a bystander saved the little brother, but the five-year-old girl …"

He swallowed hard, even now seeing the images of the flaming car. "Everyone thinks a PTSD trigger has to do with gunfire. I guess it's that way for a lot of men and women, but that doesn't bother me."

She squeezed his hand. "Is it children, then? I noticed you don't interact with the guests at all. Is that because of the children?"

Relieved he didn't have to say what sounded absolutely stupid to him, he nodded.

She was quiet for a moment as she looked toward the house. "But you just had an episode?"

He liked how sharp she was. "Yes. I was just sitting in the

family room thinking." He frowned, not happy about what that might mean. "I think I'm getting worse instead of better."

"Not necessarily. But I think you should definitely tell your therapist what happened."

He looked down at their clasped hands, feeling guilty. He'd been told he needed to get one but hadn't because it was another change in his life that he wanted to put off.

"Oh, you don't have one yet." It wasn't a question.

He shook his head, disappointed in himself once again.

Her wet hand came up and cupped his jaw. "That's understandable. Brody told me you just got home a little over two weeks ago. You had no reason to jump on that right away, especially with a new baby to care for and adjusting to your family home now turned into a dude ranch. But since this happened, it might mean that you have to move finding a therapist up on your priority list."

"Yes, I probably should. Dad keeps singing the praises of Dr. Navarro. That would be the easiest."

She shrugged. "I think you should do whatever works best for you, not your dad."

"You don't know my dad. Sometimes doing what's best for him is what's best for us."

She chuckled, lowering her hand. "And here I didn't think you had a sense of humor."

He shook his head. "I don't. I was being stone cold serious. Dad is a force unto himself, even in his wheelchair."

She cocked her head. "My dad was a big pushover, but he had three girls and didn't own a ranch. Your dad is like he is because of how he was raised. You know, when it comes to raising Tabitha, you can decide how much you want to be like your father or how much you want to be the opposite of him."

He hadn't even contemplated what kind of dad he would be, even after being handed his daughter. He just wanted to protect her. "So you're saying everything I don't like about the way my father raised us I can be sure not to do and then maybe Tabitha won't be a mess like me?"

"You're not a mess, Jackson. You're human. There's a difference."

"Yes, I am. The Army psychologist agreed with me when I said I was a mess. I'm pretty sure I'm both, a mess and human."

She squeezed his hand under the water. "Then, from one human to another, I can tell you that we can change and grow and fix our messes if we want to."

Now that was a new take on his situation. "What makes you so wise? Have you had to change and grow?"

This time, she laughed. "So many times I've lost count."

"Name one time." Even issuing the challenge had him feeling more like himself.

She kicked her feet back and forth as if she were swimming as she thought about what to tell him. It made him more anxious to hear.

"Okay, here's an example. We all have our first boy or girlfriends, right? So mine was in college. I—"

"You didn't have a boyfriend until after high school?" She must have misspoken.

"No, I didn't. There weren't many boys your height in my high school, and I was big and tall. High school boys don't like the idea of having a girlfriend who's taller than they are."

He'd never thought about that since he was always taller than everyone, or almost everyone. "That makes sense. We boys are pretty insecure in high school."

She let go of his hand and cupped her face with both her hands. "You think boys are, you should see the girls in the bathrooms." She turned her head toward him. "'Is my eyebrow line right? Do you think I need more blush? I swear, I've gained a pound this week. Does it show? Oh, my, God, I think I'm getting a zit!'" She covered her face with her hands completely, then dropped them. "It's never-ending."

"I don't want Tabitha to go through that. I want her to be as confident as you are."

"Then you can instill in her that beauty is what's on the inside and to have confidence in who she is."

"Being a father is getting harder and harder. How do I do that?"

Dani looked away as she thought. "My father always told me that I was smart and beautiful and that I could be whatever I wanted to be. Though he was gone by the time I was ten, that still might have helped me. I didn't even bother with the mirror in the bathroom at school because it just seemed like I was being vain to keep checking myself out. It kind of felt like if I did that, it meant I didn't believe my dad."

Knowing how much she loved her dad, he could understand that. "Being a father is going to be difficult."

"No one says it's easy, but it's worth it. My mom says being a parent is the hardest and most rewarding thing she's ever done in life."

Right now, all he could see was the hard part, the unknown future of fatherhood, though Dani's advice was helping. "You were going to tell me about your first boyfriend."

"So I was. That was Bill. He seemed perfect. First of all, he was taller than I was. He was also very polite and a really nice guy. Unfortunately, he didn't have a plan. He was only going to college because his parents were making him, so he didn't take his classes seriously, preferring to skip lectures and get a tutor at the last minute to help him pass, when he did pass. When he told me his parents insisted he break up with me because I was too big of a distraction, I was relieved. That's when I learned I needed to really think about what I wanted in a significant other."

He probably fell far short of what she wanted, and it was just as well since the last thing he needed was a significant other. "Did you find someone?"

For the first time since meeting her, he sensed vulnerability.

She shrugged. "I thought I did a couple of times, but for one reason or another, it didn't work out. I've decided I'm quite content on my own. There's no rule that women have to marry. Just look at all the bachelors out there. Even my boss, who's in his fifties, is a bachelor."

"Yes, Layne is a bachelor, and he's eight years older than I am."

She chuckled, lifting her hand out of the water. "That's not that old. One of the guys at work just got married this summer and he's forty-two." She stared at her hand. "Damn, we've been in here a long time. Look at the wrinkles on my fingers. It looks like I'm eighty."

He pulled his hand out and held it next to hers. It wasn't

nearly as wrinkled. "Guess I have too many callouses to wrinkle."

She pulled his hand closer to inspect it. "I see a little wrinkling, but you're right. Your skin is tougher than mine. That's because you do good, honest work, as my father would say."

He wanted to disagree, as all he was doing was feeding and changing Tabitha's diapers and some computer work, but since she'd mentioned her father, he didn't want to seem ungrateful.

She rose, and the water sluiced down her curves as she stepped out of the hot tub. He found himself wanting to lick it off her. He grasped the edge of the hot tub to keep himself stationary. Unfortunately, that meant he had a perfect view of her as she dried herself off before putting on the robe.

She stepped into her flip-flops and picked up her towel before turning toward him. "Are you getting out?"

Considering the erection he had in his shorts, he shook his head. "I'll stay in a little longer."

"Okay. I'm going to head back and change for dinner. I can't come over tomorrow because I promised Kaitlynn I'd go on the trail ride with her, and then she wants me to take line dance lessons with her. I guess you all are having a band tomorrow night, and she doesn't want me to make a fool of myself." Dani rolled her eyes, obviously not concerned.

He'd forgotten about the dancing and drinks event. Probably because it was the last place he would want to be. He just hoped it wasn't too loud for Tabitha's sake.

"I'll be over the following morning. I ordered something for you, and I should have it by then."

"For me?" He wasn't sure what to think of that, but he didn't think it was good.

"Well, it's more for Tabitha, but you'll benefit as well."

He relaxed. Anything for his daughter was appreciated. "I look forward to seeing it. Thank you for thinking of her."

Dani waved and left the pool area.

He was an idiot. He hadn't even thanked her for helping him get back to reality after what she called his "episode." He'd have to do that next time he saw her. Unfortunately, his body was telling him how it wanted to thank her. The last thing he needed was to get involved with a guest ... or was he too late?

"Fuck."

CHAPTER 9

DANI WATCHED Kaitlynn two-stepping across the floor with her latest conquest. In a way, she envied her friend's ability to enjoy life and men on a strictly physical level. In fact, she wished she could follow suit.

Taking the time to hang out with Kaitlynn and just have a girls' day had been a nice break from her puzzle-solving project that was Jackson. She needed the time to process what had happened in the hot tub. It wasn't his PTSD episode that bothered her. One of the guys at work had described his own issues with the disorder and what it was like. That was the great thing about the men she worked with. They talked—a lot.

However, Jackson's kiss had been a surprise, as had the passion he'd ignited in her. She'd forgotten what that kind of passionate excitement was like. At first, she wasn't sure whether he knew who she was, but when he held her hand so long, it told her he was very aware of her. That night, she'd even dreamed about him and what it would be like to have sex with him. A dream was all it could be because he was so far removed from her list of partner requirements that he might very well be the complete opposite of what she wanted.

So far, Jackson didn't meet seven of her eleven criteria: 1. Though he wasn't a gym rat, he was still too good-looking and would attract many women; 2. he had some serious emotional baggage from his deployment; 3. he had an ex *and* a child; 5. he didn't like to talk, though he had after his flashback, but that was a special circumstance; 6. he had no sense of humor; 7. he had an interfering family; and 8. he was former military, which meant his past was filled with dramatic events.

She could probably cross off "desk job with good earning potential" too. So that was eight out of eleven that he didn't meet. Luckily, she was interested in him only as a vacation puzzle to put together. She didn't know yet if he met two other criteria, but he did meet one, the last one, Number 11, which she'd added to her list after her third try at love—"passion."

Despite her efforts to ignore it, she was very sexually attracted to him, and it was too bad that's all it was. Still, that made him perfect for a hookup. The question was, could she have sex with no emotional attachment? She'd never tried a casual hookup before. Rocky Road was as good a place as any to try one since she lived in Show Low and had no reason to be near the ranch or Four Peaks again.

Even as she gave herself permission to try something new, the band started a slow song, and couples who'd been doing the two-step quickly embraced as more came onto the dance floor. It was easy to tell which couples were married or in a long-term relationship and which ones were still in the getting to know each other stage. One cute couple made up of maybe a ten-year-old and a nine-year-old, neither with any formal dance training, were taking their lead from the adults. There were a few who were just dancing to dance. And then there was Kaitlynn.

Dani smiled. Her friend hadn't waited until the first chorus to start kissing her partner. For the first time in a long while, Dani found herself a little jealous. Not of Kaitlynn's partner but her own inability to follow through on truly living like there was no tomorrow, the way Kaitlynn did. But it wasn't as if she could walk into Jackson's home tomorrow morning and seduce him.

Frustrated, she rose. Hanging around a bunch of couples wasn't going to make her feel better. What she needed was a brisk night walk looking at the stars. After pulling on her leather jacket, she took her bottle of beer and headed outside. Unfortunately, it wasn't as cold as she'd thought, and with her long-sleeved maroon knit top, she really didn't need the jacket. Still, she headed for the ATV road and walked toward the birthing pen, her long flowered skirt swishing against her boots.

There was something soothing about being alone outside at night or early in the morning. She took a few deep breaths. The stars were bright, and the vast sky reminded her of exactly how insignificant she was in such a big universe. Her dad had always pointed to the stars when she complained about missing him. He told her all she had to do was look up and know that he was looking up at the same stars.

A wild burro complained up ahead, so she turned

around. She didn't need to tangle with an ornery burro. Not when she was just looking for a relaxing stroll. As she headed back, the outside lights of the bunkhouses made it clear they were in a U formation, and the colored lights from the band danced behind the large windows of the clubhouse.

She walked past her bunkhouse and stepped up to the corral, though it was empty of any horses. She leaned on the top rail. She had only one more week of vacation, and she hadn't learned to rope or shoot. But she had learned to line dance, helped set fence posts, and gone on a trail ride, though the last was a reach because she'd already known how to ride from her teenage years when she went through her horse-loving stage.

She had, however, had experiences the others didn't like—

"Hold on. You need to slow down. You'll be sick. Here."

At the sound of the voice coming from the barn, she stepped away from the corral and quietly approached the open door. The lighting was low, but it was easy to see inside. The problem was, she didn't believe what she was seeing. "Jackson?"

His head snapped around, but he relaxed when he saw her. "Hi. I'm just feeding Shotgun."

She took a step into the barn and pointed. "Is that the raccoon from the trash bin?"

He nodded as he held a piece of apple out to the animal. "Yes, he adopted me, so I come out and give him some food when my father insists on grandpa time with Tabitha. As long as Isaac is there, I'm okay with it."

She took a few more steps into the barn. She'd only been

joking when she called the raccoon his pet, but here he was feeding it, a bowl of water on the hay bale where the animal sat. "Aren't they dangerous? Can't they give you rabies?"

"Wait." He spoke to the raccoon before handing it a piece of carrot. "Yes, they can on both counts, but this one is young. I think when it fell in our plastic trash bin and couldn't get out that its mother left him. He's probably old enough to be on his own, but he appears to think he can depend on me now."

She found herself fascinated by the raccoon's behavior. As soon as Jackson turned to speak to her, the little animal took advantage of his inattention and grabbed another piece of food from the small bucket at Jackson's side.

At her silence, Jackson turned back to Shotgun and tipped the bucket over. "That's all I have. You ate it way too fast and will probably be sick. Don't blame me, and don't throw up in the barn. Hear me?"

Instead of looking guilty, the little guy jumped onto Jackson's arm and settled on his broad shoulder, where it began to wash its bandit eyes.

She grinned, moving closer. With any other person, the raccoon wouldn't have been able to sit, but Jackson's shoulder was plenty big enough. "He looks pretty clean."

"He washes himself every night after dinner. Then he scurries off to see what else he can find to eat. I usually find him back here," he patted a hay bale behind him, "in the predawn hours when I go for a run. I change the water in his bowl, and he washes himself again before going to sleep."

The raccoon started washing his ears with his paws by licking them and then rubbing.

"I have to admit, you surprise me."

"Is that a good thing or a bad thing?"

"I never thought about it, but you know, I do like surprises, so that would be a good thing."

Jackson leaned back against the hay bales, which didn't seem to bother Shotgun at all. "What are you doing out here? Is the band finished already?"

She waved her hand toward the clubhouse, her bracelet catching the light in the barn as it peeked out from beneath her jacket. "No. They're still going strong. I just went for a walk. The stars in your valley are as bright as they are in Show Low, only you have more night sky to look at than I do from my house. I have lots of trees."

He turned his head toward Shotgun. "Are you done yet?"

The raccoon was staring at her.

"Hey, you done washing? I have things to do."

Shotgun chattered at him, as if answering.

She laughed. "I take it that was a no. He's one lucky raccoon."

"I think he realizes that. Every morning, he leaves me something he found on the outside windowsill of my room."

Surprised, she raised her brows. "I've never heard of such a thing, but I'm no expert on raccoons. What kinds of things does he leave you?"

Jackson shrugged, which Shotgun did not appreciate from the sound of it. "Basically, garbage. Nothing edible. A silver plastic spoon, a sparkly girl's hair tie, and a beer bottle cap. The other things were bits and pieces of something else. I have no idea if that's normal. It's just what he does."

That was actually cute. "Your family must love that."

He hesitated before responding. "They don't know he's still around, and I want to keep it that way."

She was about to ask why but decided against it. She'd already seen that Brody and Jeremiah meddled wherever they wanted. She could understand him wanting to keep Shotgun to himself. It wasn't every day a wild animal picked a human to befriend. "I promise I won't say a word."

As if Shotgun had been waiting for her promise, he climbed back down to the hay bale and looked expectantly at Jackson.

Jackson addressed him. "You look good."

As if on cue, Shotgun stood on his hind legs and sniffed the air before scrambling down and disappearing out a hole in the wall of the barn. She eyed the hole and was pretty sure it wasn't a rotten piece that had broken off but a recently cut square big enough for a raccoon to go in and out of. That Jackson had gone to so much trouble for an orphaned raccoon tugged at her heart. "Do you always befriend stray animals?"

"I've never been home long enough to. As a kid, I hung out at Layne's and then I joined the Army and have rarely been home." He was back to frowning.

He seemed to have two main expressions, serious and frowning. She had yet to see him smile. Hopefully, he smiled at his daughter, but as she thought about it, she wasn't sure. "Maybe Shotgun sensed that you would be staying for a while."

"I don't think so. Animals have many senses, but that's not one of them. I was just in the right place at the right time to rescue him. I still haven't decided if his dependence on me is helping him."

"I think it's a two-way street. You help him and he helps you."

Jackson crossed his arms. "How so?"

She moved to the hay bale Shotgun had just vacated and sat. "You give him food and a safe place to live. He gives you happiness and garbage."

"Are you saying I like garbage?" He frowned as he pushed away from the tall stack of hay bales against the wall and faced her.

"Not at all. I'm saying that Shotgun gives you joy because you are his world. He chose you. You're happy to help him. Most people would not be deemed worthy by a wild animal, but you are. Of course, that's just how I think. There's nothing scientific about it."

He set his hand against the bales to the side of her. "I like the way you think. It's different."

She smiled, very pleased by that. "Thank you."

"I also like the way you look and smell. You're unique."

Her heart skipped a beat. "How I smell?" As strange as his comment was, it still sent goosebumps racing across her flesh.

"Yes, it's ... peaceful."

Peaceful? What an interesting word for a scent. "It must be my body wash because I don't use perfume."

"Or maybe it's just you."

His look was more intense than his words, which had her body on alert. "Peaceful. That's a positive, at least. I mean, it's not like I smell confused or chaotic or ..." She snapped her mouth closed, not sure why she was rambling except for the look in his eyes. It was strange to feel as if someone were ready to pounce on her and to be anxious for it to happen.

Hadn't she just been thinking that a hookup with Jackson would make her vacation complete and allow her to test the waters of non-relationship sex? If she wanted that to happen, then now was her chance. More comfortable with action instead of reaction, she rose and faced him. "What do you smell like?"

His brows rose, and his gaze moved over her face as opposed to staying in one spot. "I don't know." His brows lowered, and his chin lifted slightly as he looked down at her. "Maybe you can tell me."

Okay, that was an invitation if she'd ever heard one. Stepping very close to him but not touching his large pectoral muscles, she made a show of taking a deep breath. He smelled clean, like basic soap, but how could she describe it in an abstract? Closing her eyes, she took another deep breath, letting her mind wander, hoping to catch the feeling of the scent. She smiled as it came to her, and she opened her eyes. "You smell like beginnings."

"Beginnings." His voice was just above a whisper as he stared at her mouth. "I like beginnings."

She licked her lips in response, perfectly willing to begin an enjoyable encounter. "I do too."

Without touching her, he lowered his head as if to kiss her but instead closed his eyes and took a deep breath.

The action almost had her rising on her toes as every nerve ending reacted to him.

His eyes opened, and he gazed into hers. "I need peace."

Those few words held a lot of meaning. He was telling

her not only that he needed peace but also that he needed her, and she could give him both. Even if she weren't already physically excited, she could no more deny him than deny they stood in a barn.

She wrapped her arms around his neck. "You can have peace." She tugged on his neck, and his mouth brushed over hers, testing her, as if not quite believing. She pushed herself against his entire hard body, the thrill of the contact setting off sparks of desire everywhere they touched.

As if her movement was exactly what he needed, he wrapped her in his arms, and his mouth came down hard on hers, his tongue thrusting between her lips.

Yes! The word sounded in her head at his invasion, and she met his tongue with her own. To say she felt wanted was an understatement. Jackson's hands roamed all over her as his mouth held hers, from her back to her butt to her head, before moving back to her butt and pulling her against his obvious erection.

Her body lit on fire with craving. She felt unable to get close enough to him. She ground her pelvis against his even as her tongue retreated and allowed him to thrust into her mouth, like she wanted to feel him between her thighs.

He groaned before breaking the kiss and crushing her against his body, which was like being crushed against a human wall. His breathing was as rapid as hers, and she couldn't tell where his heartbeat ended and hers began. Her instinct told her he was trying to regain control, but she didn't want him to. "Jackson."

He didn't move an inch. "Yes."

"I'm hot."

"Yes, you are."

She grinned against his chest. "No, I mean, I have too many clothes on." She didn't think the man's body could get any harder, but at her words, he turned into a rock.

When he did speak, his voice was gravelly. "Do you want me to help you take some off?"

"Yes."

A tiny shudder rippled through him before he loosened his hold enough to allow her to bring her arms down.

His brown eyes appeared so dark they looked black. It was as if he wanted to devour her. At the spike of need that sent to her groin, she felt moisture outside her sheath. She couldn't remember getting hot so fast for anyone else. She swallowed hard to get words out. "My coat?"

He turned her toward the stack of hay bales and pulled the jacket off her shoulders from behind. Before she could turn back, his arms came around her once more, pulling her against him, his arms wrapping around her, holding her tight. She felt his face against the top of her head as he inhaled again.

She waited for the exhale, but it was a long time coming, and when it did come, he loosened his hold, his hands moving down to her waist. "Lift."

Understanding dawned, and she readily complied, lifting her arms so he could pull the knit top off. The cool air of the barn hit her bare skin around her stretch bra. It felt good.

"Lower."

She grinned at his command. She had planned to, but he was obviously impatient. She liked that. Still, she lowered her arms slowly until they finally rested at her sides, curious how quickly he could lose control like she hoped.

He smoothed his hands down her arms until he entwined his fingers with hers, just as he had done in the hot tub. It was a gesture of comfortability, which she appreciated, considering how closed off he'd been the day they first met. Was that only a week ago?

Before she'd realized what he was about, her hands were behind her back and she felt the sleeves of her top wrapped around them, her bracelet wrapped up inside. She froze even as her heart started to race. "What are you doing?" She wasn't into bondage, having never been the submissive type.

He immediately stopped, lowering his head to speak in her ear. "I can't let you touch me. If I do, I won't be able to enjoy you. I haven't been with a woman in almost a year."

The thrill his words sent through her body hit every part of her, even her heart. Still, it made her nervous. "Okay, but only if I get to do the same with you another time."

She could feel him thinking. How could that be? How could she be so in tune with him that she knew what he was doing with her back turned? Was it being tied up that caused him to hesitate, or was it that she'd mentioned another time? She hadn't even thought that far. It had just come out. Then, before he spoke, she knew he'd made his decision.

"If that is what you would like, then I agree."

She had no chance to respond as the material tightened around her wrists. Another tie was made, and she was bound. A little panic hit her, and she tested the tie. Despite it being snug, the knit material of her top had give, and if she needed to, she was confident she could wriggle a hand out. That calmed her.

Jackson pulled her against his body once more.

She grinned as she realized her hands were in a very good place if she wished to encourage him. But as his hands came down off her shoulders over her bra to cup her breasts, she was quite sure he didn't need any encouragement. He lifted them, as if feeling how heavy they were, before brushing over them to the straps on her shoulders.

Slowly, Jackson pulled the stretchy material down her arms until he'd revealed her breasts.

The cool air hit her warm nipples, which were already on alert, making them harder.

He lowered his head, setting his chin on her right shoulder. "Perfect."

The word was spoken as if he were in awe, which had her melting inside. Anxiously, she waited for him to touch her, but he didn't, not exactly. Instead, he tilted his head down and blew air across her right nipple, sending sharp tingles of excitement to her core. Damn, the man knew how to tease.

His hands continued down her arms, leaving the bra straps where they were to find the three buttons at the top of her flowered skirt.

She sucked in her waist as he unbuttoned the top one, but that's as far as he went. She understood why as he slipped his left hand beneath the skirt and under her panties even as his right one held her hip still. She wanted to encourage him, but with her hands behind her back, there was little she could do. If she touched his cock within his jeans, he might stop altogether. He had said he couldn't handle her touching him. So she forced herself to let him do as he wished.

Luckily, he knew his way around a woman's body. His fingers brushed through the small patch of hair she left on her mons and continued downward to explore her folds. The second his fingers touched her wetness, he stopped.

It was agonizing, waiting for him to continue, but she forced herself not to move her pelvis and allow him his own pace, not something she was very good at usually, but Jackson was far different than any lover she'd had before.

She wasn't sure whether he had made a decision or simply regained control of his own body, but he finally moved his fingers along the opening of her sheath, gently touching her everywhere but not delving in where her body wanted.

Instead, he moved his fingers up and around her clit, circling it but barely brushing it.

Her insides tensed with anticipation, and she found herself making fists behind her. She tried to stand still and wait, but he was killing her. Her pelvis tilted toward his fingers of its own accord.

His chin dug into her shoulder as he complied with her unvoiced need, and his fingers played with her excited nub. Need spiraled inside her as he fiddled with her excitement, stroking, pressing, and circling her clit, preparing her for an orgasm that continued to build.

Her panting grew audible, but all she could focus on were the feelings building in her core.

Jackson took that moment to use his free hand to turn her head toward him and kiss her. There was nothing sweet about the kiss. It was hard and demanding, and it pushed her over the edge.

Her pelvis rocked against his hand as she screamed around his tongue even as he continued his pleasurable torture, prolonging her ecstasy yet sharing it with her. Then he pressed his fingers against her clit and held her there for a moment longer before allowing her to come back to reality, kissing her gently as she regained her senses.

"That was ..." She gave up. She couldn't think straight enough to find the words. Vaguely, she realized he pulled his hand from her body. As he turned her to face him, her legs wobbled, and she found herself sitting on the hay bales.

Jackson knelt before her. "You okay?"

She grinned. "More than okay. Just a little weak after that."

"Good, because I want to taste you."

She barely had a moment to comprehend his words before he was rolling up her skirt. She tried to help him but realized her hands were still tied. If this was how he made love when barely under control, she needed to find out how he did it when he had all the time in the world.

He tugged off one of her cowboy boots and had her lean to one side, then tugged off the other so he could pull down her panties until she lifted one foot from them. The man definitely didn't seem to be in a hurry. Then he nudged her legs open and again took a deep breath, his eyes closing. When he opened them, his nostrils flared.

She'd never met someone so in tune with his senses. There was something primal about Jackson that she hadn't noticed before, and every womanly part of her reacted.

His gaze met hers, and the pure need in his eyes sent a sharp ache deep inside her. She didn't want to wait any longer. "I want you inside me."

At her words, his look grew hotter, but he shook his head, though he did nothing else.

The man must be made of stone to have so much control after a year of abstinence. When she tried to rush things, he just slowed them down. Trying to find patience, she closed her eyes and counted to ten. She had just made ten when cool air on her nipple had her opening them once again.

Jackson was back to enticing her, but now that he was in front of her, he was able to blow on each nipple in turn and multiple times. They were so hard, they ached.

He leaned forward and kissed her. Another hard I-want-you kiss that literally had her body tingling.

Then he sat back on his haunches and stared at the juncture of her thighs. His hands against them pushed them just a bit wider before his head lowered and he licked from the bottom of the entrance to her sheath to the top of her clit.

Her body ignited all over again, already anxious for what he'd do next. She wanted to grab his head and hold him there, but all she could do was watch as he once again lapped at her. Then his tongue delved into her sheath, and she moaned. It was close to what she wanted, but instead of thrusting as she wished, he moved his tongue inside her and around the entrance, tasting her as he said he would.

Just when she thought she would cry in frustration, he lifted his hand from her thigh and inserted one of his large fingers inside her.

Her entire sheath closed around it in relief. As he moved

it in and out slowly, she tried to relax and enjoy the sensations, but they were so strong—unreasonably so.

He pulled his finger out and inserted two very slowly.

Instinctually, she widened her legs more, anxious to take whatever he could give. His head lowered again, and he licked at her clit. Sparks ignited, and she squeezed his fingers, anxious for that pinnacle he could take her to. As his tongue worked over her clit, she bucked at his still hand, unable to help herself, but he didn't move his fingers at all.

Her whole body was wrapped up in the sensation building in her core as she grasped for the orgasm that seemed just out of reach. The feelings intensified, bringing her to the very brink and holding her there. Suddenly, his fingers moved, and she split into a thousand atoms, bursting with pleasure.

"Now."

CHAPTER 10

JACKSON COULDN'T HOLD on any longer. He hoped she could take him, was ready for him, because he had to be in her. Unzipping his pants, he released his cock, giving him a few seconds of control. He pulled Dani up, his fingers still inside her, and pushed her against the tall stack of hay bales.

She was still coming around his fingers, grinding against his hand.

He quickly pulled his fingers from her and slowly pushed his cock into her, careful to hold back his frenzy a moment longer as her sheath stretched for him.

"Yes." The guttural word tore from her throat as her hands, one wrist still with her knit top wrapped around it, grabbed onto his neck.

Relief enveloped him, and her single word was all he needed. Lifting her legs, he thrust in again, pushing her into the hay. But it wasn't enough, not nearly. She felt so good, so warm, so wet, so tight, like she'd never let go. He needed more. Much more.

He pumped into her, not sure how long he could hold out, enjoying the feel of her but willing to push it to the brink. Her nails dug into his back, and she panted hard until she tightened around him even more and yelled. He wanted to stay, just one more thrust, just another, just—

He felt his balls tighten and pulled out just as he came, rubbing himself against her thigh as the pleasure swept over him and cooled. The feel of his jeans sliding down past his knees brought him back to reality. He should apologize for being so rough, but he couldn't seem to say the words. That's who he was.

"Jackson, are you okay?"

He opened his eyes, not realizing he'd closed them. "Yes. You?"

A wide smile filled her face. "Oh, I'm more than okay. I'm great."

She was great? She enjoyed it? Didn't mind his uncontrolled rutting? It was hard to believe. "Are you sure?"

She nodded. "Absolutely. I feel amazing."

Though she still straddled him, he hugged her tighter, unable to explain how he felt in words because to say he felt normal would sound too weird.

She looked around his shoulder. "We should probably get dressed before someone comes to investigate all the noise in here."

"What noise?"

Her brows puckered together. "Um, between my scream and your shout, I'm surprised someone didn't call 911." She gave him a sly smile.

Fuck, he hadn't even been aware he shouted. He was

always aware of his surroundings. If he weren't, he could get killed—except he was home, on the ranch, where it was safe, with Dani. Absently, he nodded, and she dropped her legs from around him, his backside immediately feeling the cool night air.

Letting go of his neck, she hopped on one foot to the lower hay bale, pulling on her underwear first, then grabbed her boots, moving them closer. She looked at him as she wriggled her top off her wrist. "I'm really enjoying the view, but you might want to pull up your jeans before someone comes. I mean, before someone arrives. We already came." She chuckled at her own joke and then set aside her top to pull up her bra.

Listening now, he heard the front door of the house close. "Better dress quickly. Someone is com—arriving." He bent and pulled up his jeans, fastening them in no time. He moved away from Dani, not in a hurry to reveal what had happened. He wasn't even sure why it happened, but he was glad it did.

Dani moved toward the wooden ladder into the hayloft, holding onto one rung as if still not steady on her feet.

Footsteps approached. Whoever it was wore cowboy boots and was in a hurry.

He scanned Dani's clothes, motioning with his hand that she had hay on her sleeve.

She flicked it off just as Brody came into the barn. "What happened? I heard a yell from inside the house. Is everyone okay?" Brody gave him the once over, not even seeing Dani.

Jackson didn't hadn't figured out what excuse to give when Dani spoke.

"That was your brother. He caught me about to climb

into the hayloft in a skirt and yelled at me. He was right, of course."

He froze, his whole body tensing, making it difficult to breathe as memories assailed him.

Brody's head, which had whipped around at Dani's voice, turned back to look at him. "Jackson? You okay?"

He tried to nod but couldn't seem to move. His throat was far too tight to speak.

Brody strode over to Dani. "Let's get you back to the dance. It's a lot more fun than my brother."

Jackson watched as Brody escorted Dani out of the barn. She looked back at him once, her brow furrowed, but Brody kept her moving.

Unwillingly, he moved his gaze to the loft. The feelings of guilt from his childhood filled his gut, only now they were twofold. He'd found peace with his purpose in the military, but that was gone now. He had no one to save, and he was still alive. His fingers curled into his palms at the change in his fate.

He closed his eyes, reliving the many missions where he'd saved his fellow soldiers, whole or wounded, and gotten them back so they could go home to their families. That had been his driving force, his personal mission, but now he was home with no way to atone, no way to make his life worth—an image of a baby, *his* baby, filled his head. Tabitha. A life for a life?

Footsteps approaching the barn had him opening his eyes, waiting. He wasn't surprised to find Brody had returned.

"Was she bothering you?"

Brody didn't often defend their family, his own need to leave the ranch usually taking precedence, but Jackson could tell by his brother's tone of voice that he was ready to warn Dani away. It was almost humorous, considering he'd found a few minutes of peace only when he was with her. He made his head move, shaking it. "No. She was actually helping."

Brody's brows rose as he clearly wasn't buying it. "What was she doing climbing the ladder?"

Though she hadn't, he was quite aware that it was something she would do. "Curiosity, what else?"

"Did you tell her what happened up there?"

This time, he had to swallow hard to make his voice work. "No."

"I can tell her to leave you alone. She's just a guest."

He appreciated his little brother running defense for him, but he was capable of doing that himself. "No, she's been helpful with Tabitha."

Brody gave him a crooked smile. "Yeah, she did order something for Tabby. I think it came in today."

He was sure whatever it was, it would be helpful. That's one thing he liked about her. She was practical. Another was that she didn't pretend to be an expert, at least not on babies. What she was an expert at was safety, and from what he'd read, she hadn't held back on her feedback so far. Tanner wasn't going to like all the issues she'd found.

"Jackson?"

"What?"

"I asked how long you have to stay with Tabby before you can work on the ranch again."

Though his family insisted on nicknaming his daughter,

it irritated him every time. "Why won't you call her 'Tabitha'?"

Brody's eyes widened. "Because 'Tabitha' is too formal. She's just a baby and my niece. She needs a friendlier name. Why? What's wrong with it?"

He gritted his teeth. Brody wouldn't understand. "It's not her name."

Brody rubbed the back of his neck. "I don't know, Jackson. I don't think anyone is going to change what they call her. None of us had nicknames, and I know Dad is thrilled to call her 'Tabby.' You know he won't stop."

Jackson rubbed at his eyes, beginning to feel his mind going back to Syria. Quickly, he stopped and focused on his brother instead. "Her mother was called 'Gabby.'"

"Oh, then 'Tabby' works perfectly, right?"

How could he explain? "No, because her mother tricked me. Gabriella Rossi told me she couldn't get pregnant because she was on the pill and yet then she did. I'm sorry she'd dead, but there is no love lost there."

Brody opened his mouth and closed it without uttering a word.

The silence continued, but Jackson was comfortable with silence—Brody, not so much.

"So you're saying if this Gabriella didn't trick you, I wouldn't have a niece, and my brother wouldn't be home in one piece?"

At Brody's question, he blinked. It was true, he'd still be in Syria, saving lives, fulfilling his purpose. But he also wouldn't have Tabitha. She simply wouldn't exist. At that thought, his heart seemed to stop. He couldn't imagine not having her in his life now. When he spoke, she looked at him, depending on him for her very life. Slowly, he nodded.

"Then I'm glad this Gabby tricked you. You are one lucky asshole."

"And you're still a little shit. Don't you have somewhere you're supposed to be?"

Brody held his arms out. "Nope, just here straightening you out."

"I don't need the runt of the litter messing with me." Jackson took a menacing step toward his brother, not that he'd do anything to him. They were blood, which was even stronger than his fealty to his soldiers.

Brody touched his temple. "I just remembered, my sweet wife-to-be was hoping for a slow dance tonight. I better go make sure the band plays one more so I don't disappoint." Brody started walking backward. "Try not to have any fun while I'm gone. Oh, that's right. You don't have fun anymore."

Jackson took two more strides toward his brother before Brody turned and ran, laughing all the way. He stopped and shook his head. At least some things at the ranch hadn't changed. He grunted, looking back over his shoulder at the stacked hay bales where he'd just had hard sex with a woman who could handle it. Obviously, "fun" was a relative term. Turning back, he continued out of the barn to rescue his daughter from her grandpa.

Jackson added more ratings to the Excel sheet. It was the most boring part of what he had to do, and his mind wandered. At least, instead of thinking about his deployments, he was fixating on his encounter with Dani the night before. He didn't understand why he was so attracted to her. She was physically the opposite of what he usually went for.

His women were always much shorter and wider with bigger curves. He liked a lot of body to sink into. Yet, last night had been some of the most satisfying sex he'd ever had. He was just glad that he hadn't hurt her and that she'd enjoyed it. Even now, he was anxious to repeat the encounter, though in a variety of different ways.

Shaking his head at himself, he refocused on the ratings. There weren't that many feedback cards left for him to go through, then he'd go back and add the comments into the appropriate categories. He'd had to create three additional categories for some of Dani's suggestions. His older brother hadn't anticipated comments on safety, ordering items shipped, or the host family. Tanner's categories were items like food, accommodations, activities, and staff.

Jackson had added a couple comments of his own about guests wandering away from activities and being nosey but deleted them after the third day. He was glad Dani had a mind of her own and followed it.

He was on the last card when he heard the front door open. He waited, hoping it was Dani. As familiar footsteps approached, he hit the enter key and leaned back in the large leather desk chair, his gaze on the open doorway of the office.

She didn't poke her head around the door frame or knock

on the door. She strode in as if she belonged there. "Good morning."

She was dressed in a pair of jeans and a purple turtleneck sweater that hugged her curves nicely. The weather had turned almost frosty overnight, for which he was thankful. Her extra-wavy hair was pulled back in a ponytail like she was ready to get to work. She hiked her hip up on the corner of the desk and set a package down in front of the computer screen. "This is for you and Tabitha."

As if she didn't already have his attention, he leaned forward, curious about the box in brown paper. "For both of us? I can't imagine what we both have in common."

She set her hand on the box. "Seriously? How about DNA, to start. Plus, anything that makes caring for her easier is something you'll both like. Am I right?"

He did like the way she thought. "You're right." He set his hand on the package, planning to open it.

Dani pulled it away from underneath him and kept it on her lap. "Uh-huh, not yet, big man. This is a reward. You have to earn it first."

He'd obey her command, but he was no one's trick dog. "You said you ordered it days ago, so that must mean I've already earned it."

She cocked her head, obviously thinking about his response. "That's true. However, I changed my mind last night."

Feeling completely out of his element and not a little irritated, he sat back in the chair. "I earn promotions, missions, and leave, not gifts. Either the box is a gift or it isn't."

"Touchy. Okay, I'll send it back." She rose from the desk and started toward the door.

"Wait." He hated being manipulated. He'd had a sergeant who'd done that, and it was an abuse of power in his mind. Did Dani have power over him? No fucking way. "Never mind." He sat forward again and flipped over the pile of feedback cards, fully intending to get back to work.

Dani didn't leave, though. She moved to the chair in front of his dad's desk and set the box on the corner.

He ignored her and started to type in the first comments. The person was raving about the food. He wasn't surprised. They'd hired a chef who used to cook for cattle drives down in Texas. The man knew how to cook. He added that comment to the Positive column, then checked for more comments. There was one more about the soap in the shower. Someone was looking for something more fragrant. On a dude ranch? He shook his head and added the comment to the Improvement column.

As he turned over another card, his gaze fell on Dani sitting there watching him. "What?"

"What happened in the hayloft?"

Though his heart hitched, he'd known she'd ask eventually since she didn't have a chance after Brody escorted her out of the barn. It had only been a week of having her around and he knew more about her than he did about Tabitha's mother. Dani was too damn observant. "Curiosity killed the cat."

"But satisfaction brought it back," she finished the rhyme. "So what happened? That you turned stiffer than a side of beef left in the freezer for two years is not that surprising since you're already stiff. But after I mentioned climbing into the hayloft, even Brody, the charmer of your family, got all bristly. That means something serious."

He set the feedback card down and gave her his full attention. "Why do you want to know?" He held up his hand as she opened her mouth. "And being curious is not enough."

She closed her mouth and looked away.

For some reason, her answer was important.

It took her a good two minutes, but she finally met his gaze. "Because I think it has something to do with who you are."

His gut told him that her answer wasn't what he'd sought. "Why do you want to know who I am?"

"How about, for starters, because we had mind-blowing sex last night."

It still wasn't what he'd hoped, but he didn't even know what he'd wanted or the right question to ask. His disappointment colored how he answered. "My brother died because of me when he fell from the hayloft."

Her whole body froze as she stared at him, no doubt thinking the worst.

If she thought the worst, then it wasn't even close to what he knew to be true. He turned back to the computer before glancing at the next comment and typing it under the Positive column.

"I'm sorry. I didn't realize it was such a devastating event."

He didn't look at her. He didn't want to think about it, so he kept his focus on typing in comments.

Though she rose quietly, he was completely aware of her

every movement, even without looking at her. So he wasn't surprised when he felt her step up next to him, put her hand on his shoulder, and drop a kiss on his head.

Then she left, her cowboy boot heels clicking along the travertine tile in the hall until he heard the front door open and close.

He finished typing a comment into the Improvement column, adding the code for activities, then turned to the stack again.

As his gaze moved, the box she'd brought, still sitting on the corner of the desk, caught his attention. Did she leave it by accident or on purpose? No, she didn't forget. She was far too purposeful. Against his will, he found himself picking it up and setting it before the computer. A similarly wrapped box had come into the general's office while he was in Afghanistan. That box had blown up, destroying the whole side of the building, but the timer on it had gone off too early. The building had been empty.

He stared at the box. It was not a bomb. It was from Dani, and she wouldn't hurt him and his daughter. He was also home, not overseas. There was no threat. Still, he hesitated to open it. Dani didn't do frivolous things. Then why had she told him she wanted him to earn it?

The pieces fell together easily. She'd planned to ask him about the hayloft, and when he told her, she would have given him the box. She knew the loft was a serious issue and hoped to persuade him. And now she knew. She'd also learned that bribery didn't work with him.

Pulling his utility knife from his back pocket, he cut the paper around the box and pulled it away, crumpling it into a small ball and dropping it in the trash next to the desk. It was a white box with a picture of a woman carrying her baby in what looked like a pink backpack, but it was worn on the front. Across the side was printed "Baby Sling."

He turned the box and found a picture of a man and his baby. The carrier fitted over the torso like a sling and held the baby close to the chest, leaving the parent's arms free. Excitement filled him. Quickly, he opened the box and pulled it out.

It was Army green.

He stared at it. She'd said she wanted to know about the hayloft because it would tell her who he was. But she already knew him better than anyone except maybe Layne. He pulled out the directions and started reading. He needed to thank her.

No, he and Tabitha needed to thank her.

CHAPTER 11

DANI STEPPED INTO THE CLUBHOUSE, feeling like a heel. She'd pushed too far. She didn't just feel it. She knew it. She wasn't stupid. The best thing for her to do was give Jackson some space. She didn't for a minute believe he caused his brother's death but knew with absolute certainty that he believed he had.

She slowed at that thought. Did she really know him that well already? He wasn't that hard to read, once she was able to get him talking.

"Hello, Dani. Did you come in to see what to do next?" Amanda strode forward in a pair of blue jeans, brown cowboy boots, and a light blue sweater, a straw cowboy hat atop her head.

At Amanda's greeting, she pasted on a smile. "Yes, I did. I'm looking for something that will take me into the mountains. I haven't been there yet."

"That's right, you never did make it to the petroglyphs."

Dani stopped before the coffee station. "No, I had much

more fun setting fence posts. Did they get all the fencing up?"

"They did. We'll have a few animals in there before everyone leaves."

Dani picked up a cinnamon roll slathered in icing. "Does your cook make all the food here?"

Amanda chuckled. "He could, but he's far too busy with the main meals, so we buy from the small businesses in town. We're hoping they will see the benefits of our operation."

Taking a bite, she closed her eyes. "Hmm, these are amazing." She opened her eyes. "I have to admit, I wasn't excited about spending two weeks here, but I'm really enjoying myself."

Amanda held her hand out toward a whiteboard on the wall. "Then let's see if we can find something you can do today that you'll enjoy even more."

"There's bound to be something." Taking another bite of the cinnamon roll, she followed Amanda to the daily activities list. It had the usuals, but they always threw in a handful of different ones. "What's this?" She pointed at the word "trevanger."

"Oh, that's Brody's brainstorm. It's a cross between a treasure hunt and a scavenger hunt on one of the peaks. I think it's the third one we've done. He and Hannah created the idea and set it up. I guess there are natural items to find, and for each one, you get a clue to the treasure's location. It will take all day."

That sounded different. "Is there anything that would help the ranch in particular?"

Amanda shook her head. "Not until tomorrow. We had a

group leave early this morning to repair a break in the north fence on the far eastern side. But tomorrow, we'll be moving the cows to the south fields. We'll also be riding the south fences. Did you want me to reserve a spot for you?"

She didn't like committing ahead of time. "No. I might want to just read a book tomorrow or take a walk." Or sit in the hot tub at the house.

"I understand. Your friend Kaitlynn signed up for the 'trevanger' today, if that makes it more enticing. Maybe you two could team up."

If Kaitlynn weren't busy with her latest interest, that could be fun. They hadn't done much together so far except eat. "Actually, it does. When do we leave?"

Amanda looked at the clock on the wall. "In about fifteen minutes. You may want to grab a jacket. The mountain can get cold fast. Everyone is meeting in the corral."

"Sounds good. Thanks." She turned and headed for the door but snagged another cinnamon roll on the way out. She could get back on track with healthier eating when she went back to work.

After returning to the bunkhouse for her leather jacket, she strode toward the corral, where people were being assigned their horses.

"Hey, Dani!" Kaitlynn waved, still waiting for her horse.

Dani walked into the corral. "Just the person I wanted to see."

"Really?"

"Yes. I heard you were going on this scavenger hunt and thought I'd tag along, unless you have someone more interesting you want to hang with." Dani scanned the group to see if there were any single men that Kaitlynn might have her eye on.

"No. He left too early this morning to go paint a fence or something." Kaitlynn pouted for about three seconds, then grinned. "But I have you here, so that's even better."

Better? She thought to ask why that would be, but Nash came over with their horses. "You ladies know how to—oh, hi, Dani. I know you can mount a horse." He handed her the reins. "How about you, Kaitlynn?"

Dani made the acquaintance of the quarter horse Nash handed off to her before mounting up. The horses the Dunns used for guests might be broken, but it never hurt to make friends. After mounting, she waited for Kaitlynn to get settled. In short order, they were all mounted.

Brody jumped up on the saddle of his horse, then stood on it to talk to them. "I hope you're all ready for a fun day of searching. We'll ride out to the base of the mountain and have us an early lunch. We cowboys like to eat early. Then I'll explain the rules while we eat, and you'll have three hours there before we return."

A man in the back yelled out, "Or earlier if we find the treasure."

Brody grinned. "I wouldn't count on it." After the laughter stopped, he pointed to the men sitting on their horses to his right. "Nash and Waylan will be with us to keep us safe. This is the wild, so there is everything from grasshopper mice to wild burros. If you see anything, be sure to give a shout. Now, I know you all have been with us a week, but if you're still not completely comfortable riding, raise your hand."

A mom, her daughter, and a man in his fifties raised their hands.

Brody nodded to them. "You three ride with me. The rest of you, follow Nash."

Dani was having a hard time paying attention. The last thing the man should be doing was standing on his saddle. That would give the kids ideas.

Just as she was about to say something, Brody jumped off the horse into a flip and landed on the ground.

The group erupted into applause before he remounted and tipped his hat. "Don't try this at home, folks. I'm a professional trained in trick riding. If you're curious how to get trained, I'll be happy to give you the name of the organization. Now, let's go see what the mountain has for us to find."

At his words, Nash moved his horse forward, and people started to follow him.

Kaitlynn leaned over. "Show off."

Dani agreed, somewhat appeased that he'd let people know he was trained. She'd be suggesting a few things on her nightly feedback card, though. She and Kaitlynn fell into place as the group started forward, with Waylon bringing up the rear.

At first, the pace was so slow, she worried she'd fall asleep, but it picked up. Still, it took a while to get to the base of the mountain. As soon as they arrived, Kaitlynn threw her leg over her horse and dismounted, stumbling a bit.

Dani jumped down and quickly moved over to steady her. "You're not used to riding. It's better to take it slow."

"Now you tell me." Kaitlynn grabbed onto the saddle, giving a slight groan.

"Are you okay?" Dani looked down to see whether Kaitlynn had landed wrong and twisted an ankle or something.

Kaitlynn grinned like the Cheshire cat. "Oh, I'm more than okay. My muscles are just tired. I was 'riding' all night." She wiggled her brows just to be sure her meaning was clear.

Dani thought about her ride. She hadn't worked her leg muscles at all with Jackson running the encounter and her hands tied. She hoped she had the opportunity to give him payback for that. Not that he was very happy with her at the moment. Unfortunately for him, it wouldn't stop her from trying to figure out why he thought he caused his brother's death.

"I'm good now. Let's go get some food."

At Kaitlynn's assurance, they moved to a table that had been set up before they arrived, and they found the cook explaining the various choices for sandwiches. They each chose a boxed lunch, and Dani grabbed a blanket from the pile set up on a small boulder. Moving to a spot in the sun since it was still a little chilly, they spread out the blanket and sat to eat.

"Hmm, I think I'd stay here another two weeks just for the food." Kaitlynn wiped barbeque sauce from her mouth. "Did you know that the owners of the ranch all cook as well?"

Dani finished chewing her bite of pastrami sandwich before answering. "I didn't know that. Who told you?"

"Amanda. I guess her brothers don't cook, but all the Dunn boys are excellent. They each take turns cooking and cleaning up afterward each day. Because Amanda married Tanner, she now cooks too. Hannah would after her Christmas Eve wedding, except Brody's leaving the ranch in

January to become one of those animal wardens for the state park system."

Dani lowered her sandwich. "Brody's leaving? He seems to love being the center of attention." Did that mean Jackson would then have to take on the responsibilities that Brody had? She didn't like that idea. He had a daughter who needed his attention, especially at not even two months old.

Kaitlynn finished chewing her bite. "I know what you mean. He does like playing host. Maybe they'll hire another ranch hand or something, though I think the head ranch hand, Layne, would make a good host. It's too bad he's so old."

Dani almost choked on her bite and quickly gulped down some water. "He's only mid-thirties, from what I heard."

"Exactly my point." Kaitlynn leaned in, a sly grin on her face. "Every night on my comment card, I tell them they should have singles only weeks so we can see who's available. I figure if two single people come to a dude ranch, then they automatically have one thing in common."

Dani nodded at her friend, not surprised that Kaitlynn had thought of that angle. "Speaking of singles, are you still interested in the man you were dancing with last night?"

"Him and a couple of others."

Dani shook her head as she plopped the last bite of sandwich in her mouth.

"Why are you shaking your head? We only have six days left and I need to make a decision, so I'm speeding up my process."

"It's not that I disapprove of your process. I'm just in awe of how you can enjoy men physically when there is no relationship. It's something I've been contemplating for myself."

Kaitlynn put down her bottle of water as her eyes rounded. "You? Ms. Top-Ten-Characteristics-That-Make-Mr.-Right?"

The way Kaitlynn said it did make Dani feel like she'd overthought the whole partner requirements idea. "It was top eleven in the end. And I told you, I burned that list."

"That's right. I forgot. For the last five years, you've been judging every man according to it. Is it hard to stop?"

Dani thought about all the ways that Jackson failed to meet the list of requirements. "Yes, a little. But since I'm no longer looking, I just ignore it. But I was hoping to learn a bit more about your process."

"Mine?" Kaitlynn's smile was wider than the Salt River. "What do you want to know?"

Dani opened her mouth to ask, but Brody called for everyone's attention. So she waited as he explained the hunt, much like Amanda already had, and then refused to reveal what the treasure was.

She and Kaitlynn threw their trash in the garbage bag and then picked up a card and pen so they could mark off what they found. For every two items they found and took a photo of, they could get a clue. Brody made a big deal of not touching anything, especially because "snakeskin" and "dead spider" were on the list and judging whether something was alive or dead could become deadly.

Dani led the way up the mountain, mainly because she'd wanted to simply hike up and enjoy the view, which the people at their table a couple nights ago had raved about.

Then again, they were from Phoenix, so the view would be very different to them.

"Hey, hold up. Isn't that an animal bone?" Kaitlynn, a couple steps behind, pointed to her right.

Dani turned to investigate. "Yes, it is. Looks like it could be rabbit."

Kaitlynn quickly took a picture and made a check on their card.

Obviously, Kaitlynn was excited about the scavenger hunt, so Dani paid more attention to their surroundings as she climbed. After a few yards, she stopped. "Wasn't there 'pink granite' on that list?"

Kaitlynn came up next to her, perusing the card. "Yes! Did you find some?"

Dani pointed to a fist-sized rock, and her bracelet clasp came undone. She quickly caught it to refasten it.

"Got it." Kaitlynn took a photo and then checked off another box.

They continued walking. It took a little longer, but she spotted something else. "There's a piece of burnt wood."

Kaitlynn quickly caught up. "I wonder what burnt wood is doing up here."

"There was a devastating fire here in the nineties. I'm surprised there's any burnt wood left. You should get two clues for finding that."

"I agree. But I doubt if Brody will agree."

Dani looked to the left and right to see whether anyone else had climbed as far as they had. Luckily, there were a couple of people, one on either side of them, who were higher. Actually, it looked like Nash might be one of them, if the rifle he held was any indication.

"Wow, check out that view."

At Kaitlynn's enthusiasm, Dani turned and grinned. "Now, that's what I'm talking about." It was stunning. The valley where the ranch sat was long and wide, stretching east to west. On the south side of the ranch, the land started a slow incline where the town of Four Peaks was nestled. It was one of those views that made humans realize how tiny they really were.

Not one to stop and smell the roses for long, Kaitlynn faced her. "Speaking of talking, you were talking about getting my advice. You never ask for my advice."

Dani stared at the scene a bit longer but knew Kaitlynn's patience was limited. "That's not true. I often ask you who you think would work best on a specific drill team or what's the best hotel in the area."

"Yeah, I guess. So what do you want to know?"

"I'm curious about your process for finding lovers. I'm thinking since I've given up on finding Mr. Right, maybe I should try it your way for a change."

Kaitlynn gave her the side eye. "For real?"

She grinned. "Yes, for real. I'm here on vacation, so maybe this is as good a place as any. What's your criteria?"

"Criteria? First of all, you need to get out of your head. I'm not *thinking* about who I want. I'm feeling. It's about chemistry, desire, passion."

She definitely had all those things with Jackson. "So once you realize you're attracted to someone, what do you do?"

Kaitlynn rolled her eyes. "Duh, you jump his bones, as my mother used to say."

She looked at Kaitlynn blankly. "Do you mean have sex?"

"Yes. If it's good, then you go back for more."

"Okay. Then what?"

Kaitlynn cocked her head. "What do you mean, then what? Then you have great sex until you don't anymore. Then you look for a new lover."

She hadn't realized it, but she'd been hoping there was a bit more to it. "So you just want to go from one bed to the next until you get too old to do it?"

"Not exactly."

"Okay, then what is the end goal?"

Kaitlynn started looking around at the ground as if she were starting the search again. "The end goal is to find that lover that you can't live without and he can't live without you."

Dani perked up at that. "Have you ever come close?"

"Once. It was a false alarm."

From Kaitlynn's tone, it sounded like the man had been the one to leave. "So you just enjoy men until one decides they can't live without you?"

Kaitlynn lifted her head. "Exactly. I figure if you have passion for each other in bed and that passion bleeds into other areas of life, then that's a keeper. Can you look at this? It looks like it might be a part of a snakeskin."

Dani inspected the opaque film. There wasn't much, but it had the markings of a rattlesnake. "Yes, it is."

In no time, Kaitlynn was back into the scavenger hunt, scanning the ground for anything on the list.

But Dani kept thinking about how Kaitlynn approached finding the one. On the one hand, Dani was pleased that, in the end, they both had the same end goal, even if she'd given up on hers. On the other hand, maybe she could try Kaitlynn's way for a while. She'd given her process ten tries over the last five years and it had bombed.

She doubted that she and Jackson would find they couldn't live without having sex together, but in the meantime, she had this week to find out, and the first night had certainly been promising. What did she have to lose?

CHAPTER 12

JACKSON RESETTLED Tabitha in the sling. It was a bit awkward, as he wasn't used to holding her so close, but he found it reassuring to feel her tiny warmth against his chest. Her round blue eyes were wide as she tried to look around even though she faced him. It also felt strange that he didn't need to support her head since it was well supported by the material.

To test out his movement, he walked out of his bedroom and into the kitchen, where Tanner was adding lunch dishes to the dishwasher. "I thought Amanda was cook today?"

Tanner looked up and frowned. "What is that?"

"It's a baby sling. I'll give you this one when Tabitha grows too big for it."

Tanner lifted one eyebrow. "I think *you're* too big for it. Is it supposed to fit like that?"

Jackson ignored the comment since he'd read the instructions and it fit fine. He moved to one of the stools at the counter and pulled it out, wanting to see how it felt sitting with Tabitha.

Starting to sit, he stopped. "Whoa, that's not good." He clasped the back of his daughter's head. Leaning forward when sitting down could cause her head or back to hit the counter. He pushed the stool out further and then sat, satisfied Tabitha was safe from harm. "It works better when standing and walking around."

"Where'd you get that?" Tanner came around the counter to examine the cloth carrier or smile at Tabitha. It was hard to say what his true purpose was.

"Dani, one of the guests, ordered it. I guess her sister has kids, so she knows a little about them. Where's Amanda? I thought she had cooking duties today."

Tanner walked back to the other side of the counter. "We traded days. She's got an errand to run and won't be back in time to make dinner. So, this Dani. Is she filling out the comment cards, or has she given you any feedback about her experience so far?"

Dani was one of three guests who gave feedback every single day, but since the cards were anonymous, he wasn't about to reveal that. "Now that's hard to tell. It's not like there are names on the cards, and we get multiple ones from each bunkhouse. But she was the one who helped us get the fencing posts in the ground for the petting zoo pen. So I'm guessing she's the one who suggested the guests do more 'meaningful' work on the ranch."

"I heard that from a couple of others, so I sent a group out to mend the north fence this morning. I just hope Nash and Vic make sure it's done right."

Jackson stood up from the stool since it was more comfortable. "You're wound tighter than I was when I found out I had a daughter. Don't you trust your ranch hands?"

Tanner sighed. "I do. It's just with all these people around who all want something different, it's a lot of personalities to handle."

"You don't have to handle them. Let your staff do their jobs. You should be coordinating, not stepping in everywhere."

"And you know this because of the last dude ranch you ran?"

"No, smart man. I know this because I was in the Army and there are good leaders and bad leaders. The good leaders trust their men to do their jobs. The bad leaders ... they just get people killed."

Tanner studied him for a long moment. "I would put you in charge if I thought you wouldn't scare away the guests."

Jackson shrugged. "Better than scaring away the staff." He started to walk out of the room.

"Did you hear something from one of the staff?"

At Tanner's panicked voice, he shook his head. "No. Just making a point. You need to chill."

Ignoring the grumble from his older brother, he headed outside to further test the baby sling, grabbing his cowboy hat on the way out. As he walked toward the corral, he kept looking down at Tabitha. Her eyes were wide as the side of her head rested against his chest. Did she see the barn? Or the two horses in the corral? Sometimes she seemed more attuned to sounds than sights.

He needed to do more research. That was one benefit of

helping the ranch from the office. He had time to research what to expect from his daughter. It was also helpful for videos on how to put on a baby sling.

He stopped at the corral and turned so Tabitha could see the horses. "I'll buy you a horse when you get older and teach you to ride. You'll be the best female rider in the whole county." He paused as another thought occurred. "Unless you'd rather do something else. Just be smarter than I've been." Again, he paused. "But no pressure. I want you to be happy. I'll always be here to catch you if you fall. I promise."

He lifted his hand toward hers, and she wrapped her fingers around his. Contentment filled him as she did so, but as usual, it was followed by a shiver of panic. He was petrified he'd screw her up. He had no sisters to talk to. He still didn't trust Amanda. He'd grown up hating her whole family. Finding his brother married to her had been more of a shock than his home turning from a cattle ranch into a dude ranch.

"I wish everything was the way it was before I left—except you." He stroked Tabitha's knuckles. Sometime in the last ten days or so, his feeling of resentment had faded. Now, he couldn't imagine not having his daughter.

Tabitha turned her head, her face against his chest.

He wasn't comfortable with that and gently turned her so she faced the other way.

Her little legs kicked once before she settled against him again.

Her trust in him gave him confidence and a lot of responsibility. He'd led men in three countries and was up for the mission, but he was smart enough to know that Tabitha would be his hardest mission yet—but maybe, if he did well, his most rewarding?

He moved away from the corral. "Let's see if we can find Dani and thank her for your new ride." Even as he headed toward the clubhouse to see whether anyone knew where she was, he imagined buying Tabitha a rocking horse when she was a little older.

Walking into the building, he quickly scanned the area out of habit. Four guests were sitting at a table playing cards, a family was just leaving out the back with towels in hand to take a dip in the pool, and an older gentleman was helping himself to one of Mrs. Silva's cinnamon rolls. The older man looked around the corner of one of the large wooden posts that held up the log ceiling of the grand room and split one side in half with a wall. "Do you have any whiskey to go with this coffee?"

"Mr. Hernandez, surely it's too early for a drink." Amanda came out from around the post and smiled at the man.

He hooked a thumb over his shoulder. "After seeing that tarantula crawling out from under the bunkhouse, I need one."

"Oh, let me take care of that for you."

She started to walk by the man, but he held up his hand. "You're going to take care of it?"

"Of course. I don't mind a pretty tarantula now and again."

The man straightened his shoulders. "I wouldn't bother it. It just surprised me is all. I should have expected it out here in the desert."

"Are you sure? I can transport it to another area of the ranch."

Mr. Hernandez shook his head. "No, no. Don't bother yourself. I'm heading out to the pool to watch the cannonball contest, though how they can get in that pool when it's barely seventy is beyond me."

Amanda laughed. "It's heated at this time of year. That makes it a lot more pleasant." She leaned in. "But what you'll really want to try is the hot tub."

The older man grinned. "Oh, I already have." He lifted the coffee and cinnamon roll as he started for the back door. "Thanks for the snack."

As soon as the man had exited, Amanda turned toward Jackson. "Is that what I think it is?" She strode forward and walked around him.

"It's a baby sling. I told Tanner he needed one."

Amanda laughed. "Oh, I bet he loved hearing that. Is it as comfortable as they say?"

He shrugged. "I don't know what they say, but it does leave your arms and hands free, and the baby seems comfortable."

Amanda stopped in front of Tabitha and gazed at her, a wistful look on her face. "She is so sweet." Her voice had lowered. "And I'd say she's comfortable because she's sleeping. She probably was soothed by your heartbeat."

He hadn't expected his daughter to fall asleep in the carrier. The last thing he'd thought of was his heartbeat. It was probably just because she usually napped at this time. "Have you seen Dani?"

Amanda's gaze immediately changed. "As a matter of

fact, I have. She went on Brody's 'trevanger' hunt." She held up her hand to forestall questions. "He claims it's a scavenger hunt and a treasure hunt in one. He's doing it on the east mountain with Nash and Waylon. They won't be back until late afternoon. Why? Did you need her to help with something? She'd been looking for a ranch task, but she settled for the 'trevanger' since her friend was doing it."

"No, I just wanted to thank her for this baby sling. She said it was a gift for Tabitha." That was true. Amanda didn't need to know that Dani said it was for him too. He didn't want his family knowing that he preferred talking to Dani over them, and Amanda would run right back to Tanner and tell him if she knew that.

"That was very kind of her. She's very different from the rest of the guests. I'm hoping she's giving us a lot of feedback."

Dani was giving far more than Tanner was going to want. Jackson shrugged. "It's all anonymous feedback, but she does seem like the type to tell us if there's something missing. I'll find her later or tomorrow, then." He didn't want Amanda to know how disappointed he was that he couldn't show Dani how well her gift worked.

"Okay, I need to get back to planning tomorrow's activities. I'm thinking maybe a bonfire. It's supposed to be pretty cold."

He had no idea what the weather would be, nor did he care. "I'm going to check on Havoc." Without waiting for a reply, he strode for the door.

Once outside, he breathed easier. Having to be civil to someone he'd been brought up to hate was wearing. But

Tanner would be furious with him if he didn't respect Amanda, just like he'd be furious if anyone didn't respect Tabitha.

He strode toward the stable, his intent to introduce Tabitha to Havoc. He couldn't imagine that Havoc was happy having the ranch hands riding him now that he was home. Stepping into the building, he immediately sensed someone was there and stopped. "Hey."

"Howdy." The response came from the far stall.

Layne. He should have known. "What's up, old man?"

Layne snorted. "I could still whip your butt if I wanted to."

"Maybe with experience, but you're too soft." He stepped up to the stall and found Layne brushing down his horse.

Layne looked up and chuckled. "Nice baby sling."

He checked Tabitha, who was looking toward the horse. At least, he thought she was. "It's comfortable, and she seems to like it." He smoothed his hand over his daughter's back.

"My youngest sisters swear by those things. They even have their husbands wearing them. Just another reason I'm glad I'm never having children." Layne pointed at him. "What you're doing right there is multitasking. It's bad for your brain."

"Fuck you. What do you think you're doing? You're brushing your horse and talking to me."

"Tsk tsk, no swearing in front of the child. She'll pick that up faster than you know it. And for the record, I stopped brushing when I spoke to you."

Holy shit. He hadn't even thought about his language.

After ten years in the Army, he'd never remember to watch his mouth. He was screwed. Crap.

"You're looking like a deer in headlights there, Jackson."

"Wouldn't you if someone handed you a baby and said, 'Here, this is yours'?"

"Shit. Is that really what they did?"

At Layne's response, he frowned. "Watch your language. Yes, that's what they did. They called me into my staff sergeant's office in Shaddadi. He asked if I knew Gabriella Rossi. When I told him I did, his aide walked in and handed me Tabitha. Then my staff sergeant scowled at me and told me it was a good thing I told him the truth because he would have had me court-martialed if I had lied."

Layne didn't even pretend to brush anymore, instead moving to the door of the stall and leaning over it. "How'd they know?"

"DNA test. They tested her and found a match with me. It was easy to figure out I'd slept with Gabby since I often traveled to Shaddadi."

"And you had no idea?"

Jackson shook his head. "She lied to me. Told me she was on the pill. Turned out she'd been trying to get pregnant for months, according to what the nanny said. The Army was more pissed that she'd been able to hide it from them. I guess when she got big, she worked from her assigned apartment, claiming sickness and other issues so she could go to meetings remotely."

"Wow, she must have wanted a baby bad. It figures the one man, besides me, who never wanted children is the one that succeeds."

He'd thought exactly as Layne did a million times over. Just his luck, his sperm was successful where others' hadn't been, whoever they were.

"It's sad that she barely had any time to be a mother after wanting it so much."

At Layne's observation, he paused. He had been so busy griping at his own lot, he hadn't thought much about Gabby, except that she tricked him. But Layne was right. She'd barely had three weeks with Tabitha. His chest tightened. At least he knew Tabitha had been loved before they figured out he was her father.

"You never said how Gabriella died." Layne looked at him expectantly.

No, he hadn't. He hadn't said much and, even now, couldn't bring himself to admit he'd slept with a superior officer. Talking to Layne was like talking to a vault. It never went beyond the man, which was how he wanted it. "She died in a helicopter crash. It wasn't even an important mission. She just needed to go to Green Village, about forty miles away. A copter was headed out to pick up wounded near there, but it was shot down before it arrived. Two were killed. She was one of them."

"Why did she have to go to this village?"

"It's a small base with multiple contingents, including an FST. There had been some problems with the SDF wanting to use the FST for locals."

Layne looked blankly at him. "Are you talking in code on purpose?"

"Just habit. Basically, we had what you'd call a MASH unit, like the old television show? They were there to take care of the wounded combatants, be they allied forces or Syrian Democratic Forces or enemies. They were not authorized to care for local women giving birth or kids with dysentery. She'd been sent there to make the lines clear."

"That sounds like if it escalated, it could have become a serious issue. I wouldn't say her mission wasn't important."

That was true. He'd visited Green Village a few times, and there were so many different groups there, he was surprised anyone got along with anyone. "I see what you're saying. So maybe when Tabitha is older, I can tell her that her mother was a hero."

"You can also tell her that her dad is a hero too. You saved dozens of people over there."

"No." The word came out fast and strong. "I'm not a hero. Promise me you will never tell her that."

Layne held up both hands and backed away from the stall door. "Okay, okay. But you know your family will."

Fuck. He'd forgotten about that. Then again ... "I'm not sure they will. As far as they're concerned, I'm like a dog who got caught stealing the rib eye off the counter and slunk into the corner with my tail between my legs."

Layne chuckled as he moved back to his horse. "No, that's how you view yourself. Your family might be giving you a little space, but not because you're a bad dog. They're giving it to you because they can see you're angry and hurting and not yourself. But your dad is thrilled with Tabitha, and your brothers are a bit in awe of your service."

They were? Was that why Brody was ready to send Dani packing? He didn't want them in awe. He wished his relationship with them was more like his with Layne. "You aren't giving me any space."

"Hell no. Never did. Never will. You're the one who decided my house was more fun than the ranch back in grammar school. You were such a pain in the ass, following me around and trying to break your own neck. Scared the bejesus out of me so many times I lost count. That gives me privileges no one else gets."

Jackson snorted. "Some privilege that is. I have no idea why—"

A loud screech, followed by the distinctive bray of an angry burro, sounded outside.

He spun and ran out the open back doors of the stable, cradling Tabitha's head against his chest. Layne was right behind him. He skidded to a halt at the scene before him. Shotgun stood on the lid of the green plastic trash barrel, his paws raised high. He dropped down on his forepaws, and low growls issued from his throat.

The burro snorted, bobbing his head before stepping closer to Shotgun.

"Fuck, I need to stop this." He looked for something nearby to shoo the burro away, but nothing was outside. He stepped next to Layne and lifted Tabitha from her comfortable position, the coolness hitting his chest almost uncomfortable.

Reluctantly, he handed her to Layne. "Here. Hold her."

Layne didn't hesitate—he'd held many a baby in his family—but he did step back from the angry animals.

Jackson edged over to Shotgun. "Hey, what's wrong?" He kept one eye on the burro as he scanned the raccoon. Shotgun stood again, and that's when he spotted the apple core. "Shotgun, did you take that from him, or did he see you with it?"

Shotgun chattered at him for a moment before getting down on all fours again and growling.

Not sure which was safer, he stepped between the two animals, his back to Shotgun. Maybe if they didn't see each other, they'd stop. But no sooner had he positioned himself than he felt Shotgun's claws as he scrambled onto his shoulder. "Well, that didn't work."

Layne, who stood far enough away to keep Tabitha safe, chuckled. "I could have told you that."

He practically growled. "No, you couldn't." Reviewing his options, he stepped back next to the trash barrel, keeping his eye on the burro. The damn thing advanced another step, issuing a low grunt.

Great. Now the burro thought it was winning. The last thing he needed was to get bitten. Without taking his gaze from the burro, he felt around and found the apple core. He held it up over his head, making sure the burro saw it. Just as Shotgun grabbed his head to reach for it, he chucked it across the ATV road and into the desert.

The burro watched, turning its head as the core fell to the ground. It turned back to him and gave a loud bray before turning to go get the treat. Meanwhile, Shotgun sat on his shoulder, scolding him.

"I'll get you a whole apple for tonight, okay?"

That didn't seem to appease Shotgun since the raccoon chattered all the way down his arm and leg before scrambling off around the barn toward the house. He finally looked at Layne, who was focused on the burro.

He walked over, anxious to have his daughter back. "I'll take Tabitha now."

Layne handed her over. "I know that burro."

He couldn't resist. "In the biblical sense?"

Layne's head snapped around. "No, wiseass. I've seen it a number of times in the past month. It's always alone. Burros tend to hang around each other in small herds, like wild mustangs. It's odd."

Jackson settled Tabitha into the sling before moving his gaze to the burro, who had already eaten the apple and was now looking in the direction Shotgun had gone. "Are you sure it's the same burro?" He looked down at his daughter and moved her head so it rested to one side. He didn't like her squishing her tiny nose against his chest. She needed to breathe.

Layne stroked his bushy mustache. "I am. He has a distinctive white patch on his forehead. It's a diamond shape."

"It could be he tried to be the dominant male and was kicked out."

"You're probably right." Layne shrugged. "Anyway, I need to head out. Mom's got a surprise party planned for my oldest niece, so I need to help set up. You good here?"

He set his hand on Tabitha's back, amazed at how much that steadied him. "'Good' is a relative term. But yes, I'm good."

Layne shook his head as they strode back into the barn. "If you want to be good in general, you should talk to that psychologist your dad always raves about. Because eventually, your family is going to start getting in your face, and you're not going to have Tabitha or Shotgun around to use as an excuse."

"Mind your own business." He scowled at Layne, irritated that the man was probably right.

"You are my business." Layne pointed at him before striding out and waving behind him.

Jackson looked down at Tabitha. "You know, your Uncle Layne has been a jerk, a pain in my butt, and downright frustrating, but he's always been right." Damn him.

How much longer before his family decided to intervene? Did he have a week, three days? The answer came quickly. Six days. He'd bet money that as soon as the last guest left, they'd turn their attention to him.

Well, that was six more days to figure things out and maybe—just maybe—enjoy Dani's company.

CHAPTER 13

DANI SAT ALONE at the picnic table in the quad, a warm cup of coffee in front of her as she twirled her bracelet, contemplating what she might do with her day. It was cold, but since it was mid-morning, the hard chill had burned off and sitting in the sun was pleasant with a jacket on.

She'd had a late night, getting in past dinner thanks to one guest spraining an ankle and a coyote scattering the horses at the "trevanger." They couldn't call for help because there was no cell service. Definitely a safety issue. Even with the remotest Mayes Mineral mine, they used two-way radios or satellite phones. Unfortunately, after the accident, Nash had to ride in to get the ATV and ride back.

She'd stayed with Hannah and Brody to gather up the few horses that had run off while Nash and Waylon brought the rest of the guests back. After being treated to dinner in the industrial kitchen, she'd gone back to her room to write up her feedback card. She'd actually used two cards, as a couple of the women never bothered to fill them out. She took issue with that. The whole reason they were staying for free was for their opinions. After that, she'd showered and gone to bed.

The ranch was pleasant without all the guests about, each having chosen their activity for the day. And what would she do? She would definitely go to the hot tub at the house. Riding after years of not doing much was one thing, but herding runaway horses was another. Her sore muscles would welcome the hot water.

There was going to be a big bonfire after dinner, which she wouldn't mind, but there was a big variable in her plans, and his name was Jackson. When she'd left him with the surprise baby sling, he hadn't been too happy with her. If he were someone she hoped to have a relationship with, she'd give it a few days and then text. But since she wasn't looking for a relationship and she had only five days left on the ranch, she might just barge into his office and see where his head was at. She had nothing to lose, except amazing sex.

"Mind if I join you?"

Putting down her coffee mug, she looked up to find Hannah, Brody's fiancée, standing on the other side of the table in a pair of jeans, cowboy boots, a blue turtleneck sweater, and what looked like a white down parka with a large mug in her hands.

"Of course." Dani held out her hand. "Are you cold?"

Hannah gave a self-deprecating smile. "A little. I grew up in the city, so this is my first year experiencing desert cold."

Dani nodded, though she'd never lived in the city, so she wasn't sure how different it might be. "That coffee will warm you from the inside out."

"That's what I'm hoping. I'm a little late getting up." Hannah leaned in as if someone might overhear, though they were the only two people in sight. "Are you sore this morning?"

"You bet I am. Haven't ridden like that in years. I'm hitting the hot tub today for sure. Jeremiah lets me use the one at the house."

Hannah looked surprised. "He does? Wow, he must like you. Tell me when you're going, and I'll tag along. I'm a new rider. I'm not sure how much help I was yesterday, but Brody knows how much I like to learn new things. I guess chasing after runaway horses counts as a new thing." She shrugged as she brought the mug to her mouth with two hands and sipped.

So that's why it looked like Hannah didn't know what to do yesterday evening. She didn't. Still, she'd tried, not even caring when she made a wrong move, simply adjusting and carrying on. She was a sweet person, which she'd have to be to put up with Brody's penchant for being the center of attention. "I imagine you're learning a lot living here at the ranch."

Hannah waved away her comment. "Oh, we don't live here. I own the property next door, and as soon as Brody graduates from the game warden school, we'll move wherever they need him. I work from home mostly."

"So you're just helping out for these two weeks?"

"Yes. Brody, though, will work here until the end of the year. It's going to get busy with us getting married on Christmas Eve and then Christmas, New Year's, and Brody going to the school."

Dani had heard people mention that Brody and Hannah were getting married soon. "Where is the wedding?"

Hannah hooked her thumb over her shoulder. "Right here. I'm keeping it simple. We'll get married in front of the stone fireplace in the clubhouse, then have dinner right there, and then instead of dancing, we're having a bonfire. That's why I'm excited about tonight. I want to see how the bonfire will look. Amanda promised one just like tonight's." Hannah's smile proved how excited she was.

"And Brody is good with your plans?"

"Of course. He said whatever I wanted to do. I'm even having tres leches cake for a wedding cake and churro ice cream."

Though the desserts were a little different, the fact that Brody would do whatever Hannah wished surprised her. She must have read him wrong. "How did you know Brody was the one? You two seem different on the surface."

Hannah grinned before taking a sip of coffee and putting it back on the table. "It was a bit of a rollercoaster. I wasn't looking for a relationship. In fact, I was grieving when he showed up at my door. Talk about something to brighten my mood. He was super nice and helpful but then started getting a little, um, too bossy. But once I showed him I didn't need a boss, he came around."

Dani blinked, trying to imagine sweet Hannah straightening out the big personality that was Brody. "So he just came into your life and you went with it? Did you think about what you were looking for in a husband?"

Hannah laughed. "Honestly, a husband was the furthest

thing from my mind. He came into my life, turned it upside down, and made it a hundred percent better."

That sounded amazingly risky. "My mom told us girls that we should think about what we wanted in a partner so we'd know him when we found him. That's how my older sister recognized her human resources director of a husband was perfect for her. She now has two children. My younger sister, on the other hand, is too busy saving lives as a paramedic to think about her future yet."

"That sounds lovely."

"It does?" That wasn't how she'd describe preparing for the future.

"It does. First, to have a mom who gave such sage advice. My mom died when I was an infant. And then to have sisters! I was an only child. But soon I'll have a sister-in-law with Amanda, and I can't wait."

Discovering so much about the woman in so few sentences had her entire assessment of Hannah changing. She was a lot stronger than Dani realized. "And someday, you'll have another sister when Jackson gets married." Even as she said the words, she couldn't imagine what kind of woman would marry him.

Hannah shook her head. "I'm not holding out that hope. Jackson is different. Brody says Jackson's broken and just needs to be fixed. I'm not so sure. We're all worried about him."

Even though Hannah's words foretold a sad life for Jackson, the caring of the family was very discernable and soothed Dani's unease. At least Jackson had them and his daughter. "Even if he never marries, at least you have a niece."

Hannah's whole face brightened. "That's right. She's only a baby now, but soon she'll be walking around. I hope that wherever Brody gets a position that we'll get to come back for holidays. I always wondered what it would be like to have a big family at the holidays."

Dani reached across the picnic table and took Hannah's hand. "You are going to love the holidays with this crew. I guarantee it." She squeezed the woman's hand and let go, with a new appreciation for how much she had in her own life. Maybe burning her Mr. Right Characteristic List was the best thing she could have done.

"Hannah, there you are."

At the sound of Amanda's excited voice, Hannah turned. "I'm just chatting with Dani."

Amanda strode forward, wearing a sleeveless fleece vest over her corduroy button-down. "A special package came for you. I put it in my room so no one would see it."

Hannah jumped up so fast, the bench she was sitting on tipped over. "Oops." She righted it, then bent over the table and whispered, "I have to go try on my wedding dress!"

Dani didn't have a chance to respond as Hannah practically ran toward the house. Part of her was envious, but mostly, she was happy for Hannah. The woman was clearly head over heels in love with Brody.

While she'd counted herself in love a few times, it had never been anything like that. Still, she wasn't sure she could go into a relationship like Hannah had. Maybe it was just different for some people.

"Dani!"

She turned around to find Hannah walking back toward her. "Yes?"

"Come with us." Hannah waved her arm toward the house.

Surprised, she wasn't sure what to say. "Me?"

Hannah cocked her head. "Yes, you. I need your opinion. You can give an opinion, right?"

Boy, could she—and she had. But on a wedding dress? Even with doubts assailing her, she rose. Why not? She was leaving in five days. If Hannah wanted her opinion, then she'd give it. "I'm coming."

"Excellent!" Hannah waited until Dani caught up. "I've just started making girlfriends in town, so I hope you don't mind."

Amanda joined them. "I'm her maid of honor, so I'll be throwing the shower."

Hannah nodded. "Yes, and Sheila, my friend in town, who is also my maid of honor, is helping with that. She's a little wild. But she doesn't close her shop until eight, so I really need another opinion."

"But I'm just a guest on the ranch."

Hannah waved off her concern. "That doesn't matter. You're a woman with a brain. That's what I need."

Dani shook her head. "You don't have very high standards for friends, do you?" She'd intended the comment to elicit more criteria.

"Don't I know it!" Hannah and Amanda burst into laughter.

Feeling out of the loop, she kept quiet until they reached

Amanda and Tanner's room. The door to the office, which was the first room down the hall, was closed. "Are the rooms arranged by order of the sons?"

Amanda answered. "Yes, they are."

She wanted to ask about Devlin's room, but it wasn't a good time. This was about a wedding, not a death.

Hannah squealed when she saw the box on the bed. "I can't believe it's finally happening."

Amanda rolled her eyes. "It's only been two months, and you already live together."

Hannah was busy taking the lid off the box. "Not the wedding, the dress." She lifted the white garment out.

Dani saw lace and beads, but that was it.

"Okay, you two go out while I get dressed." Hannah dropped the dress on the bed and waved them away, then closed the door behind them.

Amanda looked at her. "It feels a bit odd being shut out of my own room."

"Should we wait in the living room?" She wasn't sure what the protocol for this was. She'd been her sister's maid of honor and at the store when the dress was chosen. Her sister had picked it up when the alterations had been made.

"No, we better stay right here. She's going to need help, which she's obviously forgotten."

Within moments, they heard talking behind the door. "Well, sugar. That's not going to work. Amanda!"

"Excuse me." Amanda grinned and then slipped into the room.

Dani tried to wait patiently, but the urge to see whether

Jackson was in the house was too strong. Quietly, she went back to the office and opened the door.

It was empty. It was mid-morning. Usually, that's where he was, not that she'd been keeping track. After closing the door, she moved back down the hall.

A few more minutes passed, and she toyed with the idea of looking for Jackson's room. If they were in order, his would be the next one, or was it the third?

"Okay, you can come in."

With Hannah's call, her decision was made for her. She opened the door and walked in.

"What do you think?"

"Wow." She studied the fairy-tale dress with a wide skirt tastefully decorated with lace, beads, and tiny bows. "You look like a princess."

"Don't I?" Hannah turned toward a full-length mirror on the inside of a closet door. "It's exactly what I wanted, and the alterations are perfect. Mrs. Martinez did an amazing job."

The dress fit Hannah beautifully, not just in size but in spirit. She really did look like a princess. It was nothing like the style Dani preferred, but it was perfect for Hannah. She seemed to feel such joy in life. "Brody is going to be stunned."

"Do you really think so? I want him to be speechless. Do you think this will do it?"

Dani nodded, smiling widely at the thought of the cowboy being upstaged by his sweet bride. "Most definitely."

Hannah smiled with glee. "I can't wait."

Amanda moved around to her back. "Now, let's take this off. We don't want Brody to see you in it."

"Wait. Dani, could you take a picture of me? I want to be able to look at it whenever I want."

"Of course." She pulled out her phone and snapped a couple. "Which one do you want?"

After Hannah had decided on two instead of one, Dani took her number and texted them to her. "Brody is a very lucky man."

Hannah grinned. "He sure is." Her laughter filled the room.

The joy that Hannah exuded was almost overwhelming and not a little depressing for someone who had given finding a husband her best shot and failed. "I'll leave you to getting dressed. I'm very happy for you."

Hannah stepped away from Amanda and grabbed her arm. "Thank you so much." Then Hannah gave her a bear hug.

"Hannah, you'll have to have that pressed again."

At Amanda's scolding, Hannah stepped back. "Oops." Then she turned, half unbuttoned, and went back to Amanda.

Dani left the room quickly before any more hugs. She felt on the verge of tears, the same way she'd left the ranch house once before. This time, she didn't stop. She kept walking past the stable and down the ATV road toward the birthing area. Taking deep breaths, she got her emotions under control. She blamed Brody for this one. He was the one who asked her to check on Jackson. He was the one who meddled and had her learning far more about the Dunn family than she'd wanted to. She was just a freakin' guest.

Her anger took over, and she stalked down the road, not

caring where she was headed. It felt good to move, and the sound of dirt crunching under her cowboy boots was satisfying. Now all she needed was a shovel and some hard work and she could be happy. She slowed at that thought. What was wrong with her? Why couldn't she just relax or enjoy the activities the dude ranch offered?

She came to a complete stop. What if the problem with her Mr. Right list wasn't the list but her? "Damn." If that were the case, it meant there was no one out there for her. Could that be true?

The sound of horse hooves pounding the ground behind her had her spinning around. "Jackson." It figures that he'd show up when she was having a good, honest life crisis. Then again, watching him ride toward her made for great eye candy. She hadn't seen him on a horse her entire stay. So where was Tabitha?

As he drew closer, she studied him. No matter what she might say about his personality, the man was seriously built, and her riotous emotions coalesced into simple admiration.

He brought his horse to a halt not far from her and jumped down. "Hey, where you going?"

"Nowhere."

He looked about them. "Obviously. Were you trying to get to the petting area? There are only three animals in there right now."

"No." In the back of her mind, she realized their conversation pattern had reversed from when she first arrived. Was this how he'd felt then?

"Were you looking for someone?"

Was she? Not anymore. "No."

Jackson's brows lowered. "What's wrong?"

She almost smiled because she'd said the same thing to him at one time. "Nothing. Just going for a walk."

"Okay." He stood next to her, his hand holding the reins as if he expected to walk with her.

Finally, she relented. "What are you doing?"

"I came to find you."

That wasn't what she expected. "Why?"

"Tabitha is napping." He patted his phone on his hip. "And I wanted to thank you for the baby sling."

She crossed her arms as she remembered how she'd tried to hold it for ransom, not realizing she'd pried too deeply. "You're welcome. I'm sorry I asked you about the hayloft. I didn't know."

"Of course you didn't. All you knew, because you're too damn observant, is that it caused a shift in our behavior."

She uncrossed her arms. "Yes. But it wasn't my place to pry."

Jackson rubbed his fingers over his eyes with his free hand before looking at her. "No, but it's not a secret, just forgotten by most people except my family."

Feeling the need to offer comfort, she laid her hand on his arm. "Losing a brother in an accident had to have been hard."

He looked at her hand. "I was seven. Devlin was eight, going on twenty. I looked up to him. He never shied away from anything, not even a scorpion when it crawled up his pants. In my mind, he had the courage of ten men."

She didn't want to ask questions he wouldn't want to answer. "It sounds like he was born brave."

"He was. And every time he did something brave, he never got hurt. I was in awe. And then he was gone."

She felt his forearm stiffen under her hand and looked down to see his fingers had curled into a fist. Did he need to talk about it, or should she change the topic? But to what? Instead, she just kept silent, her hand still on his arm.

He raised his head and looked at her. "Tanner was in the loft that day. He was ten, and Dad told us we couldn't go into the loft until we were nine. Devlin and I hated that. So I told Devlin we should go in the loft anyway since Dad wasn't around. Of course he agreed. He never backed down from anything. We climbed up there and started to build a fort with the hay bales. Shit, those suckers were heavy back then. That's when Devlin grabbed one and swung it up onto another near the edge of the loft. He held onto the bale too long, and when it went over the edge, he lost his footing and went over with it."

Her heart stopped for a second at the scene he painted, a dull ache filling her chest at the image of an eight-year-old boy flying out of the hayloft to hit the floor below. Reflexively, she squeezed his arm even as her throat closed.

He looked away. "I yelled, and Tanner ran down the ladder. I followed to help, but he told me to get Dad. They took Devlin away in an ambulance, but he was already gone. I felt it. We were inseparable, not that he always appreciated me tagging behind. But when he hit the concrete, I knew he was gone. Later, I found out he broke his neck."

Her heart was breaking, not just for Devlin but also for the little boy that Jackson had been. "I'm so sorry."

Jackson shook his head. "I killed him. I told him we

should go up there when I knew we weren't allowed to. If I hadn't suggested it, he'd be alive today."

His words knocked the air from her, as if he'd kicked her. She took a few seconds to get it back. "You don't know that. If nothing happened that day, you don't know that he wouldn't have been killed the next. If he was that brave, then he could have said no to you. He knew as well as you that he wasn't allowed in the hayloft. He made the decision to go up there, not you."

Jackson looked at her blankly, as if he couldn't hear her.

And she knew he had gone into an episode. "Jackson?"

He jerked his arms from hers and dropped the reins.

Considering his mood at the time, she stepped back and grabbed up the reins, not sure what he would do. The last thing she wanted him to do was hurt her or his horse. He didn't need that guilt added to what he had now.

"No!" He stalked forward, away from her and toward something only he could see, a tic starting beneath his right eye. His arm swung out.

She wanted to help but didn't know how. Maybe she should call someone, but the only phone number she had was Hannah's. Should she ask Hannah to send Brody out?

Jackson suddenly raised his hands to his head. "It's wrong. I can't do this." He fell to his knees, his head bowed.

She tied the reins to a small palo verde tree and started to walk around Jackson, giving him a wide berth. "Jackson? Are you okay?"

His head snapped her way, moving with her as she walked to the front of him, but he didn't lift it. "Jackson. It's me, Dani."

"Dani." The word was whispered to the ground.

"Yes, I'm Dani. Do you remember me?"

He raised his head, and his eyes looked haunted.

She swallowed hard. "It's okay. You're okay." She stepped closer.

His gaze finally focused on her. "Dani?"

She stood next to him to help him rise, but his arms locked around her legs. Her heart broke while her own guilt settled in. She laid her hands on his head and held him to her, wishing there were more she could do.

She wasn't sure how long they were like that. It may have been ten minutes or more, but when his hold loosened, she knelt down before him. "Do you want to go home?"

He didn't say anything, but he nodded. Rising with her, he took her hand, and they started to walk back.

She stopped to get the reins of his horse. "I don't think Havoc would appreciate being left behind." She smiled at Jackson, but he didn't respond.

Silently, they strolled toward the house along the ATV road. As much as she wanted to talk, her instinct told her to let it be for now. Last time, it took him a while to get completely free of his episode. He needed help with his PTSD, more than what she could give him. He needed professional care.

When the stable came into sight, he suddenly stopped.

She halted as well and looked at him, not sure if he was still lucid or had gone back again.

Then he spoke, still facing forward. "I tried to be like Devlin, not because I was brave but because I didn't care if I lived. Layne finally sat me down and told me if I was going to be stupid-brave, then I should enlist in the Army. I went the next day and signed up. My dad was furious, but I was elated."

Jackson finally turned his head and looked at her. "I found a purpose. My mission was to save as many men, women, and children as I could to make up for what I had done. But it was never enough. I wanted to die for my country to make my life worth something. So I was stupid-brave and instead received stupid medals, but all I wanted was peace."

Her heart jumped at the thought that he'd wanted to die. "Did you find any peace?"

He looked back at the road and shook his head.

"I think you need to find some peace for Tabitha's sake."

Jackson looked out at the mountains, then faced forward again without a word and started walking again.

She walked with him. She had no choice since he was still holding tight to her hand.

CHAPTER 14

JACKSON PACED THE FAMILY ROOM, anxious for Tabitha to wake up. Every sixth step, he looked at his phone to see whether she was awake. He'd hoped that Dani would come by the barn last night, but she hadn't. So he'd waited all morning for her to stop by his office, but again, she hadn't. He'd checked the hot tub a dozen times, but she wasn't in it. Where was she?

Had he scared her away?

Not wanting to have her talk about what happened the day before, he created a plan. As soon as Tabitha woke up, he'd put her in the baby sling and go look for Dani. That way, they could talk about Tabitha instead of him but he could still be around her.

He didn't know why he liked being around her. She'd triggered his last episode, so he shouldn't want to be, but his gut was telling him it wasn't actually her but him. He just wasn't sure why. He hadn't been thinking about any of his deployments, just about the day of Devlin's death. So maybe if he didn't think about anything traumatic, he could get himself under control. He was a sergeant in the Army. He needed to pull himself together.

Checking his phone again, he halted. Tabitha was awake.

He left the family room and strode into his bedroom. "Are you ready to go for a walk with your dad?"

Her eyes turned toward him.

His heart filled. That *had* to mean she knew him. He'd read it took months to bond, but he'd swear she focused on him every time he talked to her. He stepped up to the crib. "Hey there, little one." He bent over the crib and lifted her out.

The scent of poop filled his nostrils, and he held her away from him. "Okay, we'll just change your diaper first." Laying Tabitha down on the changing table nearby, he opened her diaper. "Whoa, I've smelled better scents in the back allies of Manbij."

Quickly, he dropped the diaper in the trash can, making a mental note to change the trash as soon as they got back. Then, after cleaning his daughter up and putting a new diaper on her, he held her in his arm as he looked through the top drawer of his dresser for her sweater. He would have liked to take credit for thinking to buy her one, but it was actually Amanda who had given it to Tabitha as a welcome home gift.

Bringing Tabitha back to the changing table, he carefully added the sweater on top of her onesie. After donning the sling, he settled Tabitha inside. There was something about having his daughter flush against his chest that made him feel like he could keep his promise to always keep her safe. A promise he took very seriously.

Once she was all set, he strode from the room and headed out the front door, only to turn back around immediately. The temperatures had dropped more than he expected. After tucking a blanket around his daughter and putting on his field jacket, he grabbed up his gray felt cowboy hat and set it on his head. He was going to need a haircut soon. He'd been home for almost a month already.

Better prepared for the cold air, he stepped outside and down the steps of the porch into the sun. He looked down at Tabitha. "This is what winter is like. That means Santa is coming." He stilled. He'd never expected to say those particular words. They felt odd but not bad. "Let's go see if we can find Dani."

He headed for the stable first, but she wasn't there. Then he checked the clubhouse. A number of guests were playing games, and a couple were reading near the fireplace. He looked out the window, but no one was in the guest pool. As he came to the whiteboard with the activities for the day, he perused them, but he didn't see anything Dani would enjoy. He'd started for the exit when Hannah strode in.

"Hi, Jackson. Hi, Tabby."

He gritted his teeth to keep from snapping back that her name wasn't "Tabby." "Hi, Hannah. Have you seen Dani?"

As if she'd expected the question, she smiled. "I have. After breakfast, she said she was going to read in the bunkhouse. Most everybody who isn't here went on the hayride, so I imagine she's enjoying the quiet."

He wasn't sure whether that was a hint not to disturb her

or not, but he'd ignore it. "Thanks." He didn't elaborate but headed for the door.

"Have fun."

Confused by Hannah's phrasing, he walked back outside. Since it wasn't the first time he'd found Hannah's sunny disposition confusing, he shrugged it off.

As he stepped up onto the porch of the women's bunkhouse, he hesitated. Should he knock? Walk in? Since he hadn't been in the building since the guests arrived, he walked along the porch until he spotted Dani sitting on a loveseat with a blanket over her legs, reading.

He knocked on the window.

She started before turning to look out. When she smiled and waved him in, he felt his muscles relax. Maybe she wasn't avoiding him, after all.

Moving back to the door, he walked in and strode down the long, narrow room to where she sat near the fake wood stove that was actually powered by gas.

She had set her book on a small table next to her and looked up. "Good morning."

"Good morning. I thought you might like to see how well your gift works." He turned to the side so she could see Tabitha's face.

She pressed a hand to her chest. "Oh, she's so adorable in there. She has no idea how strong a support she has with you. You make her look so tiny."

He liked how Dani's gaze softened, turning a muted gray. "She's only seven weeks, but she's long. That's what the doctor said."

"Jackson, any child next to you is going to look tiny."

That was probably true. He remembered carrying a five-year-old in—he stopped himself. He had Tabitha with him. He couldn't afford another flashback. "Would you like to hold her?"

"Are you sure?"

He didn't even have to think about it. "Yes." Carefully, he pulled Tabitha out of the sling and bent over to place his daughter in Dani's arms. "She only weighs ten and a half pounds, but the doctor said she's on track."

"Oh, she's adorable." Dani gazed at his daughter as if she were the prettiest thing in the world.

He actually thought his daughter was a little wrinkly.

"I wonder what color her eyes will be."

Confused, he frowned. "They're blue."

Dani looked up at him. "All babies' eyes are blue. Didn't you learn that in high school?"

"I'm sure they taught it, but I didn't pay attention to anything having to do with babies." He almost added that he never expected to have one but kept that to himself. No need to remind her of that.

Dani looked back at Tabitha. "I hope she has warm, crystal-brown eyes like her daddy."

Warm crystal-brown? He'd never heard his eyes described like that. "Her mom had blue. I thought that's why she had blue eyes."

"You'll know by the time she's a year old. They could even start changing in another month, but if they don't, that doesn't mean they won't. She's going to grow fast." Dani looked up at him. "You can sit instead of towering over us. She keeps looking up at you when you speak."

Thrilled that it wasn't just him who thought that, he sank into the cushions of the loveseat next to Dani. This close to her, he could smell the scent of her that made him feel at peace, but added to it was his daughter's own scent. For that moment, all was good.

Dani had his daughter's hand wrapped around her finger. "You are such a cute little thing. I bet you grow up to be gorgeous and cause your daddy all kinds of headaches."

Tabitha's mouth turned up into a smile at that, and then she farted.

Instead of being annoyed, Dani chuckled. "You're going to get more of those smiles than real ones right now, but eventually, she'll smile on purpose more and more, won't you, Tabby?"

He stiffened. "Don't call her that."

Dani turned toward him. "Why? Because it sounds like she's a cat?"

"A cat? No." He hadn't even thought of that. "No. It sounds too much like her mother's name. Though her given name was 'Gabriella,' she went by 'Gabby.'"

"And you didn't like her mother but slept with her?" Dani's tone made it clear she was not impressed.

"It wasn't like that. I did like her. When you're in theater, you don't get a lot of time for relationships, but Gabriella and I enjoyed each other's company. What I didn't know was that she was determined to have a child and lied to me about being on birth control. I don't like people who lie to me."

"Oh. I can understand. That's a life-changing thing to lie to you about." Dani turned back to his daughter, who looked right back at her. "I don't think you'll be able to keep people from calling Tabitha 'Tabby.' Your whole family already refers to her that way."

"They'll just have to stop." Though he knew from Brody that wouldn't happen.

"Maybe if you told them why you don't—"

"No."

Dani remained silent for a long while, lightly rubbing the back of his daughter's tiny knuckles with her thumb.

"What if you gave her a different nickname? 'Tabitha' is a lot to say, and a different nickname could catch on."

"Like what? Her name is 'Tabitha.' I'm not going to call her 'Button Nose,' 'Poop-Machine,' or 'Baldy.'"

Dani laughed, and Tabitha gave a little squeal, smiling.

He pointed. "That has to be a smile she made on purpose."

"Maybe she did." Dani grinned. "I don't suppose you could call her 'Smiley'?"

He shook his head. That was a silly name. "If she has a nickname, it has to be something she won't be embarrassed by when she's older. I know my family, and they will not change what they call her. Shit, Brody still calls Amanda 'Mandy.'"

"You're going to have to stop the swearing. You don't want that to be her first word."

"I know." He let his shoulders roll forward. "In the Army, we swear a lot. It's going to take me time."

Dani knocked his shoulder with hers. "Just let everyone know you're trying to stop, and they'll remind you."

"I know they will." He gave an exaggerated sigh.

"So, Tabitha, what would you like your nickname to be?"

He gazed at his daughter, quite sure she'd be a hell of a

lot smarter than him. "How about 'Einstein'? Or is that too much pressure?"

"Way too much pressure. What's her middle name?"

"'Joy.' As much as Gabby lied to me, she was truly happy to have Tabitha. My guess is that is why she named her 'Tabitha Joy.'"

Dani cocked her head. "Hmm, 'Tabitha Joy.' How about 'TJ' for a nickname, then?"

"'TJ.' That's not bad. It sounds nothing like 'Gabby' and is definitely not a cat or other animal. 'TJ.' I don't see her being embarrassed by it either. Yes, I like it." He liked Dani too for thinking of it. "Thank you."

She faced him again, smiling. "You're welcome."

Unable to resist, he cupped her cheek and gave her a kiss. Just a gentle, grateful kiss.

To his surprise, she flushed as she turned back to his daughter. "TJ, you're going to love growing up on a ranch with so many family members around to spoil you."

He frowned, not happy at what that could mean. "I don't want a spoiled brat for a daughter."

Dani laughed. "There's only one way to avoid that."

"How?"

"Have another child." She grinned, obviously thinking it funny.

He, however, did not. "I wasn't even supposed to have this one."

She lifted Tabitha and put her in his arms. "Yes, but aren't you glad you did?"

He looked into the blue eyes staring at him. Tabitha's chubby cheeks and wrinkly skin and tiny little nose. Her image was burned into his mind. He didn't know what the hell he was doing or whether he'd do anything right, but she was his, and somehow, he'd become hers. "I'm proud to be her father."

"Well, shoot, it looks like the gang is back. I promised Kaitlynn I'd have lunch with her today." Dani looked out the window, clearly not happy to have to go.

That made him feel a little better. "It's about time for Tabitha to eat, too." He rose from the couch and set Tabitha into the sling once again.

"Thank you for showing me how well this works and sharing TJ with me. It's been years since I held such a young child, and she is a pleasure." Dani sniffed at her sleeve. "I'm going to enjoy having that baby smell on me all day."

"You mean the baby wipes smell from cleaning her bottom?" He thought they smelled too powdery himself.

"Yes, those and the scent of her sweater and just her skin. There's nothing like the smell of a baby."

It must be a woman thing, so he let the comment pass. Out the window, he noticed a number of women heading toward the building, so he moved toward the door. "I might be able to have dinner with everyone tonight."

Dani smiled. "Great. I'll look for you."

He stepped out on the porch and made it down the steps before five women surrounded him, all wanting to see "the baby." "Sorry, ladies. She just pooped. I need to change her."

As if on cue, Tabitha started to cry, and he quickly extracted himself. By the time he made the house, Tabitha was wailing. He tried to soothe her, but only formula would do that.

After dropping his hat on the entry table, he strode into the kitchen and immediately started warming her bottle. He'd just begun to feed her when Tanner walked in, slamming the front door and scaring Tabitha.

"Have a little consideration."

Tanner stopped when he saw them. "Sorry, I didn't think anyone was in here." He continued in and opened the fridge, grabbing a water bottle. "Want one?"

Jackson shook his head. "What's got your panties in an uproar?"

"One of our suppliers just texted me and said they've closed—as in for good. We've increased our herd size to try to keep up with the bigger producers, but we have to buy baleage because we don't have enough grazing land for the larger-sized herd. I'm going to need that grass, or our cattle aren't going to do well."

Tanner's single response made it clear to Jackson exactly how long he'd been away from the family ranch. He'd had no idea they increased their head of cattle. "Didn't Dad just sign a lease with Hannah? Wasn't the whole purpose so we could use that for grazing?"

Tanner took another gulp from his water bottle before answering. "Yes, but with the dude ranch needing to be completed, we made the decision to continue one more winter with the baleage. So we haven't put up any fencing yet. But we're going to need to supplement the cattle in another week. I'll have to call another supplier, but it's going to cost us. We'll be lucky if we break even on this herd."

"Does Dad still have the gas-powered post-hole digger?"

"No. Even if we had it, there's no way we can enclose the eight hundred acres needed in time."

Jackson gently wiped his daughter's mouth after she finished. Throwing a hand towel over his shoulder, he lifted her up to burp her. "But we don't have to enclose all that at first. We just need enough to feed the cattle while the north field grows, right?"

Tanner moved around the island counter and sat. "Yes. What are you thinking?"

He rubbed Tabitha's back as he spoke. "Well, we'd need a gas-powered post-hole digger."

"Mr. Hardy has them at his store. We could rent one."

Tabitha burped. "Good girl. Can I have another?" He looked at Tanner. "Then we get a map of Hannah's property and determine where we want the first fencing. I assume Brody knows where the best grassland is. We mark and dig the holes and use the manpower we still have this week to set the poles. We might even be able to start the fencing. You could have a new grazing area before Christmas."

Tanner's left eyebrow raised. "Hell, you could be right."

"Hey, watch your language around my daughter."

"Really?"

Jackson nodded, for once feeling like he knew what he was doing when it came to her.

"We'll need all hands on deck, but you're right, the guests could be helpful if they want to be."

He thought about Dani suggesting he tell his family about Gabby to get them to stop calling Tabitha "Tabby." "You could tell the guests the issue. Maybe they'll want to help, especially if they've enjoyed their stay so far."

"It can't hurt. I'd have to rearrange a few staff the rest of this week. We only have four more days with the guests, but we need a day for marking and to start the holes."

He'd heard about his brother's rule that no ranch hand could be out in the field alone since their dad's stroke. "You could also gain hands by allowing only one ranch hand to be with the guest activities. For example, for those guests who want to go for a hike instead of help, just send one hand. If anything happens, there's plenty of people with them."

Tanner stood. "You're right. This could work. I'll go call Mr. Hardy and make sure he hasn't rented out all his post-hole diggers." Tanner started through the family room toward the hallway.

Jackson stopped patting his daughter's back since she'd fallen asleep. "Let me know. I can drive in with Tabitha and pick it up."

Tanner stopped and turned toward him. "I'm really glad you came home." With that, he continued out of the room and down the hall, and the office door opened and closed within seconds.

He hadn't been glad to be home when he arrived. Now, he wasn't sure how he felt. He wasn't glad, but he wasn't angry about it anymore either. He'd have to think about why.

CHAPTER 15

DANI ROUSED herself from her comfortable seat in the clubhouse. She'd eaten so much, she couldn't even make it back to her bunkhouse. She wasn't surprised she'd enjoyed the cheese-stuffed meatloaf with all the usual sides. Her afternoon had been spent helping to build a roof for the new petting zoo area, and that was after spending the whole morning babysitting.

She'd be lying if she said she wasn't honored that Jackson had trusted her with the care of Tabitha while he and Layne marked where the new fence on Hannah's property would go. Tabitha was a joy to be around. She could see why that was her middle name. It was sad that she would never know her mom. Holding the little girl and feeding her had Dani wishing her dreams of marriage and children hadn't gone up in the smoke from the burning of her Mr. Right Characteristics List.

It also had her crossing off yet another characteristic in regard to Jackson—"open to forever." Not only was the man not open to a possible forever relationship, but he also hadn't even planned on living as long as he had. She was beginning to understand why. He'd had a lot of emotional traumas in his life, starting at seven years old. That he was still standing and breathing was to his credit. She just wished he'd bring his family in on his problems. She was leaving in a few days and was worried about him.

She wrapped her hand around her bracelet. It would be so easy to just tell Brody or Amanda or Hannah, but it wasn't her place to interfere. All she could do was make suggestions to Jackson. She was no more than a guest he had chosen to confide in and have his first sex in almost a year with. She couldn't forget that part. She hoped they'd find another opportunity to do so again before she left.

So far, he didn't make the cut on nine out of eleven of her Mr. Right characteristics. Two people couldn't build a relationship on passion alone, even if what they had was amazing. The last characteristic—"willing to admit when he's wrong"—was a moot point. The man was simply not marriageable material.

That wasn't to say she didn't like him. In fact, she did, quite a bit. She'd have to classify their relationship as more of a friends with benefits arrangement. She glanced at the clock on the wall next to the stone fireplace. Just a few more minutes and she'd mosey on out to the stable to see whether he was feeding Shotgun yet. After all, there were advantages to a friends with benefits arrangement.

"Hey, Dani! There you are." Kaitlynn strolled over and plopped in the adjacent comfy chair. "So what do you think about this whole expansion plan? Are you in?"

"I am. I've already helped set fence posts for the petting zoo, and from what I saw today, they're still holding." She grinned, having had no doubts they would.

Kaitlynn nodded. "Yeah, me too. I'm going to try and pair up with my last two contenders for my next lover." She held up her hand as if Dani would interrupt. "Not that the other two aren't also good options. It's just that these two live closer."

That was a good strategy. Would she consider dropping by for good sex with Jackson if they were closer? Hell yeah. She smirked at the thought.

"What? You don't think it's a good idea to choose based on location or on working on fence posts?"

Dani shook her head. "No, I actually think both are a great idea. In fact, I heard quite a number of women signed up for tomorrow. Layne's not going to be happy unless they send him somewhere else. I guess we'll see how many women decide to go back the next day and the next. I know I will. I'm really enjoying the physical work. So much of my usual workday is sitting behind a desk or driving to a mine."

Kaitlynn shrugged. "I don't really care one way or the other. I'll do the next two days so I can pair up with each man in my sights." She smirked. "Too bad men aren't more willing to share. I'd have both at the same time."

"Kaitlynn! Shh. There are children around."

Kaitlynn covered her mouth before scanning the room. Then she lowered her voice. "I forgot. I'm going to add that suggestion about having only single women and single men groups on occasion on my comment card tonight. I've already got three other women writing it too. A singles week is my own little campaign."

"Are you thinking of coming back here for vacation?"

"It depends." Kaitlynn lowered her voice again. "If I get a good lover from this, it may just be my go-to source." She laughed, clearly pleased at her cleverness.

Dani didn't see Tanner being excited about the Rocky Road becoming a place for hookups. She got the feeling that he wasn't a hundred percent in on the whole dude ranch thing. He seemed more excited about expanding the cattle feeding ground when he announced what they were doing the next few days. "I've been adding my two cents as well, especially around the safety issues."

Kaitlynn groaned. "You didn't."

"Of course I did. At least I'm trained in this area, and they can get things fixed before anything bad happens."

"Yes, I know. I admit to being glad you checked things out more than once before we started drilling. But you're supposed to be on vacation."

Dani rose and pulled on her leather jacket, pleased that some of her food had digested. "Oh, I am. I'm following your advice and enjoying myself. See you later." She started for the door.

"Wait, you can't drop that bombshell on me and leave."

She looked over her shoulder. "Just did. Seeya." She quickly exited the building and skirted around the corner to make sure Kaitlynn didn't follow. When her friend hadn't left after a few minutes, she took the long route around the bunkhouses instead of across the quad to avoid being seen.

The air was cold and getting colder. She wouldn't be surprised if there was frost on the ground come morning.

She headed for the barn, hoping Jackson would be feeding Shotgun. She wanted to tell him what a joy it had been watching Tabitha. Since Isaac had taken over the afternoon watch, she hadn't seen Jackson all day. As her departure drew closer, she wanted to spend as much time with him as possible.

She'd just reached the barn when she heard voices outside. Walking past the open doors, she found Brody and Hannah sitting on the bench on the porch of the house, cuddled up under a wool blanket. "Oh, I didn't mean to intrude. I heard voices."

"Don't we all?" Brody chuckled at his own joke.

Hannah waved her forward. "Don't mind him. We were just talking about the ranch finances out of earshot of Jeremiah."

She walked toward the porch. One would think that, as the patriarch of the family, Jeremiah would be involved. Then again, he was still recovering from a stroke. Her confusion must have shown on her face because Hannah explained further.

"You see, I tell Brody what I discover in looking at the books, and I make suggestions. He figures out how we should best approach it with Tanner, then Tanner and Amanda explain it to Jeremiah."

The round-robin thing made sense in an odd sort of way, but the start of it all is what had her puzzled. She spoke directly to Hannah. "You look at the books?"

"Yes. My regular job when I'm not entertaining guests is as a budget analyst. The ranch employs me as a consultant."

Dani's respect for Hannah grew tenfold. Not only did the woman lease out her land, but she also had a consultant gig with the Rocky Road Ranch. That was a good lesson in not judging a book by its cover, or rather, a woman by the man she was about to marry.

Brody chimed in. "This idea of Jackson's to start the expansion early since our feed supplier folded will cost some money. But more problematic than that is the full build-out."

Hannah nodded. "And of course we have a vested interest in it since it's our property."

"Your property."

That Brody made it clear it was Hannah's property jumped him up a notch in Dani's estimation. The "family" business was a bit complicated, but having met all the key people, she understood why. "So whose idea was it to turn this place into a dude ranch?"

"Dad's."

"Really. He seems a bit ..."

"Ornery?" Brody supplied.

"Opinionated?" Hannah added.

She smiled. "I was going to say 'persnickety,' but those work too."

Brody nodded. "He is, but he did the research and felt it was the best option."

She was about to ask where Jackson was supposed to fit when that very man stepped outside and stopped at seeing them there.

"Did I miss the memo about a family meeting?" From the look on his face, he didn't seem pleased.

The last thing Dani thought he needed was to get into an argument with his brother. "No, I just interrupted these two. I was actually looking for you."

The tension in his body seemed to relax. She could tell by the way he held his head. Instead of his chin up higher than needed, it settled into a normal position.

"I'm going to the barn to feed Shotgun. You're welcome to join me."

"I think I will." She looked at Hannah and Brody, not missing Brody's calculating look. The man really needed to not meddle in his brother's life. "I'll see you two later."

She walked beside Jackson, who had donned his jacket but hadn't zipped it up. Her leather jacket was snapped up tight and she still felt the chill. The man must run warm.

When they entered the barn, Shotgun was already waiting for them. He stood up on his hind legs and pawed the air before coming back down on all fours and chattering.

"I know. I'm late. But I brought you another apple, so you can stop begging." Jackson pulled an apple out of his pocket and held it out.

Shotgun picked it up with his hands and set it down, sitting to cover it. Then he chattered some more.

She was astounded. "Is he saving it for later?"

"That's exactly what he's doing. I guess he likes those apples the best." Jackson then pulled a small bowl and a bottled water from another pocket and filled the water bowl. He set down a piece of carrot, an egg, and what looked like kibbled dog food.

"Is that dog food?"

"Shhh, I took it from the bag Brody keeps here for Cami. But since he's left her at Hannah's while the guests are here, I figure he won't notice."

"Raccoons can have dog food?"

"A little once in a while won't hurt, but as a regular diet, no. I did a little research. Shotgun loves it, so I only bring some out once a week and make sure he has healthy food too."

"I noticed you gave him a bowl of water."

"Yes. I read about that also. They like to wash their hands and to wet their food. It has something to do with a lack of saliva. He usually doesn't drink much."

She watched as Shotgun did, indeed, dip his hands into the water before grabbing up some of the dog food. "I guess you have two children now."

"You mean the raccoon?"

"Of course. Why, do you have a possible offspring somewhere else?"

"No. I'm careful."

At his words, she remembered the sex they'd had. That's why he'd pulled out at the last minute. He'd never even bothered to ask whether she was on birth control. She understood now that she knew what Gabby had done. "I came looking for you because I wanted to tell you what a joy it was to take care of Tabitha. She's the sweetest child."

He took his attention away from Shotgun to look at her. "You did change her diaper, right?"

She grinned. "Yes, I did, and it was a full one. She also

fussed a bit and even cried, but she's still a sweetheart. My sister's babies were impossible. Trust me, you lucked out."

He stood a bit straighter. "She just takes after me."

Dani laughed. Obviously, he hadn't meant it to be a joke, but it was just the way he'd said it. "I know. Every good trait she has is because of you, and any bad traits are due to her mother."

"She doesn't have bad traits."

She bit the inside of her lip to keep from smiling. He was such a dad, proud of his daughter, and it tugged on her heart. He'd come quite a ways from the man who held his daughter on the edge of his lap. "I agree. She doesn't have any bad traits."

After Shotgun finished, he ran up Jackson's arm and sat on his shoulder to wash himself, just like he had last time.

She shook her head. "I don't think Shotgun is ever going to leave now."

"I've come to that realization myself. He's already got me trained. Every morning, I wake up and check the windowsill to make sure there's something new waiting for me there. The day after I gave the wild burro his apple core, even though I gave him a full apple, there was nothing new on the sill. It really fucked with my head. He's just a raccoon, but I thought he was gone. And I was upset by that."

She smiled kindly, liking this soft side of Jackson. "Yes, but he's your raccoon. Just hope he doesn't bring you a whole new family, or you may end up having to build him his own house."

Jackson looked shocked, and she laughed. He really

wasn't good at thinking of the future, or the consequences of keeping a pet raccoon.

"I hope he doesn't do that. I'm not ready to be a grandpa. I don't even know how to be a dad yet."

Shotgun finished his bath and ran down Jackson's arm and back to the hay bale. He stood on his legs again, made a little noise, then turned around and disappeared through the hole in the stable wall.

She touched Jackson's arm. "You're doing fine as a dad. Plus, you have a lot of support here with your family. Tabitha—TJ—is going to have a great life with all her family around her."

He covered her hand with his large one. "I know that in my head, but part of me doesn't want to share her."

Oh, it was very good that he realized how much he loved Tabitha. "I know. But it's a good thing you have your family around you. Being a single parent is tough enough, but without a support system, it can become untenable. You're lucky your family is here with you."

He pulled her closer. "I'm lucky you're here with me."

"Yes, but I'll be leaving. You need to tell your family what you've told me. Let them help you."

He released her as if she had a contagious disease and stepped away. "Why? They have their own problems. Tabitha and I aren't part of them. Tanner is hoping to make enough profit with the additional cattle to be able to shut down the dude ranch. Brody is off to become a game warden somewhere in the state. Dad is determined to make the ranch profitable while orchestrating everything around him. I wasn't even supposed to be here yet ... if at all."

She set her hands on her hips. "I don't believe that for one second. They are all thrilled you're here, and you know your father has put Tabitha on a pedestal. You've slipped back into the family ranch as if you never left, becoming a part of the operation. And look at the great idea you had for expanding the grazing area. It's time to let go of your old feelings and look around you. You have a whole new start to life. Embrace it."

He stood there scowling at her, but slowly, the scowl faded and his face relaxed. "I think you're far too observant."

She shook her head, relieved he hadn't just brushed off what she said. "Only when it comes to safety issues. Otherwise, I can be pretty clueless at times."

"You must be clueless to be talking to me. No one else will get near me except Layne. Even Tanner isn't sure what to say to me sometimes."

"That's because they sense that you don't want to talk. But you need to. Trust me on this. It doesn't have to be right now, but talk to them soon. They love you and are concerned about you."

He pulled her in close again. "Are you concerned about me?"

At the look in his eyes, her flippant reply died on her lips. "I am."

"I need you, Dani."

His words were like a spark on an oil spill. Immediately, her body became aware of him from the inside out, and she shivered with anticipation. "I need you too."

Instead of kissing her, he took her hand and started for the exit. "Not here. It's too cold."

"Where? I can't take you back to my place." She could just imagine Jackson trying to fit in her bunk, never mind all the other women in the bunkhouse with her.

"I know." He led her out of the stable and past the corral. Relieved he didn't plan to take her into the house, she followed willingly, curious about where they were going.

When they reached the clubhouse, he let go of her hand to open the door for her, and she walked in ahead of him.

He passed by her. "This way."

She followed him, as if they planned to discuss the new addition to the ranch. The few people in the clubhouse were talking or playing cards. She didn't notice anyone from the family, probably because there was no planned activity for the evening.

He led her around the coffee station, which sported sugar cookies shaped like leaves and iced in oranges, reds, and yellows. She grabbed two and a napkin and continued after him. They went around the corner, past where the food service trays were, and down a short corridor she hadn't even realized was there. At the first door, he opened it and turned on a light on the desk.

She closed the door behind her as she scanned the area. The room had a small desk with a computer, a bunch of boxes, a partly filled bookcase, and what looked like a new couch. Maybe this time, she could tie him up. The possibilities started her body buzzing.

"It's not much, but it's warm." He stepped behind her and locked the door.

She turned around and held up a cookie. "Snack?"

His gaze raked over her. "I'm hungry for an entire meal."

Her heart rate increased at his look, and she set the cookies on the desk. "So maybe we can have those for dessert."

"I like that plan." He stepped up to her and cupped her face. "I like you too."

His lips met hers, and she opened her mouth to his. Wrapping her arms around him, she tunneled her hands beneath his jacket and shirt, which was no easy task. As their tongues entwined, the heat began to build, and her clothes made her hot.

She broke the kiss and pulled her hands from him to unsnap her jacket and dropped it on the desk. Immediately, she crossed her arms and pulled her sweater over her head.

Seeing her intention, he shrugged out of his jacket as well. Then he reached behind his head and pulled off his T-shirt.

She froze in the midst of taking off her bra. Seeing Jackson's chest without a tight T-shirt covering it for the first time was a once-in-a-lifetime experience. His pectorals were large, rounded muscles atop a set of abs that looked harder than train tracks. The dog tags he wore seemed to naturally fit between the mounds of his chest. Even his waist had muscle on it. Her body reacted without even touching him. She was sure there was some scientific name for how she felt, but she didn't give a shit what it was. All she cared about was feeling him on her and in her. To hell with tying him up.

Setting her hands on his warm chest, she looked into his eyes. "Take me."

A low growl came from somewhere deep inside Jackson, and then he did.

CHAPTER 16

THREE DAYS LATER

JACKSON DIDN'T LIKE IT, but he left Tabitha with Isaac and got dressed to go to the final dinner. It was the only way he was going to be able to talk to Dani. The last three days had not gone as he'd hoped. Everyone, even Dani, had worked like dogs to set as many fence posts as possible. They were all tired, but he knew she was wiped out. Unfortunately, except for a kiss goodnight, he hadn't been with her since the night in the clubhouse.

Even as he thought of that night, his body reacted. She had been wild, amazing, and so satisfying. He wasn't sure how he'd managed to pull out despite her assurance she was on the pill. Luckily, she hadn't taken offense and had actually licked him clean, which had led to more. He wanted her again and again. He had to talk to her tonight.

He walked into the family room, where Isaac watched Tabitha in her port-a-crib. He lifted her up to give her a kiss on the cheek before holding her to his chest for a moment. "I'll be back, little one. I promise."

He looked at Isaac. "Her nighttime bottle is in the fridge and ready to be warmed."

"Got it. Go on. Have some fun." Isaac waved him away.

Fun? There were more important things than that tonight. He set Tabitha back down and moved her favorite stuffed animal next to her. He'd have to see about buying her a stuffed raccoon.

Finally, he walked into the entryway and shrugged into his jacket, leaving his hat on the table. He wasn't playing cowboy tonight. Dani knew who he was. As he walked briskly between the stable and the corral, he glanced inside out of habit. All the horses were stabled for the night.

As he turned the corner past Dani's bunkhouse, the lights inside the clubhouse made it easy to see inside. Most everyone was already there. He slowed his walk and stopped at the pink aura covering the ground. Looking up, he caught the final brush of color from the sun before the purples took over to meld into darkness. Cold and night seemed to rule at this time of year.

"Hey, hold up."

At the sound of Dani's voice, he turned. "You're not at dinner yet?"

She chuckled. "Obviously. I decided to wait until all the women had showered to take mine. It was just too noisy. How are you? I saw you ride by with a stack of poles a couple times."

"Yes. Tanner decided things could go faster if I dropped a pole at each hole instead of people having to carry them."

"That did go a lot faster. Too bad he didn't think of it earlier. You'd be done with the fence posts. How short are we?"

"A hundred and two."

Dani whistled low. "That's a lot for your ranch hands to get in, isn't it?"

"Not really. We'll get it done. You want to help?"

She smiled sadly. "Actually, I'd love to, but vacation is over for me."

And then he knew he couldn't stand to pretend to enjoy dinner and the slide show of everyone Amanda had created over the last two weeks. "Would you mind if we went into your bunkhouse and talked?"

Immediately, she grew serious and placed her hand on his arm. "Not at all."

He liked how she often touched him when she was concerned. He'd grown used to it. He opened his arm toward her bunkhouse, and she moved forward ahead of him. Even though he'd gone over everything he wanted to say while he lugged post after post, he felt it all slip away as he entered the building.

She took his hand and brought him to the loveseat near the fireplace. "Let's sit. Tell me what's on your mind."

He still held her hand where it rested on her leg. "I don't want you to go."

Her eyes widened just a bit before sadness seemed to fill her. "I have to go. I have a job to do, just like you have a job here. I have a home up in Show Low."

He knew that. "But I'm not ready for you to leave."

"I understand. You feel like you can talk to me, and I'm

honored that you've trusted me with your truths. But now you need to talk to a professional. Have you had any more episodes since that night with me?"

Gritting his teeth to keep from speaking, he looked away, into the fire. He didn't even want to think about the one yesterday morning in the shower.

"Jackson, have you called a psychologist?"

He shook his head. "Haven't had time."

She squeezed his hand. "It doesn't take long to make a call."

He didn't want to talk to a professional. He wanted to talk to her. He was well aware of how irrational that was but hadn't been able to bring himself to make a call.

"Tomorrow. Make the call tomorrow. Not just for you but for Tabitha. She's depending on you to be whole, to be there for her."

"I know." And he did, in his head. But he couldn't seem to get himself to do it.

Dani gave him a sympathetic smile. "You have this amazing family here to help you adjust. Yes, they are a bit unique, but that's what makes them yours. Trust me, I know. Next weekend, I gather with my mom and sisters for Thanksgiving, and they're going to drive me crazy, but I'll have the best time, too. That's the way families are."

He shook his head, not only because he didn't want to tell his family but also because he knew that as early as tomorrow, they might turn their attention to him. His only hope was that the expansion and upcoming wedding would distract them. "I've never told them anything. I wouldn't know where to start."

"You could start with Devlin. Or with Gabriella. You can start with the men you saved or with the reason you joined the Army. It doesn't matter where you start."

He tried to imagine telling Brody and Tanner that he had been the one with the idea of going into the hayloft. They'd hate him on the spot. He couldn't do it. "Just one more week? Not even a whole week. Just until you have Thanksgiving with your family?"

Dani let go of his hand and clasped it with her other one. "You knew that I would have to leave tomorrow."

He rose from the couch. "But I didn't. I don't think like you. I can't think like you."

"I know. You live in the present, something everyone wishes they could do. And right now, I'm here and you're here. I do care about you. I want you to feel comfortable being a dad and confident that you're not going to slip back to Syria in your head at the wrong moment."

"You make me sound like I'm broken."

She rose and put her hand on his arm. "You're not broken. You're just trying to get your feet under you after a major life change. Anyone else with your experiences would be the same way."

"And what if I can't get by without your help?"

Dani shook her head. "You can't solve your problems by being dependent on someone else. Then you're just trading one set of issues for another." She stepped back, and he felt the warmth of her hand gone from his arm. "Maybe I've made them worse."

He hated the fear in her eyes and held her upper arms.

"You didn't make it worse. I know I'm better with Tabitha. That counts for something."

This time, Dani smiled fully. "I'm so proud of you for how you've stepped into your role as a dad. Tabitha can feel your love now, and soon she will be talking and walking and wanting to be with you all the time."

At her words, he saw his little daughter in his mind, following him around the ranch. It filled his heart. "I love her."

"Yes, you do. Never stop telling her or showing her that you love her."

"I won't."

"Good. Now, shall we go get some chow?"

He pulled her closer. He didn't know what to say to make her stay and didn't have the words to tell her how he felt, so he lowered his head and kissed her, desperate to show her.

She wrapped her arms around him and kissed him back, welcoming him, and his desperation eased. But when he ended the kiss, he saw the tears in her eyes.

"I'm going to miss you, Jackson Dunn."

His throat closed as he fought the panic swelling up inside of him. Unable to speak, he stepped away, his fingers curling into fists. He stared at her, unbelieving she would be gone yet, at the same time, memorizing her face. Then, without a word, he strode to the door and left.

He walked into the night behind the clubhouse, past the pool, and into the desert, trying to stay focused on his surroundings, fighting the scenes starting to crowd his head, memories of being trapped and surrounded, with screams all around him, and there was nothing he could do. People were dying. All of them. He fell to his knees, helpless to stop it.

Why was he alive? He didn't deserve to be. Why? He'd hurt someone. No, he'd killed someone, his brother. He'd killed his own brother. No, not on purpose. But he had. He had to save everyone. It was his mission. Save them. Save his daughter. Save—

He snapped his head up. His daughter. He was alive for his daughter. He made himself stand. First, assess the area. Desert, darkness, buildings. He started for the buildings, and the fence seemed familiar. At the opening, he found a pool, and lights in the house showed a man and a baby.

Tabitha. Relief swept through him. He ran forward and opened the sliding glass door into the family room.

"Jackson, what are you doing back so soon?"

He looked at the man. He knew him. He was helping.

"Are you okay? I was just about to feed Tabitha."

And then it all made sense again. "Yes, please feed her."

He ambled toward the kitchen. He had to feed someone else. Looking around the kitchen, he saw the plastic bowl on the counter. He had to feed Shotgun. One thing at a time. That's how a man survived.

THE NEXT MORNING

Dani had her bag packed and in the back of Kaitlynn's vehicle before Kaitlynn was even awake. She'd hoped she'd run into Jackson taking his morning jog, but she must have missed him. She didn't like how he left the evening before. Now, she dragged her feet as everyone stood in the parking area saying goodbye. The whole Dunn family was there except Jackson. Well, Jackson and Jeremiah, but Jeremiah had not interacted with the other guests, only her.

That gave her an idea. Scanning the people, she noticed Kaitlynn had slipped off to somewhere more private, so Dani strode to the house and walked inside. She planned to find Jackson and say goodbye. She walked down to the office and peeked into the room but found no one there. Continuing farther down the hall, she opened the door to Jackson's room and found Tabitha asleep. Unable to resist, she walked to the crib. "Goodbye, sweetheart."

After tiptoeing out, she closed the door, undecided on where to look next. Someone must be watching Tabitha. She headed back to the front and walked through the kitchen and into the den, where she found Jeremiah and Isaac. "Hey there. Just wanted to say goodbye. It was a great stay."

Jeremiah grinned. "Of course it was. It's the Rocky Road Dude Ranch. Now, come give an old man a kiss on the cheek."

She did as he requested, but he grabbed her wrist. "Be good to my boy."

Not sure what he meant, she just nodded.

He let go of her wrist, and she looked at Isaac. "Do you know where Jackson is?"

"Yes. He went into town with Layne."

He didn't even say goodbye? "Okay, thanks." She turned around and headed out, passing by Jackson's hat on the entry table. She couldn't decide whether she wanted to steal it, smash it, or just knock it on the floor. In the end, she did nothing and left the house.

She saw Kaitlynn by the car and started to head that way when Brody intercepted her. "I want to thank you for all your help."

She frowned, not a little confused. "Isn't that what a dude ranch is about?"

"Not with the ranch. With talking to Jackson. He seems a little better."

Thinking back to the night before, she didn't agree. "I'm not so sure. He needs to see a professional, and he needs to start talking to you all."

Brody rubbed the back of his neck. "But he's been so busy with Tabby."

"TJ. Yes. So attentive that he left her with Isaac this morning and is in town with Layne."

"That's where he is? That's just wrong. He should be here to say goodbye to you." Brody shook his head. "That's Jackson, and he'll never admit he was wrong not to say goodbye. He'll just mope about. He's never admitted he did anything wrong in his life."

And there it was, the second-to-last item on her Mr. Right Characteristics List, "willing to admit when he's wrong." It figured. "It's not a big deal. I'm just a guest."

Brody looked at her intensely. "No. You were more. I really thought …" he trailed off.

She wasn't going to let that go, but just as she was about to ask what he meant, Hannah came up.

"I'm going to miss you."

The next thing Dani knew, she was being given a bear

hug. She hugged Hannah back. She looked over Hannah's shoulder at Brody. "Your bride is going to knock your socks off when you see her at the end of that aisle."

"She already does that now."

Hannah giggled and let go. "Yes, but Dani saw me in my dress. She knows." Hannah leaned in closer. "I'll text you a wedding picture."

It was probably the last thing she wanted, but she swallowed down her attitude. "I'd like that."

"Hey, Dani, are we going or what?"

At Kaitlynn's yell, she smiled apologetically to Brody and Hannah. "Thanks again for everything. Time to get back to my reality."

As they said goodbye, she made it to Kaitlynn's car and slid inside. "Let's get out of here."

"You sound like you can't wait to leave. I thought you were enjoying your stay."

"I was. But I'm done with the ranch thing. I have ice cream waiting for me at home."

Kaitlynn started the SUV, mercifully taking it slow. She didn't say a word down the entire mile of Rocky Road Ranch's driveway.

As soon as she pulled onto Mesquite Road, all bets were off. "So you going to tell me about it, or do I have to pry it out one word at a time?"

Dani shrugged, hoping to play it off. "It's nothing much. I followed your advice and had a physical-only relationship."

"No way, really? That's awesome. Was the sex amazing?"

As she thought back on the two times she and Jackson

had been intimate, she couldn't help smiling. "It was the best."

"That's a great start. Are you going to take him as a lover?"

"No. He lives too far away."

Kaitlynn turned onto Black Spur Road, the first paved road on their journey northward and home. "That sucks. I can see why you're anxious to leave. It's no fun finding a great lover and not getting to continue to explore it."

Not interested in talking more about her own experience, Dani used her distraction tactic. "What about you? Last I heard, you were headed for a threesome."

Kaitlynn laughed. "I wish. I finally chose one, and he's all for continuing what we have."

Relieved that they could focus on Kaitlynn during the three-hour drive home, she asked the key question. "That's wonderful. Are you going to tell me all about him?"

As Kaitlynn launched into detailing every moment she'd spent with Mike, Dani kept her attention focused on listening. The last thing she wanted to do was analyze why she felt so sad about her physical attraction to a man who ticked off not a single Mr. Right criterion except sex.

CHAPTER 17

TWO WEEKS LATER

DANI SAT in her hotel room in Summit, Arizona, and rubbed her bare wrist. How could she have not noticed her bracelet was missing? Tears filled her eyes and ran down her cheeks. Everything seemed to be falling apart since she'd come back from vacation. This was the final straw.

The first was leaving Jackson. She couldn't seem to concentrate at work. She'd thought it was vacationitis, but it was far more than that. People had started remarking on her lack of concentration. On top of that, over Thanksgiving weekend, her younger sister had been hospitalized after being hit by a car while attending to an accident victim in Flagstaff. She was going to make a full recovery, but it had shaken the whole family. Then the drill site in started reporting far too many injuries. And now this—her bracelet from her dad was missing.

She'd noticed as she'd been packing to come to Summit.

She usually took it off and left it at home when going to a drill site and staying in a hotel for a number of days, but she didn't have it on. It could be anywhere. The last time she remembered wearing it was at the Rocky Road Ranch two weeks ago. It could have fallen off there, in Kaitlynn's car, at the hospital in Flagstaff, or anywhere in between. She'd searched every inch of her house, even taking drains apart and looking in the lint screen of the dryer. It was gone.

She already missed her dad's presence in her life, but now it felt like she had a hole in her heart that would never heal. Her head said she was being silly. He'd been gone eighteen years now. She told herself he was always with her. She had her memories. Yet the ache in her chest wasn't going away. She'd cried on the entire two-hour drive, having to pull over twice because she couldn't see the road. She was a blubbering mess.

Was this how Jackson had felt when he first came home? Should she take her own advice and talk to someone? To clear her head? Would they think her weak for grieving all over again over a simple bracelet?

The key card clicked in the door, and it opened. "Hey, roomie. Glad you finally got— What the hell?" Kaitlynn sat on the bed next to her and wrapped her arm around Dani's shoulder. "What's going on? I've never seen you cry. What's wrong?"

Dani leaned over and grabbed a tissue from the box on the nightstand. She blew her nose, trying to think of something to tell Kaitlynn that made sense, but she didn't have enough brain power left. "Everything."

"Oh, no. No, it can't be everything. You have me here, and that's a huge something."

Dani laughed at that, thankful for Kaitlynn's sense of humor. "That's true."

"I'm going go out on a limb here, but a famous person by the name of Danielle Hubbard once said, 'I can't help if I don't know what's wrong.'"

Dani nodded. How weird it was to be on the other side of her own words. "That's also true."

Kaitlynn moved farther onto the bed and sat cross-legged. "So spill."

Dani sat back against the headboard and faced Kaitlynn. "What's really kicked me in the gut is I lost my dad's bracelet. I don't even remember when I lost it. The last time I know I had it was on the Rocky Road Ranch."

"Oh, Dani. I'm so sorry. I know how much that bracelet meant to you."

She felt a little better at her friend's words because they told her she wasn't an emotional mess for no reason. "I'm devastated." When Kaitlynn didn't reply but just studied her, she knew something was up. "What?"

"You always know where that bracelet is. I've seen you take it off and put it in that little bag for safekeeping. When did you notice it was gone?"

"Just as I was packing for this trip."

Kaitlynn gave her the side-eye. "It took you two weeks to realize your most precious possession was missing?"

"My sister went in the hospital."

"Nope. That was a week after we left the ranch, and it's been almost five days since your sister left the hospital."

Dani knew Kaitlynn was right. "I've just been having a hard time concentrating. And with this problem site—"

"Don't forget you forgot that paperwork on the Olsen mine and then drove to Rock Crusher instead of Rockhaven Mine earlier this week. Good thing they weren't far apart. What's going on? And don't tell me you have vacation brain, because I know you. You always can't wait to get back to work. Besides, I'm the only one allowed to have vacation brain."

"If I knew what it was, I'd fix it." She reached for her left wrist and, finding it bare, swallowed against more tears.

"Dani, is it that guy from Rocky Road? The one you said you had great sex with? Could it be that he was more than just a physical relationship?"

And there it was, the fear that had been gnawing at her for the last two weeks, interrupting her concentration and leaving her feeling exhausted every night. "I don't know."

"Which one was he? Maybe I can tell you if he's worth it or not."

She would have chuckled at that if she'd had the energy. "Jackson Dunn."

Kaitlynn let out a low whistle. "Wow, you go right for the hottest guy there. Okay, let me see if I can remember what I heard about him." Kaitlynn looked toward the ceiling, as if recalling every conversation she'd had there. Finally, she lowered her gaze. "Nope. I got nothing. No one talked about him, and as far as I know, you're the only one he spoke to besides his family."

Dani grabbed the pillow next to her and held it to her face and groaned. And there was the problem in a nutshell.

The reasons she'd left were still valid, but her heart had been captured and wouldn't let go of a lost cause.

Kaitlynn peeled the pillow back. "Hey, do you remember any of your Mr. Right list? Maybe he checks some of the boxes."

"He doesn't. In fact, the only box he checked was for passion." She buried her face in the pillow again. How long before she got her brain back, her life back, her heart—she groaned again.

"Okay, this calls for ice cream."

At Kaitlynn's pronouncement, Dani lifted her head. "Don't bother. It won't help."

"Well, shit. This is bad. I'm going to have to find something very special. We don't have to go to the site until tomorrow. There's got to be something I can find to make you feel better tonight. You just hang tight here. I'm on a mission. I may not be back right away, but I'll be back, and you *will* feel better." Kaitlyn rose.

She just looked at her friend, too tired to lie and agree with her.

"You just stay right there." Kaithlynn buttoned her suede jacket and left.

The dreary hotel room grew worse with the fading light outside, so Dani turned on the light next to the bed. On the nightstand, next to the tissue box, was a hotel pen and a pad of paper with the hotel name written at the top. She wrote out her Mr. Right Characteristics List:

1. A tall, average-looking man, not too muscular (no gym rats)

2. No emotional baggage
3. No children or an ex-wife
4. Desk job with good earning potential
5. Willing to talk
6. Sense of humor
7. No interfering family
8. No heroes—military, first responder, etc.
9. Open to forever
10. Willing to admit when he's wrong
11. Hot chemistry between them

She studied the list. For Number 1, Jackson was definitely handsome and overly muscular. But he didn't act like he knew he was attractive and definitely didn't invite other female attention. And to be fair, his muscles weren't from the gym but were used in the Army and on the ranch, so she could give him that one.

He had so much emotional baggage, there was only one possibility of carrying it all, and that was with a therapist, which he did not seem keen on going to. So even though she understood why he was struggling, unless he got help, he failed to meet that criterion. He didn't exactly have an ex-wife, and since Gabby was deceased, she didn't count. He did have a child, but how could she hold Tabitha against him? She couldn't. So while he technically didn't meet the criteria of Number 3, she could bend on that one.

Number 4 was a "desk job with good earning potential." He was a cowboy, but for his daughter, he had, in essence, taken a desk job. She had no idea what his pay was, but his family owned a significant spread in her eyes. She'd added

Number 4 after dating a bartender who lived with three roommates. So Jackson met Number 4 in the spirit of the reason behind it. Number 5 was "willing to talk." Though she'd quickly crossed that one off, Jackson had begun to talk to her and only her. She had to give him that one.

Now, Number 6, a "sense of humor," was one Jackson definitely didn't meet. She'd never even seen him smile. But she had seen Brody and Tanner joking around a few times, which meant that Jackson had the potential for a sense of humor, even if she hadn't seen it. Given all he'd gone through and done, it may simply come with time and therapy. But Number 7 was "no interfering family," and he definitely had one. Even he would admit that was true, which was probably why he wouldn't talk to them. But after being around his family for two weeks, she'd noticed they all really cared for and looked out for each other, so the intent was to help more than *interfere*.

There was no getting around Number 8, though. She didn't want a hero type for a husband, and Jackson was that in spades. Not only had he been in the Army, but he'd made a mission out of risking his life to save others. Then again, he was no longer in the Army, and she didn't see the profession of cowboy as a high-risk job, so in hindsight, he actually did fit the criteria. Then there was Number 9, "open to forever." Jackson couldn't even think ahead, never mind thinking about forever. Of course, that didn't mean he wasn't open to it, just that he didn't think about it, which was better than being closed to a forever relationship, wasn't it?

The second to last criterion was "willing to admit when he's wrong." Brody said Jackson never had and never would, but that was Brody talking. She hadn't actually experienced Jackson doing someone wrong and not admitting he had, so she couldn't judge him on that. And the final criterion, "chemistry," he aced. Not only did he have a body that sent her own into orbit, but he was also very attentive to her without being weak, and his hard lovemaking thrilled her. It just made her feel so desired.

She set the pad of paper with her tiny note scribbles next to each characteristic on the blanket in front of her. Upon reviewing it based on looking back, there was only one criterion he definitely didn't meet, and it was big. He had a lot of emotional baggage that he had to come to terms with. So was he her Mr. Almost Right? Was that a thing?

More importantly, if she had reviewed her list a second time for the other men she'd had relationships with, would they have come out better, or was it just Jackson? Why was she working so hard to make Mr. Wrong Mr. Right this time? It didn't take a rocket scientist to figure that out.

"I love him."

Even as she said the words aloud, everything she was thinking and feeling clicked into place. Her head cleared as if she'd been cured after living with a bad cold for weeks. Still, her sister had been in an accident, and at work, the mine had too many safety problems, both of which were worrisome. And worse, her father's bracelet was missing. But knowing that she loved Jackson made her feel as if she could handle it all.

Except the part about loving Jackson. She was sure he needed her, but did he love her? If he hadn't tried to contact her in two weeks, then he probably didn't. Though it hurt, it was better than not knowing why she felt so horrible.

Throwing off the blankets, she rose and pulled her phone from her jacket pocket. She would tackle her two biggest loves in one call. She'd call Rocky Road Ranch and ask whether they'd found her bracelet. If Jackson learned she'd called, which she was quite sure he would, he might reach out to her.

And if he did? She sat back on the bed, holding the phone but not dialing. Then they would have a talk. Maybe many talks, on the phone. The one criterion he didn't meet was a huge one with him. Getting the therapy he needed to think beyond today. Forever. He had to decide that, not her. Taking a deep, cleansing breath, she closed her eyes for a moment, then slowly exhaled. Opening her eyes, she went to her contacts and hit the number.

"Rocky Road Dude Ranch, how may I help you?"

"Is this Hannah?"

"Yes, it is."

"It's me, Dani. I was—"

"Dani? Hey, Amanda, Dani's on the phone. Go ahead, Dani, I have you on speaker."

Not sure why Hannah sounded so excited, she hesitated. "Hi, Amanda."

"Hi, Dani. What's up?"

"I was just calling to find out if anyone turned in a bracelet of freshwater pearls. I think I might have lost it while I was staying there."

"Oh."

She had no idea who said that, but they didn't sound as excited to hear from her.

"Dani, this is Amanda. We'll take a look in the bunkhouse for you and tell the ranch hands to keep an eye out wherever you went. I know you went to the petting zoo area and helped with the expansion fencing. Oh, and you did Brody's 'trevanger.' Can you think of other places you may have lost it?"

Crap, there were so many, but if they were willing to look, she'd try to remember. "I was in the clubhouse, both by the fire and in the office there."

"You were in the clubhouse office?"

At Amanda's question, her mind searched for a plausible reason. "Yes, I had been looking for someone to help me decide what I wanted to do the next day, but no one was about." She grimaced. It was pretty lame, but she had nothing else.

Hannah spoke. "We'll scour the whole building for you." Her cheeriness was back.

"I was also in the stable, but not in the hayloft. Oh, and I was in the hot tub at the house, and in the office in the house, and in Jackson's bedroom taking care of Tabitha. I think I was everywhere. If everyone can just keep an eye out for it, I'd be grateful. It means a lot to me."

"We will do more than that. We will actively look, right, Amanda?"

"Right. If it's here, we'll find it, Dani."

A little surprised by how determined they were, she felt the need to be clear. "Honestly, I'm not sure if I lost it there, or at Thanksgiving, or at work, but the last time I know I had it on was there."

"We understand. We will give it our best effort."

"Thank you so much. Bye."

She ended the call. Now, she might as well call the hospital and her sisters. Checking Kaitlynn's SUV was something she could do tomorrow after they got back to the hotel. Once home in Show Low, she had run errands, so she could try to retrace her steps.

The door lock clicked, and in walked Kaitlynn. "You're never going to believe what I found. It's two desserts in one."

"A pudding cake?"

Kaitlyn shook her head, her hand inside a brown paper shopping bag. "Nope, try again."

"A cake made out of cupcakes?"

"Never mind, you're never going to guess." Kaitlyn lifted out a tub of ice cream. "It's cheesecake ice cream! Isn't that awesome?"

Cheesecake ice cream. That was the flavor Jackson wanted her to try. She'd even suggested it on her comment card but never asked for it. She forced a smile. "I'm intrigued."

"Good because it's yours." Kaitlyn handed her the half gallon of local ice cream and a plastic spoon.

"What about you?"

Kaitlynn lifted a pink bakery box out of the bag. "Brownies and"—she reached in again—"a little Irish cream to make it all go down smooth."

She shook her head. "We have to work tomorrow, so keep

it to a minimum. I don't want to have to cite you for being drunk."

"Nah, I won't have that much. I want to save most of it for tomorrow night when I meet Mike. Oh, sorry." Kaitlynn returned the liquor to the bag. "That was insensitive."

"Don't put that away. I could use a drink about now."

Kaitlynn grinned. "I'll get the plastic cups out of the bathroom."

Great. Here she was heartbroken, eating ice cream in a dreary hotel room while drinking from a plastic bathroom cup. It could only get better, or so she hoped.

CHAPTER 18

ONE WEEK LATER

JACKSON WALKED OUTSIDE toward the stable, Tabitha securely against his chest, his field jacket zipped to cover her to her neck. Every time he put on the baby sling, he thought of Dani. Every time he walked into the office or the stable, he thought of her. He even thought of her when he got undressed at night or went for a jog in the morning. Shit, he thought of her all the time.

"I think I really messed up, Tabitha, but it wouldn't be the first time or the last. I know I'll do it with you too, but you need to know I'm trying. I'm just not sure how to get past this one with Dani."

Tabitha's head nodded against his chest. "I'll take that nod as an expert opinion, even if it's just my bouncing stride that caused it." He wasn't sure whether talking to his infant daughter like this was odd, but that was the least of his problems.

Reaching the stable, he opened the door and stepped inside.

"About time you showed up." Layne sat on a hay bale, his foot resting on another he'd moved to block the hole in the stable wall.

"What are you doing? You need to move that hay bale. That's how Shotgun comes in and out."

"Just close the door behind you, and I'll explain."

Jackson turned and did as he was asked. He hadn't even realized how odd it was that the stable door was closed in the middle of the day. That just proved he was thinking of Dani way too much. "Okay, it's closed. Now explain." He moved forward and leaned against the stall wall opposite Layne, unzipping the jacket a bit so Tabitha could see the stable.

"Your furry friend is up there." Layne pointed to the hayloft. "I caught him carrying a key ring. So I went up there to investigate. That critter has got pieces of tinfoil and some of those new nails we used for the fencing up there."

"Yes, he's given me a couple of nails and a ball of tinfoil too."

Layne's brow furrowed. "What do you mean, he gave it to you? He brought it down from there and handed it to you in exchange for his dinner?"

"No, every morning, he leaves me something on the windowsill of my room. He must see me in there at night when I put Tabitha down. I usually open the window and take his gift and dispose of it or put it back from where he took it. The stuff he finds would surprise you."

"You do realize you have a pet raccoon and that's weird, right?"

He shrugged. "At least I don't have a lovesick heifer who won't move a muscle without me nearby like Tanner. But what does all this have to do with why you blocked Shotgun's hole?"

Layne stroked his mustache on one side with his thumb. "Well, it appears our burro friend is back and looking for a snack, so I decided to keep these two apart until George moved off."

"'George'? You gave that burro a name?"

"Yeah. It's easier than saying, 'that wild burro that Shotgun picked a fight with.'"

"Hey, you don't know that Shotgun instigated it."

Layne raised his brow but didn't say anything.

They both knew it had probably been Shotgun since he was such a troublemaker. "Okay, so maybe he did. I picked up another bowl for him while I was in town this morning. I'm going to try to train him to eat his food from the bowl instead of from the bale of hay."

"How'd it go at the doctor's?"

"It went. Since he put me on that medication last week, he wanted to know if it had made a difference in how I felt. Now that he's evaluated me, he wants to start something called PE, where he has me talk about the memories that come up the most. He also told me to keep a list of when I lose it. Those are my words, not his. He's very particular to not say I'm crazy, though we all know I am."

"That sounds like a lot more help than you got while you were in the Army."

Jackson looked down at Tabitha to see that her nose was against his chest again. Carefully, he turned her head toward

Layne. "That's because the Army just wanted a diagnosis. This guy is supposed to help me cope. I did notice he never says he'll fix me."

"Maybe that's because you aren't broken."

Jackson rubbed his eyes and blinked. "I don't know. I feel like I'm broken."

Layne glanced at the hayloft before getting up to open the back stable door a crack, peering outside, and then closing it again. "Maybe you feel broken because Dani is gone. She was the person you talked to the most, even more than me."

"I know. There is a no-nonsense way about her that made her easy to talk to. She didn't judge me. She was smart, though. Everything she said was right, at least according to my psychiatrist."

"Like what?" Layne settled back on the hay bale.

"Like she said I needed to talk to my family more about my circumstances. Once the psychiatrist learned I had Tabitha, he was all about building my 'support network.' As we built a plan, we agreed that keeping Tabitha safe was paramount. But when I bring up Dani, he doesn't address it."

"Maybe that's because she's gone. I'm sure your doc is more concerned with what's happening to you now."

Layne was probably right. "But she *is* here. She's in my head even more than my last tour is. I think about her hourly, if not more. I don't know what to do about it."

Layne grinned. "You know what I always say."

"Yes. Be patient, and things will work out the way they're supposed to. But where does that leave goals, desires, and dreams? I don't want to be battered by change. Been there, done that. I do much better when I'm in control."

"Then take control. What would you change?"

That was a stupid-easy question. "I'd have Dani here."

Layne snapped his fingers. "Then make it happen."

"It's not that easy. She lives in Show Low, and her job takes her all over northeastern Arizona." He wasn't going to even bring up the fact that he'd never said goodbye.

"There's always Christmas. I hear miracles happen at Christmas." Layne rose again and looked outside. Apparently, George the Burro was gone, so he opened the stable doors. "All I'm saying, Jackson, is if you don't want to wait around for something to happen and you want things to change, you have to do something about it. From what I see, you've already started taking control by getting this doctor and talking to your family more. When you were young, you always ran to me and my house to avoid your problems. Now, you're facing them. I'd say that's a step in the right direction."

Layne was right. He had started taking steps, baby steps. He'd done so for his daughter and because Dani had asked him to, which was a way to feel closer to her. Now, he needed to take another step because it was torture having her in his head but not with him. He didn't want her to be a "trigger," as the doctor called it. But he wasn't sure what to do about it. "I've taken a few steps, but the next step is a big one. I don't want to screw it up."

"Good point, but you'll have to talk it over with someone else because I have to take a drive into town myself. Got an appointment with my barber."

Jackson purposefully looked at Layne's thick hair, which came down his neck, and then at the very bushy black mustache. "Is your appointment an hour long?"

"No, wiseass. The appointment is only fifteen minutes. The other forty-five is shootin' the shit."

As Layne walked past him toward the other set of doors, Jackson had to get in one parting shot. "So, in other words, you're literally getting *a* hair cut."

Layne laughed as he strode outside. "Exactly."

Jackson looked down at Tabitha, who seemed to find Havoc across the way quite interesting. Moving closer to his horse, he swore he saw her eyes light up, but when she smiled, his heart warmed. She was definitely going to be a cowgirl.

Havoc, however, was not as impressed. He snorted and then turned away back to his oats.

Jackson took that as a sign for him to figure out what he needed to do. Talking to Tabitha or Havoc wasn't going to help much. He zipped his jacket up higher to protect his daughter from the cold, then strode outside toward the house.

"Hey, Jackson!"

At Brody's yell, he turned to find his brother coming from the "guest quad," as they all called it now.

"Can you give me a hand?"

Since Brody was motioning toward the quad with his arm, Jackson reversed direction. "What do you need?"

"I need to get this coffee table moved, but whoever ordered it—Mandy—never thought about how heavy it would be. I looked at the base. I think the damn thing is a chunk of granite."

"I'll help you, but you need to watch your language." He pointed to Tabitha.

Brody frowned. "TJ is under all that? And here I thought

you'd just gained weight." Brody stepped to the side as if expecting a punch.

The reaction reminded Jackson that he'd done exactly that many times in the past. Sometimes he felt like a completely different person. "Whatever, wisea—guy."

Brody grinned as they started for the clubhouse. "We're going to have to come up with a new vocabulary. 'Wise guy' is a good one. Maybe 'fudge' for your favorite word?"

That was actually a good idea. "And 'shoot' for yours?"

Brody opened the glass door. "That might be tricky since shooting is going to be a regular occurrence here starting in another month or so when the first real guests arrive. Then again, I won't be around much, so that could work. Hannah says 'sugar,' and I guarantee you, I'm not going to use that."

At the reminder that Brody was leaving, he felt a tightening in his chest. Strange that he could live halfway around the world and not miss his brothers, but now that he lived in the same state as them, suddenly he needed them. "Don't be too scarce, or Tabitha won't know who her Uncle Brody is."

Brody stopped, a huge smile on his face. "I do like the sound of that. Uncle Brody is going to spoil that little muffin so badly you'll have a brat on your hands."

And just like that, the feeling of missing Brody disappeared. "Not going to happen."

Brody grinned before stepping over to a coffee table that looked like a roughhewn slab from an ironwood tree affixed to a stone base. "I'd just slide this thing across the floor, but Mandy said it would scratch it, so we need to lift it."

He looked around for a spot to put Tabitha.

"It's over by the office."

Confused, he glanced across the room toward the hall that led to the office where he and Dani last enjoyed each other. "Is that a playpen?"

"Mandy ordered it for a family who's coming in the spring with a one-year-old. She says it's best to be prepared rather than scramble at the last minute to accommodate a guest."

It wasn't perfect, but it would work for Tabitha for a few minutes. Jackson headed for the playpen. When he reached it, he tested it for sturdiness. Finding it acceptable, he brought it out into the main area. "Where are we moving the coffee table to, and why?"

Brody pointed to an area on the other side of the room. "Over there. And the reason is because we have to get this place ready for my wedding. Remember, I'm getting married next weekend?"

He'd completely forgotten. One of the biggest days of his little brother's life and he was so self-involved, he'd forgotten. That needed to change. "Are you excited or nervous?"

Brody laughed. "Both. I'm nervous that I'll be good enough for Hannah. She's such an amazing person. But I'm excited because she'll be mine forever. Weird, huh?"

"Not really." Jackson set the playpen down, then unzipped his jacket, lifted Tabitha from the carrier, and placed her on her back in the playpen. Immediately, she squealed and closed her fists. He'd like to think she was excited by the playpen, but he had a feeling she was just pooping.

He straightened and walked toward Brody. "I'm the same

way with Tabitha. I'm nervous I won't be a good enough father, but I'm excited I have her."

"Shi—oot, Jackson. I never thought of it like that. I'm going to have to think long and hard about when to become a father."

"You may have to consult your wife about that."

Brody's face took on a dreamy look. "Wife. I'm going to have a wife."

Jackson took the opportunity to give his brother a light punch in the arm. "Come on, Romeo. If we don't get this monstrosity moved, you won't be getting married, at least not in here."

"Right."

Brody moved to one end of the coffee table, and Jackson took the other. It always felt good to be doing something productive. Now that the guests had left and he'd been seeing his doctor, he hadn't been doing as much around the ranch. He liked spending so much time with his daughter, but the lack of physical work was a problem. He could hire a woman to watch her part of the time, but for some weird reason, it felt like he was betraying Tabitha.

"This is ... good."

At Brody's breathless statement, he realized the coffee table was severely tilted, with his own end much higher than his brother's. Carefully, he set it down.

Brody pulled a bandanna out of his pocket and wiped the sweat from his neck. "I swear that thing is heavier than a South Devon bull."

"Either that or you're getting weaker in your old age."

"Hey. I don't have to be muscle-bound like you to do my job."

He studied Brody, realizing for the first time that his little brother had packed on some muscle since he'd been deployed. "That's true. You look strong enough to wrestle a mountain lion to the ground. I'd just think about another strategy if you run into a bear."

"Thanks. I'll keep that in mind." Brody folded up the bandanna and stuffed it back in his rear pocket.

Jackson looked over at Tabitha, who seemed to be happy looking up at the rafters. "It looks like I have a little time before the next diaper change. You need anything else moved?"

Brody's brows lifted for a moment before he gave a nod. "I sure do. All this furniture needs to go there, there, and there. Then I need fifty folding chairs set up facing the fireplace with an aisle down the middle. And over there"—he pointed to the area where the guest buffet was usually set up—"I'll need to arrange folding tables and even more chairs."

He envisioned the whole setup. It made sense except for one thing. "If you move all this furniture to the side, your chairs are going to be crammed. What if you used the lounge seating to make your rows before the fireplace? Your guests would be more comfortable, and it would leave more walking space around the area for people to gather."

Brody studied the area. "Do we have enough?"

"Let's count."

Jackson couldn't believe it took them three tries and they still didn't come up with the same number, but the number was higher than fifty. So he spent the next hour rearranging furniture to Brody's specifications. When they had it arranged, they stood with their backs to the stone fireplace to view their handiwork.

Jackson wished Dani could see it. She would definitely approve, but would Hannah?

"I like it." Brody smacked him on the back.

"Good. I need to feed Tabitha and put her down for a nap. But if you want, I can come back and help you set up the rest."

"I can use a break myself. Let's do that."

He gave his brother a nod and walked over to the playpen, where Tabitha was starting to scrunch up her face and make unhappy noises.

Brody stepped up next to him. "Yeah, she's definitely fussing."

Fussing? "She's hungry and definitely needs a diaper change from the smell of it." He picked her up and set her back against his chest. The calmness he felt with her against him was welcome.

"Are you sure you don't want to stand up with me? I ordered you a tux because it might go to Tanner's head if he's the only one with me, like he's the 'best' man or something. I really prefer two best men since Hannah is having two maids of honor."

The offer, made for the third time, just made him more confident in his decision. "No. I want Tabitha to attend, and that can only happen if I have her with me. If she gets 'fussy' or needs her diaper changed, I'd have to step away. I'm all she's got, and she's my world."

Brody's hand came to rest on his shoulder. "I know she's

your world, but she's not all *you've* got. You have all of us, as mixed up and as imperfect as we are. You know Tanner, Dad, Hannah, even Mandy, and I have your back."

Remembering they all had his back wasn't easy after separating himself from his family for so long. But in his head, he got it. "I know it. I just have to learn to remember I'm not alone in this, or so I'm told."

"By who? Dani or your doctor?"

"They both said to remember I've got family. I wish Dani didn't have to leave. Again, I understand she did, but my heart doesn't like it."

"Then why don't we invite her to the wedding? We can have her down for the weekend. We have plenty of room. She could have the whole bunkhouse to herself." Brody gestured toward the quad.

"Do you think she would come? The last she saw me, I wasn't in very good shape, and I'm not a hell of a lot better."

Brody wagged his finger. "You're not a *heck* of a lot better. But you are, and you're taking the right steps. Everyone has to start somewhere, and Dani seems to be the type of person who would understand that. But you'd probably have to apologize for not saying goodbye."

"I can do that."

"You can?" Brody gave him the side-eye.

"Apologizing for that is the least of my worries." He looked away. Despite the truth of his statement, he felt as if hope started to sputter to life.

"And can you admit you love her?"

He snapped his gaze back to his brother. "Tell her I love her?"

"Really, Jackson? We could all see it. You're head over heels for her, and I think she feels the same about you."

He'd known Gabby for two years and hadn't loved her. How could he have met Dani and fallen in love in two weeks? "I don't know."

Brody threw his arms up and started to walk toward the door, then stopped. He turned around. "Tell me something. Would you take a bullet for Dani?"

"Yes. I took two for my men."

"You did?" Brody's gaze swept over him as if he were trying to figure out where, then he shook his head. "If she were sick, would you cook for her and take care of her? If she lost her job, would you give her a place to stay? If she were upset, would you try to make her feel better? If she wanted you to sew up a hole in her shirt, would you?"

"Of course. I'd do that for Tabitha too."

"Do you love Tabitha?"

He sighed. "You know I do."

"So then ..."

But did that mean he loved Dani? "Why did you ask if I'd sew a hole in her shirt?"

"Because, brother, it's those little things, not just the heroic ones, that show your spouse you love them on a daily basis. It's what I would do for Hannah and what Tanner would do for Mandy. If you would be there for Dani in the tough times and in the easy times, then there's a really good chance you love this woman." Brody strode back toward him. "Tell me something. Can you imagine waking up next to her every morning, eating breakfast together, grocery shopping together, and giving Tabitha a bath together? If you can, then that is the future you want."

The future. He wasn't good with the future. Dani had pointed that out. But everything Brody said, as he'd said it, became a clear image in his head. "I love her." The words, though whispered in awe, settled into his chest like a feather floating to the ground.

"That's what I thought. Now, I need to have Hannah invite her to the wedding. Hopefully, she won't mind the late invite." Brody turned and walked away.

Jackson stood silent for a moment, the realization of his love for Dani quietly, slowly filling every corner of his being. He wanted the life, the normal life Brody talked about, and he wanted it with Dani.

Tabitha started to wiggle against him as she pushed her face into his chest. Without even thinking, he gently turned her head. Then she let out a loud squeal.

His heart jerked, and he quickly moved to the exit. Even as he strode across the quad, his heart raced with both excitement and dread. He was excited to see Dani again but dreaded that she might turn down the invitation. What he felt was almost worse than how he'd felt before Brody suggested Dani come to the wedding. But he wouldn't lose his courage now.

Once inside the ranch house, he changed Tabitha, fed her, and put her down for her nap before wandering out into the kitchen, where everyone had gathered for lunch. Everyone except his dad, who he could hear complaining to Isaac.

Amanda saw him first. "Jackson, I made meatball subs for lunch. Would you like one?"

He felt the tension in the room even before he answered. That was his fault. He rarely ate lunch with them all. "Yes. After helping Brody, I'm starving." He pulled up a chair next to Hannah, who sat at the island counter with Brody.

Tanner stood on the other side, where his wife placed shredded cheese in a sub roll, filled it with meatballs and sauce, and put it on a plate. She slid it across the counter. "Here you go."

He took a bite, appreciating the flavor of the sauce and the spices of the meatballs. "This is good."

"Thank you." Amanda smiled at him.

He probably didn't deserve the smile. Though he'd seen how much she loved his brother and how hard she worked to make the dude ranch a success, he'd let their past color the present. It might take time, but he'd make an effort to change. Taking another bite, he nodded to show his appreciation.

As sauce dribbled over his hand, Hannah passed him a napkin. "They're great but messy."

"Thanks."

"Brody said he wants me to invite Dani to the wedding. Are you okay with that? I'd love for her to be here but only if you're comfortable."

He finished chewing and wiped his mouth. "Yes. I want to see her. Please invite her."

Hannah practically glowed. "Wonderful!"

He quickly took another bite, not wanting to get involved in the conversation, but he listened intently as they discussed the wedding and the reservations starting to come in for

February, when the dude ranch would open to general paying customers.

As soon as he finished eating, he left them all to their plans and checked on Tabitha. After making sure his app was working, he left the house, itching for a short ride. Having everyone in the house while his daughter slept was reassuring. Stepping into the stable, he stopped to allow his eyes to adjust from the bright sunlight outside to the darker interior.

Shotgun ran across the floor to his hole and then outside.

"What's the rush?"

Shotgun turned around at his voice. In his hand was another shiny object.

"You know you're obsessed. Obsession isn't good. What do you have?" He crouched down and held out his hand.

The little bugger came forward and then ran up his arm to his shoulder.

Jackson rose. "I can't ride with you on my shoulder." He moved to the hay bales where the raccoon usually ate. "Here."

Shotgun didn't move, but he did chatter.

"I have a feeling I don't really want to know what you're saying."

The chatter continued. Obviously, he was pretty upset about something.

A bark outside made everything clear. That's right, Brody had his dog, Cami, with him, and he must have let her out. "Okay, I'll close the doors. Cami can't get in here with them closed." He closed the ones closest to the house first. Brody and Hannah would probably go to the clubhouse to talk over more arrangements, and Cami would go with them.

After closing those doors, he walked down the aisle between stalls to the other end and closed those ones as well. Shotgun held on the whole time.

Jackson moved to the hay bales once again and put his hand on top of the pile that was chest high. "Okay, you're safe now. You can get down."

Shotgun chattered some more but did crawl down his arm. The raccoon didn't go any further, playing with what he had in his hand as he made small noises in the back of his throat.

"Hey, it's okay if you stay in here. Just don't go outside until after dinner."

Shotgun put down his trinket and jumped onto the next-highest hay bale.

"What's this?" Jackson picked up the shiny object. It wasn't that it was shiny but that it was white. It was Dani's bracelet!

Did she know she'd lost it? She had to be upset if she did. He hated the idea of her upset. Slipping the bracelet into a pocket on his jacket and zipping the pocket up, he went in search of someone who would know Dani's number. Actually, it should be on the computer. He headed for the house to see who was left inside. The afternoon would be busy as the wedding planning went into high gear.

The first person he saw was Amanda, who was cleaning up after lunch. He stopped out of habit, then made himself move forward. "Amanda, do you happen to have Dani's number?"

"Dani's number? I don't, but Hannah does. She's in the clubhouse with Brody."

He started to turn and then stopped. "Do you think it would be in the computer?"

Amanda brightened. "Of course. I have her reservation. Let's go see."

He followed her down the hallway, reminding himself that she was a Dunn now and no longer a Hayden.

When they got to the office, Amanda slipped behind the desk and, in a few keystrokes, was looking over the reservations. "Do you know what her last name is?"

"It's 'Hubbard.'"

Amanda looked up from the computer. "Any chance you can tell me why you need her number?"

"Yes. I found her bracelet and want to text her a picture of it."

"You found her bracelet? We've been looking all over for it! Where did you find it?"

That meant she knew she had lost it. His gut tightened, knowing how much she treasured it. "Shotgun had it."

Amanda frowned. "It was in a shotgun? She didn't even go to the range."

Shit, he'd forgotten only Brody, Layne, and Dani knew about his raccoon. It was probably best everyone knew, so they didn't shoot it. Though he felt like he was five years old again and had asked to have a rabbit. "No, 'Shotgun' is the name of my pet raccoon."

Amanda scrunched up the right side of her face. "You have a pet raccoon?"

"I do." He waited for the laughter or censure, not sure which would come.

"Well, you better keep Cami away from it. Raccoons

don't like dogs. Is Shotgun somewhere safe? Cami's outside somewhere."

Surprised and relieved by her response, he explained the stables being closed and the hole to go in and out.

Amanda nodded. "That's good. He should be fine in there. So your raccoon found Dani's bracelet. She's going to be thrilled. She called about a week ago, and Hannah and I searched. Wait until she hears a raccoon had it."

"I want to be the one to tell her. She knows about Shotgun. I just need her number so I can text her the picture and let her know."

"Oh, I see. Of course." Amanda looked back at the screen. "Let me see. Dani Hubbard."

"It's actually 'Danielle Hubbard.'"

Amanda glanced at him, a soft smile on her face. "That's right, 'Dani' is her nickname. Let me see. Here it is." Amanda wrote the number on a piece of paper and handed it to him. "Hannah already texted Dani the invite to the wedding. I hope she comes."

So did he, but he couldn't quite get himself to say so to Amanda. "Thanks."

"You're welcome." Amanda rose. "Now, I have to see if I can get your dad to do his exercises. He's been a bear about it lately. There's so much excitement right now."

Jackson stepped out of the room and allowed Amanda to walk down the hallway ahead of him, itching to use the paper in his hand. When they both arrived in the family room, he stopped her. "I'm going to be helping Brody with the wedding setup this afternoon. If Tabitha wakes, would you have time to watch her, just until I get back in?"

Amanda's eyebrows rose even as she smiled. "I would love to."

"I appreciate it." Not wanting to make it into a big deal, he turned on his heel and headed back outside. After setting the bracelet on the porch railing, he took a quick picture and then added Dani to his contact list. That was the easy part.

He sat on the porch bench and tried to figure out what to say. Finally, he just wrote, *Shotgun found it. I knew you'd be worried. It's safe with me.* He attached the picture and sent it off.

Would she respond right away? In a few minutes? Would she be awkwardly polite or real? Maybe she would decide to—

His phone vibrated. He had a response. He opened the text. *Thank you so much. I was heartbroken I'd lost it. Please give Shotgun a special treat from me.*

Real. She was real. He wrote out a message telling her she could give him a treat herself when she came down, then erased it. Instead, he simply typed, *I will.*

He waited to see if she'd say anything else, but no more messages came in. Finally, he rose and clipped his phone onto his jeans again before scooping up the bracelet. At least she hadn't told him to send it to her. That had to be a good sign, unless she contacted Amanda and asked her to send it.

"Stop it." He said the phrase the psychiatrist told him to use when he started going off in what he referred to as "a spiral."

He was good at thinking only of the present. The wedding was still a week away. That was too far into the future to worry about. So much could happen in a week.

CHAPTER 19

DANI KEPT her SUV at a crawl as she made her way down the Rocky Road Ranch's dirt driveway. She drove slowly, partly to save her vehicle but partly because she still wasn't sure she was doing the right thing. Seeing Jackson again might make her heart feel worse.

When she'd received the text from Hannah asking her to come to the wedding, she was surprised. She understood that Hannah was friendlier than most, but it was supposed to be a small wedding, the last she'd heard, so why invite her? Unless Jackson had asked her to be invited. But that wasn't necessarily a good thing. He was caught in his present-day issues and had Tabitha to think about. He didn't need any distractions.

Plus, she was supposed to go to her sister's for Christmas, and with the wedding on Christmas Eve, that would mean a long drive to Tempe on Christmas Day. However, as much as she wanted to watch her nieces and nephew open their gifts from Santa, she wasn't sure she could hold it together, seeing her sister's family so happy when she was miserable and the man she loved not ready for a relationship.

But then Jackson had texted her with the bracelet photo and the news that Shotgun had found it. The feelings that tumbled through her were chaotic, from thrilled to relieved to excited to content. It was as if her father were trying to tell her something. Not that she believed in stuff like that, but she'd never lost the bracelet before, so it was an unusual circumstance that called for an unusual response. She was so thankful for that adorable critter.

She'd gone back and forth on whether to have them send the bracelet and turn down the invitation or accept, retrieve her bracelet, and see Jackson again. Because she was weak and concerned about him, she'd caved. But now, as she limped along the driveway, she wanted to turn around and go back. What if it was even harder leaving this time?

The sun was already setting before her because the days near Christmas were so short. The oranges and yellows reflected off the snow-brushed mountain tops, making them glow. The ranch house came into view behind the fencing with the open gate, welcoming people to the end of their harrowing journey down the drive. And there at the gate stood a man in shadow, highlighted by the colors streaming behind him.

Her heart rate went into overdrive even as she pulled in, put the vehicle in park, and turned off the engine. And then there he was, opening her door for her, offering his hand.

The second she took Jackson's hand, all her doubts about coming washed away as her heart calmed. She stepped out and into his arms as he pulled her in and kissed her. It wasn't a desperate kiss or a gentle kiss. It was a welcome kiss.

She kissed him back, letting him know she was happy to see him.

He lifted his lips from hers and straightened. "I missed you."

"I missed you too."

And then there was silence. It was heavy, as if too much needed to be said.

He broke it the easiest way possible. "Let me get your bag for you."

"That would be great." She opened the back door, and he pulled out her bag.

"You're going to have a bunkhouse all to yourself. Because Hannah doesn't want Brody to see her tomorrow before the wedding, she's staying here in his room, and he's going back to her casita."

She didn't mention Devlin's room. She had a feeling it hadn't been used since he died. "It will be nice to have my choice of showers."

He lifted her bag, and they headed toward the bunkhouses.

"So how's Tabitha? Has she grown a lot in the last month?"

His gait changed slightly, becoming less stiff and more like a cowboy. "She has, and now she can lift her head when she's on her stomach. I can tell she's going to be strong like me. She also smiles, and she makes noises. I've been doing a lot of reading about her development. She's right on target."

"Oh, I can't wait to see her. I missed her too, you know."

He looked at her. "I understand that. I miss her just when I have to work on the ranch for a few hours."

They walked past the corral, and he turned toward the family bunkhouse, which was the two-story log building as opposed to the one-story one she'd stayed in.

"I'm not staying in the single woman bunkhouse?"

Jackson shook his head. "No. There's no one staying here who doesn't live here except you. The entire wedding party is here now, but everyone is going home tonight. So you can have this whole building."

Curious, as usual, she couldn't wait to see inside.

Jackson opened the door, and a large open room was before them. Off of it were six doors. He moved toward the first one. "I thought you'd like this room because it's close to the activities, but if you prefer something in the back, you can have it."

She stepped inside to find a king-sized bed in the left corner of the room. She liked it already. "Close to the activity suits me just fine."

Jackson moved to a door and opened it. "This is your bathroom."

Inside was a large walk-in shower, two sinks, a toilet, and a bathtub. "Wow, families must have loved these accommodations." She walked back out. "Then what's that door to?"

Jackson set her bag down on a dresser. "Open it."

She did and found a small room with two sets of bunk beds. "Ah, the kids' room. They can't sneak out without going by Mom and Dad. Very clever."

"That was Brody's suggestion. He was always sneaking out at night when he was a teenager."

She smirked. "Really, to go where? To visit the cows?"

"That's a good question. Definitely something to ask in front of Hannah."

"Ah, you expect there to be a little embarrassment involved. I'll try to remember. First, I should probably hang up my dress for the wedding."

Jackson stepped to the door. "I'll be right out here."

"Who's watching Tabitha?" She didn't want to keep him away from his daughter too long, but she also didn't want him to leave.

"Amanda. She's working on some party favors in the family room and has Tabitha in there."

Amanda was watching Tabitha? That was a new development. Last she knew, Jackson wasn't fond of Amanda because of an old family feud. "That's great that Tabitha is getting in a little girl time."

Jackson nodded and left.

Quickly, she pulled out her dress and hung it up, then she unpacked the rest of her things.

After leaving the room, she found Jackson sitting on one of the couches, his jacket slung over a nearby chair. The room sported a large gas-burning stove in the center, so no matter which couch one sat on, it would be comfy and warm. Without hesitation, she joined him.

He took her hand immediately, and she thought it was to hold it, but instead, he set it on his thigh and looped her bracelet around her wrist, clicking it closed. "I had to get a new clasp for it. The other one was broken. You also might find a couple of teeth marks or scrapes on the pearls. I think Shotgun had it for quite a while. Layne found a stash up in the hayloft. I think Shotgun gathers items up there and chooses one to leave on my windowsill at night."

She held her hand up to gaze at the new clasp. It looked far sturdier than the old one. "Thank you. I was devastated when I realized I'd lost it."

He took her hand in his and touched the pearls. "It's a precious gift. I'm going to give Tabitha something just like it on her tenth Christmas."

His words touched her, and she squeezed his hand, letting him know without saying anything.

"Dani, you were right about what I needed. I couldn't see beyond each day. For so long, I lived day to day while in the military, just happy to be able to put my head down at night and sleep in a safe place with a full belly, knowing none of my men were killed that day. Then everything went to shit."

When he paused, she didn't interrupt.

"Though honorably discharged, I was basically thrown out of the Army with a baby I didn't know I had fathered, told I had PTSD, and sent home, where I discovered our cattle ranch turned into a dude ranch, my father in a wheelchair, and my brother married to our enemy's daughter. It was too much change at once. I felt like a dust particle in a valley-wide haboob."

His imagery painted a clear picture of how helpless he'd felt, and she sympathized with him.

"Then I met you, always somewhere you weren't supposed to be, making it easy to talk about things, and too damn sexy to resist."

She grinned at that because he wasn't smiling and had obviously truly been bothered by that.

"But you said a lot of smart things that I didn't want to hear. And then you left."

Her chest constricted at that. "I had to."

He nodded. "I know. And it was good that you did."

That shocked her. Did that mean he was trying to tell her that he was moving on after this weekend? That would be good and what she'd hoped for. But after realizing her feelings for him ... no, whatever he needed to do, she'd support. She loved him that much. "Then I did help?"

"You did. I want to thank you."

Yes, this sounded like a breakup, even though they weren't together. She swallowed down the lump in her throat. "You're welcome."

He kissed her on the cheek, then rose, her hand still in his. Was that on purpose or from habit?

"Everyone is gathering in the clubhouse for the rehearsal dinner. After the rehearsal, I'm pretty sure the wedding is not going to go smoothly. Cami, Brody's dog, ran off with the ring when she saw a squirrel near the window, then Hannah tripped coming up the aisle, which threw Layne off balance, and he knocked over a loveseat. Brody couldn't remember more than three words at a time of what he was supposed to say, and Sheila, one of Hannah's maids of honor—she had two—swore when a spider landed on her arm."

Despite her somber thoughts, she felt for Hannah. "What did the officiate say?"

"Vic? She was laughing."

She must have heard wrong. "Vic, as in the cowgirl, is the officiate?"

"Yes. Hannah was adamant. She wanted only people she

knew and loved at her wedding, so when Brody mentioned that Vic's resume had 'justice of the peace' listed on it, they convinced her to officiate. I'm quite sure dinner tonight will go more smoothly."

Dani walked with Jackson since he still held her hand. "Wait, our coats."

After helping her on with her coat, he threw on his and grabbed her hand once again as they exited the building.

Okay, so maybe it wasn't just a habit that he held her hand. Then why'd he thank her as if he didn't need her anymore? She was thoroughly confused.

When they entered the clubhouse, almost everyone was there. Hannah was the first to spot them and squealed before running over and giving Dani a hug. "I'm so glad you could come. Say you don't hate me for the late invitation."

"I could never hate you." That got her another squeeze.

Amanda approached with Tabitha next. "Here you go, Jackson, as you requested."

Dani stared at Tabitha, impressed by her alertness and growth. "Can I hold her?"

"Of course." Amanda handed the baby over.

"Hey there, little one. You're growing up too fast." She cradled the child in her arms and smiled at her, loving everything about her, from her big round eyes and her chubby cheeks to her baby powder scent.

Tabitha made eye contact with her and didn't stop staring.

Dani wrinkled her nose, and the corner of the baby's lip quirked up. So Dani did it again, longer, and Tabitha grinned, gurgling as she flayed her arms. She laughed as the baby giggled.

"Hey, don't forget about your dad." Jackson rubbed Tabitha's belly with his finger.

The baby's gaze immediately went to him. She giggled some more, and her feet started going too.

"That's my girl." Jackson lifted his daughter and settled her into the baby sling. "I swear I'm addicted to this thing. I can't go a day without her in it."

Dani checked the adjustments and could see they were at their maximum. "You're going to need a bigger one. She's growing fast."

"Maybe you can help me order one?"

Though he asked for her help to simply buy something, his gaze was saying so much more. She just didn't know what. The moment ended abruptly as Brody, followed by everyone else, came over to say hello. But by the time they sat down, Tabitha in her port-a-crib next to Jackson, Dani had a clear idea of how the wedding would proceed—happily and chaotically.

Dinner was much the same, with everyone chatting with everyone else. As the father of the groom, Jeremiah wheeled his way around the table, talking to everyone. When he got to her, he winked. "Nice place we got here, huh?"

"Yes, it is. I heard you designed most of the buildings."

The man straightened in his wheelchair. "I did. Tanner made sure they were built as I specified. He's going to do well running this place."

"I agree. Is he completely on board with the dude ranch now?"

Jeremiah motioned yes and no with his head. "Enough for now." Jeremiah patted her hand. "Good to see you here." And with that, he rolled away.

She turned her attention back to the table just in time to hear Layne speak to Jackson. "I think I'm going to need one of those pills you got from the doc after this ceremony is over. Now *I'm* going to be traumatized."

Nash and Hannah, who were sitting closest, laughed.

Concerned, Dani looked Jackson over. "Are you okay?"

Before Jackson could answer her, Hannah, who must have heard her question, waved her hand. "Oh, he's not hurt. He's seeing a psychiatrist."

Not a little surprised that not only was Jackson getting help but his family also knew about it, she looked to him for confirmation.

"Yes. I took your advice and found a professional. I hope I never made you feel as if you should fix me. I never meant to put that kind of pressure on you. I was just so messed up, I couldn't fully understand all that you were telling me."

So that was why he had thanked her. "I'm so glad you can talk to someone who knows how to handle this."

"I'm glad too. When you left, I finally understood that I wasn't going to figure this out on my own. So I called an Army buddy of mine, who told me about a guy in Cave Creek who not only treats veterans but is a vet himself. It makes it a lot easier because I don't have to explain the whole Army combat side of things."

She looked around them, and Layne, Nash, Hannah, and Brody were all smiling at them. Brody lifted his beer toward his brother. "He's not telling us anything about what happened over there, but at least he's talking to us."

"And don't forget insulting us." Nash pointed to Layne. "Between him and Jackson, I'm lucky I have an ego left."

Hannah put her hand on Nash's shoulder. "Poor Nash. Just think of how sorry all the ladies will feel for you."

Nash raised his brows. "I hadn't thought about that. Bring it on, then."

As people laughed around them, Dani noticed Jackson's lips quirking up a little. She held her breath, expecting a smile, but Layne spoke to him, and he turned his head. She looked across the table at Hannah, who nodded toward Jackson and winked.

Dani lifted her glass of iced tea to take a moment to process everything. In the month they'd been apart, he'd taken major life-changing steps to help himself. She hadn't thought it possible. So much of his trauma went so far back. He wasn't heroic just in his military service. He was heroic in his personal life too. Though she was sure that he wouldn't see it that way.

She set down her glass, realizing that he was working on the one Mr. Right characteristic he hadn't met. Not that her list mattered anymore. It was obvious she'd used it as an excuse to break off relationships that weren't right. But Jackson was right for her.

Whether she was right for him was the new question.

As the dinner ended, she was anxious to get Jackson alone. But first, there were goodbyes to be said to those heading out, and then Brody invited whoever was left to sit around the fire he had set up in the quad.

Isaac, who had been at the dinner, came over with Jeremiah before they went outside. "Would you like me to put Tabitha to bed?"

Jackson looked down at his daughter in his arms. She was already sleeping. "I suppose it's that time."

"I'll take her," Jeremiah put his arms out. "There's not a damn thing wrong with my upper body strength."

Jackson frowned even as he settled Tabitha in his dad's arms. "No, but there is with your mouth. Watch your language around her. I don't want her first word to be 'damn.'"

At Jeremiah's surprise, Dani stifled a chuckle.

"Fine. I'll just use 'dagnabbit' and 'bull hockey.' That better?"

"No. But we'll come up with a few you can use. I promise."

She held her smile until Isaac and Jeremiah turned away. "'Dagnabbit'? What's that supposed to be?"

Jackson shook his head. "Damned if I know, but I don't want my daughter being a laughingstock at school. Can you imagine an eleven-year-old saying that?"

She laughed before realizing he'd mentioned a future milestone. That was new too. She was getting a glimpse of what it was like to come back and find things had changed. The change in Jackson was remarkable. Did that mean he was better without her to lean on? The new thought sobered her.

"Come, let's grab a couple of the comfortable chairs around the fire before Brody does."

They donned their coats and headed outside. Tanner and Amanda were already there and had commandeered two of the six "comfortable" chairs, which were just folding canvas chairs as opposed to logs.

Layne and Nash each chose logs, but Vic grabbed a canvas chair. Brody and Hannah took the last log, one big enough for two. Immediately, Brody started joking about how the wedding couple was not getting preferential treatment.

Tanner spoke up. "You need to respect your elders."

Vic pointed at Layne. "Then he should be sitting on a throne."

Everyone, including Layne, laughed. "I can still outwork any of you except maybe him." He pointed to Jackson. "But that's what comes with age. When you're thirty-six, you know when to work and when to relax." He stretched out his legs and crossed them at the ankles. "That's called wisdom."

Tanner threw a bottle cap at Layne, who caught it in midair. "Layne, you're way too set in your ways for your age."

"Don't see any reason to change 'em either."

Brody raised his hand as if they were back in school. "I'm looking forward to change. I'm starting the new year with a new career and a new wife." He kissed Hannah on the cheek.

She pulled his hand down, brought it to her lips, and kissed it. "And I'm starting the year with a new husband and a new life somewhere in Arizona."

Amanda looked over at her. "Aren't you a little worried about where Brody will get a position?"

Hannah shook her head. "Not at all. I love the mystery and the excitement. I lived my whole life in Phoenix until I inherited the place next door. I love learning new things, so living in a place I've never even visited has so much potential."

"Not me." Layne grinned. "I'm perfectly content where I am. I have my own home and my own space as a bachelor. I don't need a wife and definitely not children. My family has enough kids to populate a football team. Though I was contemplating getting another horse."

Tanner chimed in. "You've been saying that for three years now. You're not getting a new horse. It's added work."

Layne stroked one side of his mustache with his thumb as he thought. Then he smiled. "Not if I stable it here."

"Oh, no. I'm not taking care of your horse too." Vic shook her head. "All these extra horses for the guests are plenty, thank you."

"Next year, we're hoping to get some good news." Tanner reached over and took Amanda's hand. "It hasn't happened yet, but we're hoping that soon our wish for a baby will be granted."

Amanda rolled her eyes. "In the meantime, he certainly doesn't mind the trying part. Wait until he gets to change the diapers."

Dani was surprised that Tanner actually blushed. He definitely was the more strait-laced of the brothers.

"I'd be happy just to have a steady girlfriend," Nash complained.

Vic reached over and patted him on the shoulder. "I'm sure it will happen for you, buddy. Keep the faith."

"You think?" Nash gave Vic a nod to come over.

"Not happenin' with this girl, dude."

He put on a super disappointed look.

Dani joined the others in laughing. Nash seemed like one of the good guys.

Vic pointed to Jackson. "What about you, big man? What are you looking forward to next year?"

Dani tensed, worried the question would be too much for him in front of so many people.

Jackson turned toward her. He reached over and placed his hand on hers where it sat on the arm of her chair. "I'm looking forward to Tabitha and me living with Dani, if she's willing."

Her heart skidded to a halt before picking up again. "But I live in Show Low, and the company headquarters is there. I couldn't do that kind of commute." She felt as if everything she wanted had been offered and then taken away.

No one around the fire said a word.

Jackson turned his whole body to face her. "I don't care where we live as long as you're with us. I don't need you in my life, like I thought. I *want* you in my life. I love you, Dani. I want a future with you."

Her vision started to blur as her love for the amazing, imperfect man before her offered her everything, including him and his daughter. "I love you too. I would love a future with you and Tabitha."

Brody yelled across the fire, "Don't forget what your mother said. If you have love, everything else will work out."

She sniffed, smiling through her happy tears. "Yes. Yes." She threw her arms around Jackson, knocking her chair over into him.

He caught her to him in his strong embrace and whispered in her ear, "I love you. You've made me happier than I've been since I was seven."

At his heartfelt words, she lifted her head to find him smiling. He had the most beautiful smile she'd ever seen and even had a small dimple.

As applause erupted, she was pulled from the moment. Jackson steadied her and her chair back into a functional position.

"I knew it." Brody wrapped his arm around Hannah's shoulders. "Didn't I tell you?"

"Yes, you did."

Dani gave Brody the side-eye. "How did you know?" She squeezed Jackson's hand, sure that Brody would say something outrageous.

Brody shrugged. "It's simple. Tanner knew that Amanda was meant for him when she filled the dishwasher just like our mother did, which is very particular. Then Hannah here folded our napkins just like our mother did."

Dani interrupted him. "And I told your dad that love would make everything work out, and that's what your mother said. But I told you that the first week I was here."

"I know. But my mom was a very wise person and always looked out for her sons. I think she brought us the best women." Brody looked upward. "Thanks, Mom."

Tanner and Jackson looked up as well.

Into the silent, reverent moment, Layne spoke. "Brody, remind me not to tell you what my mother says. She's still alive and would love nothing better than to have another daughter-in-law."

Jackson smirked. "Too late. I already know what your mother says."

At Layne's groan, everyone laughed.

Dani squeezed Jackson's hand. She was as happy now as she'd been helping her dad on Christmas Eve, this very night, so long ago. She looked up at the stars for a moment. "Thank you, Dad."

"And thank you, Shotgun."

At Jackson's comment, she turned and smiled. "Yes, what would we do without that meddlesome critter?"

"Think he'll like it in Show Low? I know George wouldn't mind if that raccoon left." Layne gave Jackson a look that spoke volumes, but Dani had no idea what it meant.

They had a lot to discuss, but for tonight, she just wanted to bask in the happiness of being with Jackson. "Think anyone would mind if we left now?"

His gaze grew intense, causing her body to take notice. "I don't think I care if they do."

"Hey, what are you two whispering about?" Amanda drew everyone's attention to them. "Don't make any plans without us, now."

Jackson stood. "Okay. We're planning to go to the bunkhouse and make love. Any suggestions?"

Amanda's eyes rounded before the men started making rather startling suggestions on how they should do it.

Dani could feel herself blushing.

Vic yelled over everyone, "TMI, people!"

Jackson pulled her up from her chair, then gave the group a regal nod. "I will take all your thoughts under advisement."

Even as they turned their backs and headed for the bunkhouse, she could see Jackson's lips twitching as new ribald comments followed them. She wouldn't be surprised if Tanner eventually put a stop to it.

As they stepped into the building, the quiet was welcome. Finally, they were alone.

Jackson helped her off with her leather jacket. "I have a favor to ask you."

She turned to face him. "If I can help, I'd be glad to."

"Brody wanted me to stand up with him at the wedding. He even rented me a tux. But I told him I couldn't because I wanted Tabitha to be there and if she started to fuss, I'd have to walk out."

Dani put her finger over his lips. "I would love to bring Tabitha to the wedding so you can stand up with your brother."

He kissed her finger before taking her hand. "Thank you. Tonight, I'm going to show you exactly how much I love you."

Her heart did a little dance at his words, but her practical mind quickly took over. "Will Tabitha be alright?"

He nodded. "She's got Isaac, and soon Amanda will go inside. Our daughter will be fine. Tonight is about us."

Then, before she knew what he was about, he scooped her up in his arms and headed for her room.

She grabbed onto his neck. "Ack. Give me some warning before you do that."

He stopped before her door. "I don't know what the future holds, but I'm told I should celebrate the little successes in life. Tonight was a life-changing success, that you have agreed to live with Tabitha and me. I may carry you across the threshold of our home one day. But this is about right now. I can carry you across the threshold of this room that signifies the start of our life together."

Her heart melted at his words, her eyes tearing up again. She pressed her lips to his and kissed him with all the love welling up inside her as he carried her into their new life.

CHAPTER 20

AS JACKSON CROSSED the threshold of the room, it felt as if his psyche were cleansed and everything was fresh and new. Though he was well aware that wasn't the case, he enjoyed the feeling anyway. Why couldn't he get a do-over with the strong and caring woman in his arms?

He broke their kiss to walk to the bed. Letting Dani's feet down when he got there, he was pleased she kept her arms around his neck. He looped his arms loosely about her. "I want to celebrate every day with you and be there for you as you've been for me."

She stroked the back of his head where the hair was cut so short, it was barely discernable. "I want to do the same, but no prolonged time apart. Knowing how I felt about you and not being able to be with you these last two weeks has been hell. I don't know how my mother did it."

He ran his hand over her back, ready and willing to soothe her worries and step into his role as hers. "You won't have to do anything like that. I want to be your rock."

She gave him a sly grin as her hand smoothed its way over his shoulder and down to his biceps. "Oh, you already are."

"If you keep looking at me like that, you'll find yourself naked in seconds."

"Oh, I like the sound of that."

Never one to pass on a dare, he unlocked his hands and pulled her navy blue sweater up. She willingly lifted her arms, and he tossed it on the dresser.

"Now you." She took the bottom of his T-shirt and pulled it up, but she wasn't quite tall enough to get it over his head, so he bent his knees.

As she chucked his shirt on top of hers, he took the opportunity to lock his fingers under her stretch bra and divested her of that too. In the two times they'd been together, he'd never touched her breasts, too anxious to know everything about her inner sheath. But now he wanted to love her the right way. To know all of her.

He unbuttoned her jeans and unzipped them before pulling them down, crouching at her feet as he pulled off her boots while she held onto his shoulders. He held her jeans down, and she stepped from them. Then he ran his hands up the side of her legs until he reached her panties and pulled them down as well.

At her ready scent, he inhaled before rising. "I know I've told you I love you, but now I'm going to show you."

So attuned to her, he noticed when her breath hitched. She unbuttoned his jeans but didn't unzip them. "I would like that."

He placed his hand over hers and leaned down and kissed her. She opened to him, and he tangled his tongue with hers, loving her taste and the feel of her lips. Slowly, he pulled away. Backing up a step, he toed off his boots and dropped his jeans to the floor. Then he pulled her naked body against his.

His erection pressed into her belly, and her breasts pushed against his pectoral muscles, softness giving into hardness. "You feel so good."

She lifted her head from his shoulder to gaze at him.

Without a word, he held her tight, spun them around, and fell back on the bed.

She let out a yelp before laughing. "You're full of surprises tonight, aren't you?"

She lay half on top of him, and he rolled her over. "No. I have no surprises. No more secrets. You can know everything about me."

Her eyes started to tear up. "I will always be an open book to you too. I promise."

"I like that. I want to start reading right now." He leveraged himself over her to kiss her forehead and her cheek. Then he kissed her nose and left a soft kiss on her lips. Next, he moved to her chin and her neck, just beneath her ear. He inhaled, her scent filling him with peace.

Her hand lay on the back of his head, holding him to her as he moved lower to her shoulder, where he nipped, and her collarbone, where he licked. She tasted so beautiful. The more he knew her, the more love he felt.

He laid kisses down her arm, in the crease of her elbow, and at her wrist, giving her bracelet a light tug with his teeth.

Her hand on his head moved under his chin, nudging

him to look at her. She didn't say anything, just stroked his hair before laying her hand on his shoulder.

Free to proceed, he kissed her waist and her abdomen, licking her navel before moving upward.

He felt her breath catch as he positioned his head over her breast, then he lowered it and licked at her dimpled areola. Her nipple grew hard as he licked it before swirling it with his tongue. It was the perfect texture, making it impossible not to suck. As he did, her body arched, pressing her breast against his face.

He burrowed his hand beneath her back, holding her to him as he sucked and nipped, certain he could do so all night and never tire.

Soft moans came from deep in her throat as she held onto his shoulders.

Her moans filled him with happiness, so he moved to her other breast and gave it the same attention, holding her to his mouth as he tasted and played. Taking her hard nub between his teeth, he rolled it back and forth.

"Yesss."

Her hiss of pleasure filled him with need, but he wanted to know all of her. He forced himself to let go, licking her nipple before kissing his way over her round breast and down the center of her stomach, past her navel, and to the top of her mons.

He knew her sheath intimately already. He spread her legs, lowering his head to breathe in her readiness, but moved his lips to her inner thigh, then down to the side of her knee, the side of her ankle, and finally, the top of her foot.

Well aware that her breathing had slowed to a more

normal level, he worked his way up her other leg, over her hip, and along her waist, kissing the side of her breast on his way back to her lips. "I can say without a doubt that I love this side of you."

She gave him a soft smile. "It really is my best side."

He cocked his head. "I will have to investigate all sides, but I have a feeling I may love all your sides equally. Next, I want to love you inside."

Her lips parted slightly as she took in a sudden breath. "Love me, Jackson."

He lowered his lips to hers even as his hard cock touched her moist folds. He slipped his tongue inside her mouth as he lowered his hips, sliding into her slowly, fully.

She tilted her hips, moving her legs around his ass, and he sank a bit deeper.

She was warm and welcoming and felt so good, but it wasn't enough. He loved all of her. He lowered his arms so he rested on his elbows. Their bellies connected, and he understood what he had to do. Slipping his arms beneath her, he touched her everywhere, making them truly one.

Her arms wrapped around him, holding him just as close, feeling what he felt. He could tell. Then he lifted just his hips and sank into her again, tightening his hold, feeling her around him.

He moved his hips again, faster this time, holding her tight even as he began to pump into her, becoming a part of her while she became a part of him. Her breaths were as rapid as his own, and soon tiny moans came from her chest. He could feel them! Excitement, joy, happiness filled him as he moved in her, faster and faster, her nails digging into his back as she held onto him as if he were all she had to keep her safe.

He would always keep her safe.

Suddenly, she tightened around him, her ecstasy coating him before she yelled out her pleasure. The sound, the feel, the scent combined, and he filled her, losing himself in her, with her, together. He felt as if lifted on a cloud, wrapped in her arms as bliss swept through him again and again. Peace filled him even as his body continued to pump his release into her. He was hers ... always.

Dani held on as her world spiraled beyond her reality, the man in her arms the only thing solid in the pleasure rifling through her body. And then she felt it. His release, inside her, love, ecstasy, and belonging filling her to bursting. As she was swept away in his arms, she held tight, never wanting to let go.

When her senses returned, though her breathing remained ragged and her arms still held tight, she felt tears of joy run down her face. Never had she known such love or that it could feel so amazing.

Jackson moved slightly, pulling his arms out from under her to rest on his elbows, but he kept himself deep inside her. "You're crying."

She blinked, looking at him through a blur. "I'm happy." She sniffed.

He gave her a soft smile. "Me too. That happy."

That he understood just sent more tears flowing, and she laughed. "I didn't realize love would make me cry so much."

He kissed the tears on her cheek before lifting his head. "As long as it makes you laugh and smile even more, it's good."

"Oh, it's very good."

He moved his hand to her head and smoothed her hair from the side of her face. "If I had known you would be in my life, I would have lived it differently."

She shook her head. "No. It's because you lived your life the way you did that you became the man you are and the man I love."

He responded with a tender kiss that went straight to her heart.

Without warning, he rolled them over so she was lying on top of him. Luckily, she'd already had a tight hold on him. "Again with a surprise?"

"I didn't want my weight to be too much. I'm not light."

That was true, and yet she hadn't even noticed. That was surprising because the man probably weighed close to a hundred pounds more than her and it was all muscle. "We're going to have to work on you giving me a heads-up."

"You can have your head up. Just sit up."

At first, she thought he'd misunderstood, but from the quirking of his lips, he knew exactly what she'd meant. Two could play that game. "Good point. I think I will."

As she brought her legs up to sit, she felt him inside her, even though he couldn't possibly still have an erection. She looked down at his chest before her and put her hands on his pectoral muscles, which were larger than her palms. "Oh, I like this view."

"So do I."

At his words, she moved her gaze to his face and found his eyes fixed on her breasts. Her nipples hardened almost instantly. How did he do that? "Do you see something you like?"

"I do." His hands came up and cupped her breasts. "You taste good."

Though his mouth was far from her, her nipples got harder. It was the anticipation of his touch. "Do I feel good?"

"Yes." His thumbs moved across her nipples almost lazily, as if he had all the time in the world, which he actually did.

It was mesmerizing watching his roughened thumbs moving back and forth and feeling the roughness against her soft skin. Her nipples grew so hard, they became painful, yet it excited her, sending tiny zings to her sheath.

He switched fingers, using his index fingers to circle her areolas before bringing his thumb back to hold her nipples. He squeezed lightly, and her sheath tightened around him. When he held on and rolled her hard nubs to the right and left, she arched back, thrusting her breasts toward his fingers, already feeling need building inside.

Then he stopped and brushed her nipples with one fingernail, first one and then the other, until she arched further, wanting far more. She set her hands on his legs behind her to better arch against his hand, closing her eyes to indulge in every pulse of excitement. The next thing she knew, his other hand was sliding along her tummy, down over her mons, and to her clit, where his finger started to play.

Her body bucked toward him, wanting more, and he didn't disappoint. While one hand began rolling her nipple, the other rolled her clit. Her pleasure skyrocketed as the pressure in her sheath grew even as he hardened within her.

Then she felt his body shift, and he lifted up, his mouth latching onto her nipple, sending her over the brink. She grabbed hold of him as her body bucked against his finger, tightening around him inside as he sucked harder, holding her to her bliss until he released her and allowed her back to Earth. She fell against him, panting.

Wrapping his arms around her, he lay back down and turned his head toward the back of hers, holding her close. When she was finally able to take a decent breath, she sat up again. "Oh." He was still hard and deep inside her.

"I thoroughly enjoy watching you fly apart." His smile was wicked.

"I'm happy to please you in that way, then."

His brows rose. "That's what I want to hear. Come here."

She lowered herself to give him a kiss, and he rolled them over again. This time, she just laughed. "Can't decide which position you like better?"

"Oh, I know what position I like."

"Tell me."

He shook his head. "I'll show you." He pulled completely out of her.

She was about to protest when he rolled her onto her stomach and pulled her hips up. She pushed up with her arms, knowing exactly what came next and excited to have it.

As he held her hips, he slid into her from behind, slowly.

"Now that's good." She practically purred her words.

He pulled out to his tip. "Very good." He pushed back in a little faster.

The thrill of excitement it sent to her core tightened her sheath, making his pullout just as pleasurable. When he next pushed forward, it was faster yet. Her body started to spiral already. Then he pumped in faster, banging into her, throwing her into another whirl of ecstasy. She yelled as she exploded around him, a bright light flashing in her head, existing in pure joy.

Her arms gave out, and she slid to her stomach, Jackson on top of her, not breaking their connection.

As she pulled air into her lungs, she felt his racing heartbeat against her back and smiled inside. They were a pair, perfect together.

Eventually, he rolled off her and pulled her against him.

She rested her head on his chest and entwined one leg with his, content to lay in his arms, completely sated.

He stroked her arm. "Now that I have investigated all sides of you, I can confirm that I love them all equally."

She smirked. "You certainly did."

His laughter filled the room.

Happiness filled her. It was a new sound for a new beginning.

EPILOGUE
NEW YEAR'S DAY

DANI WATCHED as Jackson studied the ground about four hundred yards in front of Mesquite Road. Looking toward the Rocky Road driveway, she'd estimate they were equally far from that. What was he thinking? "Jackson, don't you think this is a little too far back? I don't think your dad meant quite this much land when he said we could have some to build on, do you?"

His head came up, and he reached his hand out to her.

She walked over and took it. "I just don't want to cause problems when he's being so generous."

"Oh, he's not being generous. He's being selfish. You heard him. He just wants his granddaughter nearby. In fact, he told me this morning when I came in from my run that we can have a hundred acres as long as the ranch has an easement to fifty of it in case it needs it."

She stared wide-eyed at him. "A hundred acres?"

"Exactly. But I think we should just take the fifty, then

it's ours with no restrictions. My father can be manipulative when he wants to be. I told you what he did to Brody."

He had, and she'd thought it so terrible that she'd asked Hannah about it, only to have it confirmed. "I like that idea." She looked around where they stood. "So you're thinking this would be a possible place for the house?"

Jackson chuckled, a sound so new to her, she doubted she'd ever tire of hearing it.

"No, I was trying to envision the driveway. I'm definitely going to have it graded and maintained, but I was also looking at elevation and where water might undermine it. Since you said your one stipulation was land near Mesquite Road so your commute wouldn't involve driving down the Rocky Road driveway, I want to make sure our own driveway is perfect for you."

How could she have ever thought of him as not up to par as Mr. Right? But at the mention of a commute, her doubts started in. "That is, if I have a commute. I'm worried about finding a new job. Even though there are so many more mines south of here, they are owned by just a few companies."

He pulled her in for a side hug. "I have no doubt you'll find a job. You're very good at what you do. What did your friend Kaitlyn say when you told her you were handing in your resignation?"

She chuckled, remembering the text she'd received just three days ago. "She's already sent her resume to every mining company down here. Her plan is that whoever gets hired first gets the other one of us hired."

"I didn't realize how smart she was. From her activity while here, I thought her interests lay elsewhere."

There was no censure in Jackson's voice, so she didn't feel the need to defend her friend. "Let's just say that she approaches relationships differently than most women. But if it weren't for her, I would have never slept with you."

He ran his hand over her shoulder to touch her breast. "Then I owe her my gratitude. As I recall, there was no sleeping about it."

She ducked from under his touch, the feelings that he sent through her body making it hard to concentrate. "As I was saying ... we are going to tag team the job search. She'll probably get hired before me simply because every mining company needs a lot of labor but rarely do they need more than one safety officer."

"You already have a temporary job with Rocky Road. I bet you are hired before that ends. Then you'll be complaining you don't have enough time to do both. If that happens, we'll just have Tanner change your contract. You're family now." He took her hand again, as if to punctuate that sentiment.

Hearing that she was family did release some of her worry. "I suppose I could do more consulting like I am for your family. I'm pleased that my many comments about safety in my feedback were taken seriously. It won't take long to have the dude ranch operation running safely, with so many people giving input on solutions. I suppose if I get enough consulting gigs or even temporary contracts, that could work until I land a permanent position."

"It won't take that long, and it's not like we'll have a mortgage, so there's no immediate pressure."

She stepped away and faced him. "How do you figure

that? The realtor we talked to might have said I can get double what I paid for my house, but I've only been paying the mortgage for six years. That's not enough left over to build a house for three."

"I forgot about that money." Jackson lowered his brows.

She stared at him. "What do you mean, you forgot about it? What were you planning to build our house with?"

"My savings. I was in the military ten years. In all that time, they paid for almost everything. I've been investing my income and have enough for a three-bedroom adobe ranch, a barn, fencing, and a playhouse for Tabitha."

She was shocked. She'd thought Jackson was dependent on his family, but he had more money stashed away than she would after the sale of her house?

"Now, if you want another bedroom or a pool, we'll probably need some of the money from your house sale. Or I can take out a loan for those additions and pay it off slowly with my Army pension."

She shook her head and crossed her arms. "No, of course not. I'm happy to contribute. When were you going to tell me you had this fortune stashed away?"

His brows rose. "Hmm, now?"

Was she upset that he hadn't told her or that he had more money than she did? It was definitely the latter. It had been only a week since they decided to live together, and much of that time had been spent discussing whether to move to Show Low or live on the ranch and, if so, how. She uncrossed her arms and grinned. "It's not like we've had a lot of time to talk about this between Brody and Hannah's wedding, Christmas, and now."

His gaze softened. "I liked having you for Christmas."

"I admit, I enjoyed Christmas with you and your chaotic family. Can you imagine what it will be like once Tabitha is old enough to understand? I hope Amanda and Tanner conceive soon so the presents are at least split between two grandchildren."

"I agree. I'd like our daughter to have a cousin close to her age to learn to ride with."

She found it telling that he spoke of riding together instead of playing together. She liked that. It reminded her that he'd talked about building a barn. She scanned the area where they stood. If he could see a slope to it, he had a better eye than she did. "You mentioned a barn?"

"I did. Here's what I envision. The drive comes off Mesquite Road around this way. Then I'm thinking over there by that large patch of brittlebush, we place the barn." He took a few steps forward and to the right. "Then the house could be near the saguaro and face the road. I'm just not sure where I want the corral."

She was still trying to find the saguaro. He really had excellent eyesight. "I have a suggestion. I think I'd like it if the house faced the direction of town so the backyard and pool could face the Four Peaks like it does at your family's house."

He looked to the mountains, which still had a dusting of snow on them since the temperature up there had not risen above freezing since Christmas. "I see your point. If we do that, I might like the barn in similar proximity to the house."

"Speaking of the barn, are you planning on horses?"

He walked over to her and took her hand. "I am. I'd like Havoc here. Plus, I want to purchase a horse for you and for

Tabitha." He gave her a hopeful smile. "I'd also like to have Shotgun here if he wants to be."

"Oh, yes. We must have Shotgun in our family." She held up her other hand, the sun shining on the freshwater pearls of her bracelet. "I wouldn't have my bracelet, or you, if he hadn't found this."

"Me?"

She faced him, taking his other hand. "I wasn't going to come to the wedding, but when you texted the bracelet was found, I guess my gut saw it as a sign. Either that or you were just too hard to resist."

He suddenly pulled her in tight, her head against his shoulder. "Shit, to think I wouldn't have you in my arms right now. I can't."

At the tension in his body and voice, she ran her hands over his back. "It doesn't matter what could have been. All that matters is now."

He pulled back slightly and gazed at her. "No. What matters is now and our future together."

She smiled. "Exactly."

He lowered his head, and his mouth brushed hers before he deepened the kiss.

Just as her toes started to tingle, his phone made the sound of an alarm clock. She jerked her head back. "What's that for? From what I can tell, you're fully awake."

He let her go and unclipped the phone to turn off the alarm. "Yes, but I knew if we came out here, I'd get lost in making plans and forget about the meeting."

"Oops, I did forget about the family meeting."

Jackson shook his head. "No, it's not a family meeting. It's a ranch meeting."

They started walking back to his truck, which was parked on the driveway. "Is there a difference?"

"Yes. And it's a big difference. A ranch meeting means handling ranch business. A family meeting means something serious has happened and we all need to be there to support whoever it affected. The last one of those we had was after I went to my first appointment with the doc. It was my homework, so I called the meeting."

"I imagine they were nervous about why you called it."

"They were, but I was more nervous. My doctor told me to tell them everything I was comfortable sharing and then five more things I wasn't. That was harder than going after one of my wounded soldiers while tanks were firing at us."

She halted. "You had tanks firing at you and you went toward them?"

He stopped with her. "Yes. That was my personal mission. To save as many men as possible."

The fact that he was still alive and here with her swamped her, and she found herself having a hard time breathing.

"Hey, you okay?" He cupped her cheek. "You got suddenly pale."

She nodded, her throat too tight to speak.

His hand moved to her neck, and his fingers rested against her speeding pulse. "Shit, Dani. You need to take a deep breath in through your nose for ten seconds and out through your mouth. Come on, you can do it."

She focused on doing as he asked, and after three deep

breaths, her heartbeat returned to something more normal. Her throat loosened, and she finally replied, "I guess the thought that you could have died hit me hard. Maybe I need to go to your doctor."

He pulled her in for a hug, his chest vibrating with his chuckle. "You're welcome anytime." He loosened his hold.

She stepped back. "We better keep walking. I don't want to be late for my first ranch meeting."

In no time, they'd made it to the truck, but their pace was slowed by the driveway. As it was, they walked into the clubhouse just as everyone was taking a seat. Tanner sat at the head of the table with Amanda to his left. Jeremiah sat at the other end. Brody and Hannah sat next to Amanda, leaving the last two seats for them.

Tanner started off. "I'm pleased to announce that not only has Dani agreed to consult with us on safety problems and solutions, but Hannah has also agreed to officially help Dad and get the finances figured out while she and Brody are still in town."

Brody turned to Hannah. "Good luck with that."

Tanner frowned at Brody. "Good thing you married a woman who can actually add two and two together."

Brody just grinned.

Tanner continued. "I've gone through the feedback from our guests, and based on that, I believe we need to change the start of our regular operations for guests."

"Why? What'd we do wrong?" Jeremiah was not pleased.

"It's not that we did anything wrong, but based on the feedback, we can do a lot of things better, and I'd prefer that we get it right."

Amanda, who sat in front of a laptop, explained. "While Tanner would prefer we don't officially open until March, there are some reservations already for February, when we thought we would open, so we'll need to honor those. Luckily, there aren't many since we told Brody to hold off on the marketing plan he'd created until after the holidays."

Brody spoke to Amanda. "Someone else is going to have to follow through on that. I'll be in school."

"We know." Four people said it at the same time, and Dani couldn't help chuckling.

Brody gave them a self-deprecating smile. "Okay, okay. Just checking."

Amanda continued. "Tanner and I discussed it, and we think it would be best if the operations were split between the cattle ranching and the dude ranch. So he's going to continue to oversee the cattle ranch side of things, and I'm going to take on the dude ranch."

Dani almost clapped. "I think that's an excellent idea."

"Me too." Jeremiah pointed at Amanda. "She gets it."

No one disagreed. Still, Dani glanced at Jackson to see if he felt left out, but he didn't reveal his feelings.

Amanda smiled at everyone. "Thank you. My first order of business, however, is to steal Layne from Tanner."

"What?" Tanner looked at his wife. "Layne's my right-hand man."

"Yes, I know. But since you'll be able to focus on the expansion, I'm going to need him for the month of February."

Tanner's left eyebrow rose. "The whole month?"

"Yes, the whole month. We have unique guests who have booked the entire month of February."

"Who would want to stay on a dude ranch for a month?" Jackson asked the question they were all thinking.

Amanda gave them all a secret smile. "You'll never guess, so I'll tell you. One of our guests posted pictures of the petroglyphs on the east mountain, and some scientists saw them. They want to stay here so they can study them."

Dani immediately understood why Amanda was excited. "If they find anything of significance about the petroglyphs, that could well put Rocky Road on the map." At her observation, everyone began to smile.

Tanner, though, wasn't happy. "But why Layne. Why not Nash or Waylon or—"

"Because, first of all, these are women scientists, and Layne is easy on the eye."

"Excuse me?" Tanner pulled in his chin, obviously very affronted.

Amanda laughed. "Oh, you are too, and much more, but you're married. A little charm from a good-looking single cowboy could go a long way in them having a positive impression of our operation. Plus, I need a more mature guide who will not only respect their work but will keep his thoughts about their work to himself. Layne may have deep-rooted opinions, but he knows when to share them and when not to."

Dani nodded, understanding Amanda's point. "In other words, you don't want someone who thinks studying drawings on a rock is a waste of time and says that."

"Yes, and since one of the scientists is an ancient alien theorist, I need someone we can count on."

Brody barked a laugh. "An ancient alien theorist? You have to be kidding. Is that really a thing?"

Amanda rolled her eyes. "And that proves my argument right there."

Tanner scowled at Brody. "Fine."

Dani bit down on her lip to keep from laughing.

"Do we have anyone else scheduled for February?" Tanner was obviously anxious to change the subject.

"Not exactly, but I'm thinking that we should open reservations just for the weekend of Valentine's Day and try one of the suggestions we received. Actually, we had many people request a singles-only weekend."

Dani knew exactly where that came from. "Were there any specific activities suggested?"

"There were." Tanner looked at his wife, obviously not comfortable with sharing.

Amanda, though, clicked on her laptop and started reading. "Yes. Let's see ... water volleyball, a red and pink dance, tickle the pickle—whatever that is—secret lover—it says here 'like Secret Santa'—a wet T-shirt contest for both sexes, hide the pickle, men vs. women contests such as riding, pole dancing class, pie eating, twerking—"

"I think we get the point." Tanner's face had grown red.

Dani wasn't surprised. He must have figured out that the pickle was a part of a man's anatomy. She looked over at Jackson, who was holding back a laugh.

Amanda shrugged and went back to her own plan. "My thought was we could try this singles weekend and possibly invite the town for a Valentine's dance."

Jackson shook his head. "I'm not sure that would be a good idea. If Valentine's falls on the weekend, then Boots 'n Brew will have a band, and The Stampede always has a couples' pool tournament on Valentine's. At least they used to."

Brody confirmed it. "Yes, they're still doing that."

As everyone mulled that over, Dani had another idea. "What if you had a gathering for the town separate from when you have guests? It could be like an open house of a new business."

Brody grimaced, and Tanner frowned.

That wasn't the reaction she expected. "What?"

Jackson looked at his brothers and then at her. "Among cattle ranchers, a dude ranch is a bit of a joke."

"Really? I thought it would be the opposite since you're running two businesses at once, plus people are paying you to work for you. To me, that's damn smart."

Hannah spoke up. "I thought that too. But cattle ranchers are a breed unto themselves."

"Actually, I think Dani's idea is perfect."

Everyone turned toward Amanda, including her husband, who gave her a look like she'd lost her mind.

"Hear me out. What better way to smash that stigma? We have an event here and invite everyone. We can barbeque and get a band."

Hannah jumped in. "Yes, and if we use the services of people in town, they'll be even more interested in coming—like if we order ice cream from Mrs. Silva and invite her. Instead of having our cook do it all, we could order pork pies from Mrs. Barker and invite her. Oh, and we could order more picnic tables from Mr. Hardy and invite him."

Brody laughed. "If we give Mr. Hardy the flyers, everyone in town will have one by the end of the day."

Jackson directed his comments to Tanner. "I think the ladies are onto something. What's the worst that could happen? You hear a few snide comments, but in the meantime, everyone who is part of it begins to see the value."

Jeremiah slapped the table. "I agree."

Tanner, who was about to say something, probably another objection, reconsidered after his dad's statement. Finally, he shrugged. "Amanda's in charge of the dude ranch operation, so if she can fit a party for Four Peaks in the budget, it's her call."

Hannah pointed to herself. "We'll talk."

Once that was settled, the topics turned to the cattle ranch side of things. Dani didn't have a lot to add to that, but Jackson offered up a few good ideas. By the time the meeting was over, she felt as if she were truly part of the family.

She and Jackson left the clubhouse shortly after Brody and Hannah, leaving Jeremiah, Tanner, and Amanda to go over a few odds and ends. The sun was just starting to reach the top of the four peaks. "Do you think Layne will be pissed to have to escort scientists for a month?"

"He won't be happy about it, but Amanda's right. He's the only one she could count on to handle the situation, especially with a bunch of people who probably don't even know how to ride a horse."

She thought about what he'd said on Christmas Eve. "Well, at least he'll be able to go home at night. He'll have some time away to decompress from all his flirting."

Jackson stopped in front of the bunkhouse, where they

were staying for a while. "I'm going to feed Shotgun now. I need to get his food from the house. Would you get Tabitha from our rooms and tell Isaac we'll take it from here?"

"I'd be happy to."

As Jackson strode off toward the house, she climbed the steps to the family bunkhouse and stepped inside. Isaac had Tabitha in her port-a-crib in the big room.

Isaac rose from the comfy chair next to the baby. "She woke up about thirty minutes ago. I changed her diaper. It was a double-bagger. Whew."

She grinned. "Yeah, I've changed a few of those myself. Thank you."

"You just stopping in before dinner?"

Dani shook her head. "No, I'm taking her to the barn. Your evening is all yours."

Isaac chuckled. "You mean all Jeremiah's. Luckily, he falls asleep early, and I'll have control of the big TV."

"Now that sounds like a relaxing evening. Enjoy."

After he left, she picked up Tabitha. "I do think you've gained another pound this week. I bet the doctor will be impressed."

The baby looked at her as if she understood, then kicked her feet.

"You're happy with yourself, are you?" She moved to the changing table and put an adorable rabbit coat, complete with a hood that had ears, on the baby. "We're going to see Shotgun. Are you excited?"

Tabitha turned her head to the side.

"Is that a no? I disagree. I think you'll be very excited."

She wrapped a blanket around the baby and lifted her in her arms, quickly exiting the building.

When she stepped into the barn, Jackson was already there with Shotgun.

She kept a good distance between them just to be safe, because she was always safe. "Are you ready to meet Shotgun?"

Tabitha turned her head to the side, and Dani moved her position so the baby could see the raccoon. An immediate squeal filled the barn, and Shotgun ran up Jackson's arm at the sound.

Jackson laughed. "You're such a coward. She's no bigger than you are."

Shotgun chattered, clearly not happy.

Tabitha, on the other hand, was reaching toward the critter.

"I think TJ likes Shotgun more than he likes her. Though to be fair, that wasn't the best first impression."

Jackson coaxed the raccoon back off his shoulder with another piece of food. "I'm sure he'll get used to her." He left a few more pieces of food on the hay bale and then walked over to them.

Wrapping his arm around her shoulders, he and Dani watched Shotgun wash his hands and take another piece out of his bowl. "To think that four months ago, I was braving bullets overseas without a care for my own well-being, and now I have a family of four to care for."

She leaned into him. "That's a big change. Are you okay with it?"

"I am. I have three more reasons to love. Three more

loved ones to protect. And for the first time in my life, I can see a future and look forward to it."

Dani lifted her gaze to view his profile, so strong, so handsome, and so vulnerable. "Four months ago, I gave up searching for Mr. Right. When I met you in here the first day I arrived, I never expected you would be the one, but I'm so glad you are."

He turned and looked at her. "When I heard you in here, I was angry that a guest had intruded on my privacy. Don't ever stop intruding. You give me hope." He leaned down and kissed her.

As his lips touched hers in a gentle kiss, Tabitha cooed in her arms.

Jackson chuckled and kissed his daughter on the cheek. "There, now is everything alright?"

Dani smiled. "Everything is so right."

ALSO BY LEXI POST

Rocky Road Ranch
Between a Rock and a Cowboy
Hard as a Rock Cowboy
Rock-A-Bye Cowboy

ABOUT THE AUTHOR

Lexi Post is a New York Times and USA Today best-selling author of romance inspired by the classics. She spent years in higher education taking and teaching courses about the classical literature she loved. From Edgar Allan Poe's short story "The Masque of the Red Death" to Tolstoy's *War and Peace*, she's read, studied, and taught wonderful classics.

But Lexi's first love is romance novels, so she married her two first loves, romance and the classics. Whether it's sizzling cowboys, dashing dukes, hot immortals, or hunks from out of this world, Lexi provides a sensuous experience with a "whole lotta story."

Lexi is living her own happily ever after with her husband and her two cats in Florida. She makes her own ice cream every weekend, loves bright colors, and you'll never see her without a hat.

Vist her website: https://www.lexipostbooks.com
Lexi Post Updates: http://bit.ly/LexiUpdate
Email Lexi: lexi@lexipostbooks.com

www.ingramcontent.com/pod-product-compliance
Ingram Content Group UK Ltd.
Pitfield, Milton Keynes, MK11 3LW, UK
UKHW040836130525
5886UKWH00017B/128